CRIMES OF MEMORY

Books by L.J. Sellers

The Detective Jackson Series
The Sex Club
Secrets to Die For
Thrilled to Death
Passions of the Dead
Dying for Justice
Liars, Cheaters & Thieves
Rules of Crime
Crimes of Memory

~~

The Lethal Effect
(Previously published as *The Suicide Effect*)
The Baby Thief
The Gauntlet Assassin

CRIMES OF MEMORY

A DETECTIVE JACKSON MYSTERY

L.J. SELLERS

 THOMAS & MERCER

Printed in the United States of America.

Published by Thomas & Mercer
PO Box 400818
Las Vegas, NV 89140

ISBN-13: 9781477809471
ISBN-10: 1477809473

Library of Congress Control Number: 2013906872

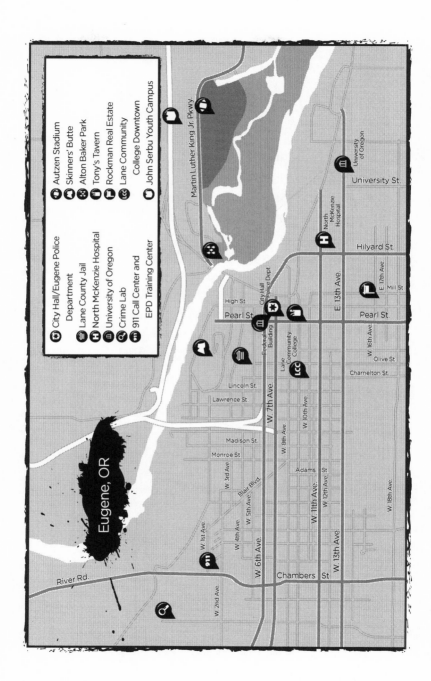

Eugene, OR

Legend:

- City Hall/Eugene Police Department
- Lane County Jail
- North McKenzie Hospital
- University of Oregon
- Crime Lab
- 911 Call Center and EPD Training Center
- Autzen Stadium
- Skinners' Butte
- Alton Baker Park
- Tony's Tavern
- Rockman Real Estate
- Lane Community College Downtown
- John Serbu Youth Campus

Martin Luther King Jr. Pkwy.

University of Oregon

University St.

North McKenzie Hospital

Hilyard St.

High St.

City Hall Police Dept

Pearl St.

Federal Building

Lane Community College

E. 13th Ave.

E. 17th Ave.

E. Mill St.

Pearl St.

W. 16th Ave.

Olive St.

Charnelton St.

Lincoln St.

Lawrence St.

W. 7th Ave.

W. 8th Ave.

W. 10th Ave.

Madison St.

Monroe St.

W. 3rd Ave.

Adams St.

Blair Blvd.

W. 11th Ave.

W. 12th Ave.

W. 8th Ave.

W. 1st Ave.

W. 4th Ave.

W. 5th Ave.

W. 6th Ave.

W. 13th Ave.

W. 2nd Ave.

River Rd.

Chambers St.

Cast of Characters

Wade Jackson: detective/Violent Crimes Unit
Kera Kollmorgan: Jackson's girlfriend/nurse
Katie Jackson: Jackson's daughter
Jan: Katie's aunt/Jackson's ex-sister-in-law
Carla River: FBI agent
Jamie Dallas: undercover FBI agent
Rob Schakowski (Schak): detective/task force member
Lara Evans: detective/task force member
Michael Quince: detective/task force member
Denise Lammers: Jackson's supervisor/sergeant
Sophie Speranza: newspaper reporter
Rich Gunderson: medical examiner/attends crime scenes
Jasmine Parker: evidence technician
Joe Berloni: evidence technician
Rudolph Konrad: pathologist/performs autopsies
Victor Slonecker: district attorney
Jim Trang: assistant district attorney
Ed McCray: ex-cop, private investigator
Craig Cooper: homicide victim, ex-con
Jane Niven: Craig's sister
Todd Sheppard: Craig's neighbor
Danny Brennan: robbery suspect, deceased
Maggie Brennan: Danny's widow
Jenna Brennan: Danny and Maggie's daughter
Patrick Brennan: Danny's brother
Chris Noonaz (Cricket): Love the Earth founder
Adam Greene: Love the Earth member
Russell Crowder: Love the Earth member
Charlotte Diebold: youth psychologist
Ted Rockman: business owner, bombing target

CRIMES OF MEMORY

CHAPTER 1

Tuesday, March 12, 8:22 p.m.

Jerry came too quickly, but before he could mumble an apology, he heard a thump downstairs in the factory. He pushed himself off his scowling mistress, leaped from the couch, and grabbed his pants.

"What's your hurry?" Candy complained. "Jesus, Jerry. I don't know why I bother with you."

"I heard a noise. Someone's in the building." He yanked up his pants, not bothering with his boxers, which he couldn't locate. Jerry regretted getting naked from the waist down. They usually just went at it on the desk, him with his pants around his ankles and her with her skirt pushed up.

Shuffling sounds, like someone moving quickly and quietly, raised the hair on the back of his neck. They weren't the heavy footsteps of the plant foreman coming back to check the day's production. Someone sneaky was in the building. "Get your clothes on and get out of here," he snapped at Candy, who'd sat up on the couch and now looked concerned.

"You think it's Ricardo?" She was married to the foreman and had reason to worry.

"I don't know. Just go."

Jerry dropped to the couch and pulled on his shoes. His socks never came off, unless he was in the shower. Listening hard, he tried to determine where the intruder was. In the break room? Maybe hoping to steal iPods or drugs from the employee lockers? It didn't sound like that corner of the building, but what else made sense? The factory filled plastic bottles with local spring water, using standard production equipment. Why would someone come in here?

A protester, Jerry realized. That was why the owner had recently asked him to work an overnight watch shift. Mr. Rockman was worried about the environmentalists, even though they hadn't been out front recently. Something must have happened to make the owner nervous.

Jerry crossed the small upstairs office and peered through the glass at the factory floor below. With the overhead halide lights off, the production area was illuminated only by small wall lights that cast weird shadows on the machinery. He scanned the floor but didn't see anything.

When he turned back, Candy had her skirt and heels on and was reaching for her pink leather jacket. "How do I get past Ricardo if he's coming up here?"

Jerry had to think. "Stay under the stairs until it's clear." *Would she be safe? Would their affair get him fired?* "I don't think it's Ricardo. Stay under there until you hear from me."

Jerry grabbed his giant flashlight—heavy enough to kill someone if he knocked 'em upside the head—and led Candy out of the office and down the stairs. As a watchman, Jerry wished he could carry a gun, but the owner wouldn't allow it. Rockman had added a weekend drive-by security detail after protesters picketed the place last year, but all had been quiet. Then recently something had spooked the owner, and he'd added a night and weekend on-premises watch. Jerry hadn't had any trouble in the two weeks he'd been in the new night position. Not wanting to go back to working the line, he was almost grateful for an opportunity to prove he was needed on the watch shift.

At the bottom of the stairs, Candy turned and slipped into the built-in closet underneath. Jerry moved down the short hallway to the door leading to the factory. Should he call the police now or wait to see what he was dealing with? He didn't want to risk getting both himself and Candy into hot water with their spouses over a supervisor coming back in for something he'd forgotten.

Jerry stepped into the factory and flipped on a row of overhead lights. "Who's here?"

The cavernous room was quiet except for the hum of the halides. Jerry moved toward the break room. If it was an intruder, how did he get in? Had Candy left the door open when she came through?

Jerry strode past the bottling line and toward the short hall leading to the break room and employee lockers. A squatting figure jumped up and bolted out of the dark. The man in the ski mask shoved past him, brushing his shoulder. Jerry swung his flashlight and missed. The intruder ran for the side door. Jerry reached in his pants pocket for his cell phone and dialed 911.

"What is your emergency?" The dispatcher's voice was calm, almost bored.

"This is Jerry Bromwell, night watchman at the Rock Spring bottling plant. We have an intruder."

"Are you in danger?"

He had her attention now. "No, just get some cops out here to catch him. He's wearing a ski mask and dark clothes." Jerry stepped into the hall where the man had been kneeling, but realized he'd passed the light switch, which was just outside the opening to the hallway.

"What's your location?"

"Rock Spring Drive, just off Laurel Hill." He flipped on his flashlight and squatted.

"Any other description of the intruder?"

Jerry couldn't process what she was saying. The thing on the floor had his full attention. His heart skipped a beat as he realized what he was seeing. "I think it's a pipe bomb."

"Get out of the building and get clear," the dispatcher commanded. "I'll send the bomb squad."

Jerry was already speed-walking toward the side exit. The overhead doors were closer, but they took too long to unlock and open. He wanted to run but was afraid. Afraid of what? That his pounding footsteps would set it off?

He wasn't ready to die. He had a lot of hunting, and screwing, and Duck football left in his life. *Oh shit!* Candy was still in the closet. Jerry stopped. Was it safe to go back for her? How much time had the bomber given himself? Just enough or maybe a good five minutes?

Fuck! Jerry spun and ran past the hallway and down the bottling line.

"Candy! Come out. We gotta get out of here!" He yelled at the top of his voice, needing her to respond to his panic.

As he approached the stairs, the closet door opened and she stepped out. "What's going on?"

"There's a bomb!"

"No shit?" She trotted toward him.

Jerry grabbed her arm and ran toward the exit, pulling her along. He hated passing the hallway, but it was the fastest way out. Like most factories, this one had no windows.

Jerry's adrenaline pumped so hard he could have made it to the red Exit sign in five seconds flat. But Candy wore heels and a skirt and didn't know how to run. She slowed him down, and he wanted to let go of her.

But he couldn't. Her whimpering brought out his protective side.

Something snapped and Candy went down, making him stumble and let go of her. She let out a cry as she landed on her knees on the concrete floor.

"My heel broke." She sobbed and pushed to her feet.

Gritting his teeth, Jerry grabbed her hand and started to run again. With a broken heel, Candy shuffled even slower. Jerry fought the urge to curse at her.

Finally, they reached the door and he grabbed the wide metal handle. He pushed it open with one hand and pulled Candy through with the other.

Behind them the pipe bomb exploded inside the factory.

"Holy shit!" Jerry instinctively covered his head.

The noise of the blast made Candy trip and fall again. She landed on her hands and knees on the asphalt this time.

Jerry helped her up and saw blood dripping down her shins. "Are you all right?"

"Yes. But shit! How will I explain this?" She gestured at her scraped knees.

"You fell. It happens. Now get out of here before the cops come."

She gave him a look.

"Get in your car and go. If anyone learns you were here, it could ruin both our marriages."

Jerry pulled her toward her car. Once she was inside, he noticed the dirt smudge on her face and reached to wipe it off. She slapped at his hand. "I can't go home like this."

"Go get cleaned up. Buy a pair of pants before you go home. Just go. We can't get caught." Jerry couldn't bear the thought of his wife leaving him and taking his little girl.

Once his mistress was on the road, he breathed a sigh of relief. Now he just had to get his story straight. He'd saved Candy's life by going back for her, but he couldn't ever tell anyone she had been there. So much for being a hero. Disappointed, he glanced back at the factory. Still standing. Damn. He wouldn't even get some time off out of this.

CHAPTER 2

Tuesday, March 12, 8:35 p.m.

Jackson pulled up behind the blue patrol car and cut his engine. He braced himself, then climbed out into the damp night air. A group of young people stood on the sidewalk watching the house. Anger flared. He wanted to yell at them to go home, that there was nothing to see. Jackson trudged up the sidewalk toward the old, two-story building. Students likely lived here and attended the University of Oregon, only three blocks away. The party had dispersed, and the neighborhood was relatively quiet, but every light in the home was on and a few stragglers sat on the wide porch.

A man in uniform greeted him halfway. "Officer Will Meadow. We met once on the Walker case." Jackson remembered him, but even more vividly, he recalled the bodies in the house. At least no one here was dead, he reminded himself. Meadow had called twenty minutes ago, interrupting a rare, private moment Jackson had been enjoying with his girlfriend.

"Hey, Daddy. Did you come to rescue me?" His daughter's voice came from the roof over the porch. The slurred words and taunting tone made him cringe. Katie was drunk. Again. He had to get her some help.

He glanced briefly at Meadow. "Thanks for calling me."

The patrol officer frowned. "I still have to report it."

"I understand."

Jackson moved toward the porch. "Would you go inside, please?" he said to the young people smoking on the steps.

"What if I don't want to?" a young man called back.

Before Jackson could respond, the officer strode over. "Get in the house or I'll arrest you all for contributing to the delinquency of a minor."

They scattered like frightened mice, two rushing for the front door, while the mouthy young man ran across the narrow yard and down the street. He apparently didn't want to be questioned. Jackson wondered if the little shit had given alcohol to his fifteen-year-old daughter. If he hadn't, someone else would have. After her mother's death, Katie had spun quickly through the cycles of shock, anger, and depression. Now she was just out of control, and Jackson knew it was about punishing him.

He looked up at his now bone-thin daughter, dressed in black and illuminated only by the neon glow of the nearby restaurant sign. What had happened to the sweet, funny, round-faced little girl he loved more than life itself?

You killed her mother, the voice in his head echoed for the hundredth time. Jackson pushed through his pain. "What are you doing, Katie?" He'd dropped her off at a friend's house two hours earlier.

"Just having some fun. I like it up here."

"The neighbors complained that you were screaming. Are you hurt?" He'd learned to approach her gently.

"Physically? No." She laughed, a high-pitched sound that made his skin shrivel. "But thanks for your concern." Her drunken slur crushed what was left of his heart.

"Please come down before you get hurt." He wondered how she'd gotten up there.

"But I want to party!" Katie stood and raised her hands to the dark sky.

"The party is over. They've all gone home." Jackson looked around for a way to climb up. He would talk her down if it took all night. He couldn't physically drag her off the roof. He couldn't physically do anything to her. She was fifteen, and the law was not on his side anymore.

"Then I'll find a new party." Without warning, Katie jumped straight at him.

Jackson opened his arms to catch her, but it happened too fast. She knocked his six-foot, two-hundred-pound frame to the ground, then rolled away, unscathed, in typical drunk fashion. Jackson's ribs felt cracked, and he was glad he'd left his weapon in the car. He pushed to his feet and winced in pain as his daughter laughed and ran for the sidewalk.

"Katie!" He chased after her and grabbed her arm. "Let's go somewhere together. We'll see a movie or something."

"Hell no." She jerked free and stumbled down the sidewalk. He noticed she was barefoot.

Jackson made a decision. He turned to Officer Meadow. "Arrest her and take her to the juvenile justice center. I need to get her into treatment."

As Katie cursed at him, Jackson got back in his car to block out her voice. He knew that forcing her into the system was the right thing to do, but it made him queasy with guilt and anxiety.

She would hate him even more than she already did. But Katie needed to know what her life would be like if she didn't stop drinking and using drugs. If she didn't finish high school. She needed to stand in a courtroom and be held accountable. It was the right thing, he told himself again. He knew it was bullshit to hand the responsibility to someone else, but Jackson couldn't make himself be the one to put her in lockup.

A warm sensation on his lip made him look in the rearview mirror. His nose was bleeding where Katie's elbow had slammed him. He found a tissue and glanced at the mirror again, feeling old. He'd discovered his first gray hair that morning, conspicuous in a sea of dark brown, and he was reaching for his reading glasses more and more. Not to mention his retroperitoneal fibrosis, which he didn't want to think about.

Jackson's phone rang and he cringed. Instinctively, he knew it was his boss. But maybe a new case was just what he needed. His date with Kera was already shot, and if he went back over there, he'd just burden his girlfriend with his daughter's troubles. He grabbed his phone and looked at the caller ID: *Sergeant Lammers*.

"Jackson here."

"Sorry to ruin your night, but we've had a homicide."

Jackson was torn. He wanted a new case to occupy his mind, but a homicide would suck up his time nearly around the clock for the next three days. Katie needed him to appear in court and petition for treatment rather than incarceration. "Can someone else take the case?" He'd never said that before and it felt wrong . . . and weak.

Lammers hesitated. "I don't have anyone else. I just sent Quince and Schak out to Rock Spring on a firebombing, and even if I assign this one to Evans, she still needs some help."

All Jackson heard was *firebombing*. "Was anyone hurt?"

"I don't know yet. The night watchman called it in, so probably not." Lammers cleared her throat. "I know you've been through a tough time, Jackson, but at this point, you're either in or out. If you can't take cases, then put in for retirement and let me bring someone else into the unit."

The ultimatum hit him like a fist to his kidney. What the hell was he supposed to do? His gut tightened in a painful squeeze. The fibrosis was growing again, and his doctor had increased his prednisone dose. The medication made him more emotional, and he fought it. In his head he formed the words, *I'm done, then. I have too much at stake with my daughter.* But what came out of his mouth was, "What's the location?"

"Safe and Secure Storage. It's just off Highway 99 on Jessen Drive. A man is dead, possibly stabbed."

Safe and secure? Jackson let out a bitter noise. There was no such thing. "What else do we know?"

"Nothing yet. But Evans is already on her way, and the ME should be there soon."

"I'll head out." He couldn't give up his job. It was too much a part of his identity. Maybe he would get lucky and find the perp hiding in the bushes with the bloody knife. It happened sometimes.

"Thanks, Jackson. I wish I could expand the unit, but you know our budget constraints."

"I'd better get going." He clicked off, wishing he could have cut his boss more slack. None of this was her fault. The crime rate in Eugene kept escalating, yet they were the least-staffed law enforcement agency in Oregon, which, in turn, had one of the lowest rates of officers per population in the country. Oregonians were mostly progressive, except when it came to taxes to pay for services.

Jackson didn't bother to go home first or stop at the department. He was still in his slacks and jacket and driving his city-issued car because he'd gone straight from work to Kera's. Once he was out of the downtown area, he called Kera and told her about Katie's incident. She was her usual supportive self.

"You did the right thing. This is Katie's third drunk episode in the last five weeks . . . that you know about. She's becoming a danger to herself."

"I know. But this will only make her more angry with me."

"You have to worry about her future, not how she feels about you. She'll come through it. She loves you."

Jackson wasn't sure he believed that anymore. "I'm on my way to a homicide, so I don't know when I'll see you next."

"Damn. Who is it this time?"

"A man stabbed near a storage unit. Could be a burglary gone bad."

"I wish you'd taken more time off."

"The Violent Crimes Unit is understaffed, and I'm hoping this will be an easy one."

Kera was silent. He'd taken three weeks of leave after his officer-involved shooting, and it had seemed like forever. In the month he'd been back, Lammers hadn't given him any challenging cases. He knew it was time. "I'll be in touch."

"Take care of yourself."

Jackson drove out Highway 99, an ugly strip of road in West Eugene made bearable by the cover of night. The route had been improved recently with trees and sidewalks, but the road ran parallel to the railroad tracks—never good for property values—and the outdated mishmash of buildings hadn't changed. Except for the new apartments built by the Sponsors program. The units were freshly painted in rich fall colors and seemed a little too nice for the ex-cons and recovering drug addicts who occupied them.

In the distance Jackson spotted the busy glow of high-powered flashlights. He hated working crime scenes in the dark, but a late-night scene with a still-warm body was better than bright daylight and a rotting corpse. The sooner they acted on the evidence, the more likely they were to make an arrest.

He turned on Jessen, then into a small cul-de-sac, and parked on the street. The storage business didn't have or need a parking lot, and two patrol cars took up the space in front of the office. It seemed like an odd place for a homicide, and Jackson wondered if the altercation had started at the nearby Lucky Numbers tavern. The tavern owner, Seth Valder, was in jail for filming pornography with a minor, and Jackson hoped the tavern manager was stealing Valder blind while he did his time.

Jackson climbed from the car and it started to rain. *Oh fuck me*, he thought, pulling his waterproof gear from the backseat, along with his leather carryall bag and a heavy-duty flashlight. As soon as he had the gear on, the rain stopped. He unbuttoned the jacket but didn't take it off. He knew Eugene weather in March.

He walked toward the silver Airstream that served as an office for the storage company, and a patrol officer approached. "Welcome to the night shift."

"I'm familiar with it." He knew he sounded tense, but that was the job. "What have we got?"

"The body is in the third row." The officer pointed to the left, where small lights illuminated the ends of ten narrow metal buildings.

The units were visible through a metal fence. "Any witnesses? Who called it in?"

"No witnesses so far. And the guy who called didn't give his name. Dispatch says the call came from the tavern." The patrol officer pointed again.

Jackson didn't have to look. "We need to find him."

"Detective Evans is over there now."

That was why he loved working with her. Evans was often a half step ahead of him and willing to do the grunt work. Her instincts were good too, but sometimes she moved too fast after a single suspect. "What unit is the body near?"

"C-13."

A car pulled up on the street and they both turned. Two people climbed out, and despite the dark, Jackson sensed they were an older man and woman.

"That must be the owners," the patrol officer said. "Ezra and Sally Goldstein. I had dispatch call them. We might need to unlock some units and check the renters."

"Good work. Find out who rents C-13 and the other units around it. I have to look at the body first." Jackson jotted down the owners' names—his first case notes—and headed for the open gate.

Made of metal like the fence around the property, the gate had wheels and rolled to the side. He stopped and flashed his light at the security device mounted on the fence. Operated by a keypad, the code was likely given to everyone who paid money to rent a storage unit. Did the owners keep track of who came and went? Jackson didn't see a camera.

He studied the fence. About eight feet tall and easy enough to scale for anyone physically fit. But you couldn't get back over carrying a TV, so it probably prevented most theft.

He turned between the C and D buildings and walked down a long row of overhead doors and thick padlocks. He kept to the side and flicked his light back and forth, looking for footprints or anything the victim or the perpetrator might have dropped. The area, which likely didn't see much foot traffic, was clean. Or at least it looked clean in the dark.

About halfway down, an officer stood with a flashlight pointed at the ground. Jackson could see the outline of the body and, nearby, the silhouette of a bicycle. Surprised at first that only two officers were on the scene, he remembered the firebombing at the bottled water company. The other late-shift patrol units were likely over there. If a traffic accident or other mishap occurred, they'd have to call in officers for extra shifts. *They probably already had*, he mentally corrected.

A light blinded his eyes as the officer lifted his flashlight to check him out.

He announced himself and strode forward, ducking under the crime scene tape.

The victim's head was toward him, and raindrops glistened on his bald spot. Jackson pulled on latex gloves, squatted, and took in the big picture. Early fifties, pale skin, jeans and a gray zip-up sweatshirt. Five-nine or so and gaunt. Stab wound to the throat with blood that was still sticky. Jackson touched the side of the victim's neck. Relatively warm. His death had occurred in the last few hours.

He looked up at the patrol officer. "Do we have an ID?"

"Craig Cooper, according to his state ID. Age forty-five."

He was younger than he looked. What had the victim done to attract or piss off his attacker? Jackson pulled back the sweatshirt and white T-shirt underneath, looking for more lacerations. Usually knife fights resulted in multiple wounds, but he didn't find any. He shone his light around the black asphalt. If there had been blood from the assailant, the rain had washed it away.

He searched Cooper's pockets and found only a small folding knife. No cell phone. Jackson flipped open the knife but saw no blood or tissue that would indicate it had been used in a fight. Cooper could have wiped it clean. Then calmly put it back in his pocket while his assailant lunged for him? Not likely.

Jackson lifted one of the dead man's hands. Thick, calloused, and scarred, like someone who'd worked with wood or gutted fish for a living. Yet the skin had not seen much sun lately. The fine black hair on the back of Cooper's hand was damp from the intermittent rain. No wounds, no blood.

Jackson lifted the other hand and spotted a crude black tattoo in the shape of a clover. Was it significant? Jackson grabbed his camera and took a close-up shot, hoping the flash would be enough. Normally, he would have taken a dozen photos by now, but in the dark it seemed pointless. The medical examiner would set up bright work lights and get better images.

Jackson reached up and took Cooper's ID from the officer. State-issued, but not a driver's license. Remembering the bike, Jackson stood and turned. Leaned against the wall between two units, the bike was an older model that had taken a beating. The rack over the back tire held a backpack. The assailant hadn't taken either the bike or the pack, so it seemed unlikely robbery had been the motive. A sense of dread washed over Jackson. Unless the witness who'd called in the body had blood on him and they found him soon, this homicide wouldn't be easy like he'd hoped.

"Here's his wallet. It was in his front pants pocket." The officer hadn't moved from his post.

The canvas wallet was so thin it made Jackson sad. He opened it to find seven dollars, a Social Security card, a picture of a woman in her twenties, and a key. The name on the back of the photo was Jane, dated 1998. He wondered if she'd be recognizable now.

Headlights illuminated the scene and Jackson breathed a sigh of relief. The medical examiner's van drove slowly toward them between the buildings and stopped about thirty feet away, well outside the crime scene tape. Maybe they would still be able to process a footprint. Jackson was glad the officers hadn't driven their vehicles into the storage area.

A thought hit him. "Was the gate unlocked when you got here?"

"Yes." The stocky officer chuckled. "I sure didn't climb the fence."

Whoever discovered the body must have left the gate open. Were they a renter here? Or had the killer left the gate open on the way out? More important, had Cooper left it open on the way in?

Rich Gunderson, the medical examiner, climbed out of the van. Dressed in all black, his face floated like a pale ghost in the dark. Jackson noticed he'd cut off his gray ponytail. Gunderson was probably looking for a job, now that the state had lost funding for his position. As the ME stopped next to the body, Joe Berloni, a short, stout crime scene technician, joined them. Jackson was disappointed not to see Jasmine Parker, who usually attended suspicious deaths, but Joe was competent and pleasant to work with.

The rain started again as Jackson filled them in. "The victim is Craig Cooper, according to his ID. He has a neck wound, likely made by a knife, and is still a little warm. No self-defense wounds."

"Do you still need me to do this?" Gunderson was always a little testy, but his pending layoff was making him bitter too.

Jackson ignored it. "There's no weapon in the immediate vicinity." He glanced at the patrol officer for confirmation.

"I walked the length of this corridor and didn't see anything." The uniformed man had stepped back to let the crime scene people set up lights and evidence trays.

"What's behind the property?" Jackson nodded toward the far end.

"A fence, then a field, then more buildings. Likely a business." The officer clicked his flashlight on. "Should I begin a wider perimeter search?"

"At least along the edge of the field. We'll get out here again tomorrow when we have more light."

The officer took off toward the back of the property, and Jackson turned to see a slim figure slipping past the ME van. Detective Lara Evans. Even in the dark, he recognized her small, muscular build.

"Hey, Jackson. I went to the tavern to find the guy who called in the body, but they said he left. What can I do to assist?"

"Go ask the owners if Craig Cooper rents a unit here." Jackson glanced at the overhead door on the nearby storage unit and saw it was padlocked. "Then get the key if they have one."

While he waited for Evans to return, Jackson stepped toward the nearby bicycle. He pulled off the bungee cord and lifted the nylon backpack, surprised at how heavy it was. He peered inside with his flashlight: thick flannel shirt, heavy-duty bike lock, brown paper bag with the remains of a lunch, and a library copy of *The Stand*. In the zipper pocket was a key, gold with a round head, like a post office box key. Worth checking out. Jackson slipped the key into an evidence bag by itself and put it in his pocket for easy access.

A moment later, Evans walked up carrying a sledgehammer. "Yep, C-13 is Cooper's rental."

Joe looked over at the door. "Want me to fingerprint it first?"

"Sure." Jackson knew it was probably a waste of time. The victim had most likely been killed moments after he rode up on his bicycle. Jackson remembered the key in Cooper's wallet.

While Joe dusted the lock and the area around the door handle, Jackson dug into his pocket and produced the key. "This will be easier."

"Damn." Evans set down the sledgehammer, then drew her weapon. "The killer could be hiding in there."

Jackson opened the lock, pushed up the overhead door, and stepped to the side.

A small animal rushed out, and Joe made a startled noise. "Was that a cat?"

"I think so." Jackson edged forward. "Eugene Police. Put your hands in the air and come out."

Nothing in the dark space moved.

"Can we take one of the work lights inside?" Jackson asked.

The ME grumbled but gestured to go ahead. Joe grabbed a tripod and moved it into the storage unit. Once they had light, Jackson and Evans holstered their weapons.

Except for a cat litter box near the door, the space was nearly empty. The front half held a futon mattress with a stack of blankets, and behind it in the shadows were a small dresser and a couple of boxes with food items. Next to the bedding they found a lantern and a canvas folding chair.

"I'll be damned," Evans said, holstering her weapon. "He lives in here."

"This can't be legal." Jackson didn't understand how someone could spend much time in the tiny windowless space with no heat and no lights. But maybe it was better than sleeping under a bridge.

Joe handed Evans a UV light and began to spray the walls and floor with luminol. While Joe and Evans looked for blood that may have been wiped up, Jackson riffled through the bedding, searching for a weapon or anything that might help explain the murder. Under a stained pillow, he found a dark-purple drawstring bag. Inside the fabric that had once held a bottle of Crown Royal whiskey was a collection of keepsakes. A beaded bracelet, a white rabbit's foot, and an old yarn toy.

The dresser was next, but it held nothing but clothing, all of it faded and worn, except for an unopened package of white socks.

Jackson half expected to find drugs, but there was no evidence of any. On the surface, Craig Cooper's life seemed simple and Spartan. Was his murder a random act of violence?

"Check this out." Evans, who'd been searching through a cardboard box, handed him a book with the cover torn off.

Jackson flashed his light on it. "A Bible." He noticed it was missing the first few chapters as well. "It looks like it's been torn."

"Maybe a struggle?"

"Or just something he found that way."

A muffled cry echoed through the damp night. Jackson and Evans both snapped their heads toward the sound. Where had it come from? Jackson pulled his weapon, ran out of the unit, and turned left—with Evans right on his heels. The ME and the evidence tech had stopped and turned to face the front as well.

Jackson slowed and listened intently, but the only sound he heard was the light patter of rain on metal buildings.

The cry had sounded so close. A homeless person along the road? A drunk in the tavern parking lot? Jackson took three more steps toward the front, then heard the noise again. No, not the same lament. Similar, but less woeful. And it came from the unit ahead and to his right. He hurried to the far side of the door and shined his light. Unit D-7. The padlock was not engaged.

Evans moved next to the door on the opposite side.

"Open up, Eugene Police!" Jackson yelled.

Silence.

Louder this time. "Police. Open up."

They heard another sleepy cry, then shuffling.

"Put your hands in the air. I'm opening the door." Jackson quietly set down his flashlight.

Sig Sauer in one hand, he reached for the handle with the other. He turned, shoved upward, and stepped to the side as the door clanged open. With his back to the building, he called, "Step out here with your hands in the air."

Evans was in a similar stance on the other side, and the pounding footsteps of the uniformed officer charged their way.

For a moment, the storage unit was silent. Jackson visualized a desperate man with a knife waiting in the dark, just inside the door. Adrenaline pulsed in his veins. If he didn't lead, Evans would. Jackson lunged sideways, weapon straight out.

And nearly collided with their suspect. A giant man had stepped out of the storage unit. The patrol officer aimed his flashlight at the man's face. It was smeared with blood.

CHAPTER 3

"Hands in the air!" Jackson yelled. The suspect raised his long, ape-like arms, stopping at shoulder height. Heavy eyelids half covered his dazed eyes. Jackson moved quickly behind the man. "On your knees."

"I'm not armed. Don't hurt me." The suspect dropped to one knee, then the other. Even kneeling, he was tall.

With Evans covering him, Jackson holstered his weapon and quickly cuffed the man. He thought about his stun gun, which he'd left in the car and now wished he had with him. The guy probably weighed three fifty, and even cuffed the suspect could do damage if he decided to rush them.

"You got this under control?" the patrol officer asked.

"Not yet." Jackson wished his longtime partner, Schak, was there too. Evans was smart and fast and had excellent fighting skills, but her small frame and heart-shaped face weren't intimidating. "Check the unit for anyone else. I heard crying sounds."

"That was me." The man hung his head. "I was sleeping and had nightmares."

The patrol officer stepped cautiously into the dark storage space.

"Sleeping? Is this your unit?" Jackson asked.

"Yeah, this is my home."

What the hell? How many other cold, dark storage spaces served as homes? And how long had this been going on? "What's your name?"

"Todd Sheppard."

"What happened here tonight, Todd? Why did you kill Craig Cooper?"

"I didn't." The man shook his head vehemently. "Craig was my friend."

"There's blood on your face. Just make it easy on yourself and tell me what happened."

"I had a nosebleed. I have high blood pressure."

Jackson wanted to get this suspect into a bright room where he could see his face and watch his body language. But Jackson wasn't ready to leave the crime scene. "Let's go into the office and talk."

The patrol officer stepped out of Sheppard's unit. "It's clear, but you've got to see it."

Jackson turned to Evans. "Take Mr. Sheppard to the office. I'll be there in a minute."

Disappointment registered on her face. "I'm on it."

She gestured for the suspect to get up and steered him toward the front. He was twice her size, at least six-five, and it looked a bit like a child leading an adult. A fearless child.

Jackson stepped into the storage space and switched on his flashlight. A heap of bedding took up an area near the front, but beyond that items were piled to the ceiling. Old paintings, beat-up dressers stuffed with shabby clothing, and boxes filled with pots and pans, candles, and every kind of knickknack. Jackson's first thought was that these were stolen goods. But, just as quickly, he realized this was junk, probably left at the curb by people who didn't want it. Garage sale items that hadn't sold or were priced for a nickel. One box contained packages of cookies, bread, and peanut butter. A small tire held a ceramic pot with a sickly-looking plant, and a small battery-powered lantern sat alongside the bedding.

Jackson wondered how long the man had lived like this. Where did he shower and eat most of his meals? At the Mission?

"It's kind of sad, isn't it?" The officer pointed his light at the yellowish plant.

"But it's a place to get out of the weather, and it offers more privacy than the Mission." Jackson rather admired Sheppard for trying. Unless the suspect had stabbed their victim over a broken toaster. "Let's do a quick search for the weapon, then I'll let the crime scene people know this area is next for evidence collection."

The patrol officer looked up. "Too bad there's no lightbulb in here, but I suppose that would be too expensive for the owners."

"My team will conduct a thorough search tomorrow in the daylight."

A cursory search of the bedding, boxes, and drawers produced several knives, none of which looked bloody or even damp from the rain.

"He probably tossed the murder weapon," the officer said. "I'll get back to the perimeter search."

Jackson headed for the front office. He found the first patrol officer standing outside with the owners under a halide light. Jackson realized the trailer didn't have room for them once Evans took their oversize suspect inside.

He introduced himself but didn't offer his hand and instead pulled off his latex gloves. The older gentleman said, "I'm Ezra Goldstein and this is my wife, Sally."

"Do you know the victim, Craig Cooper?"

"Not personally. He is a client though."

"What contact information do you have for him?"

Sally spoke up. "He gave us his sister's address and said he was looking for his own place." Sally handed him a piece of yellow lined paper. "I wrote it down for you."

"Thanks." Under the light, Jackson could make out the name *Jane Niven*. The woman in the photo from Cooper's wallet. "How long has Craig Cooper rented the unit from you?"

"Only about six weeks." Sally shook her head. "It's so tragic. I don't know how it happened. We have decent security."

"What about cameras?" Jackson asked.

"Just one here in front." Ezra Goldstein pointed to a camera mounted at the end of the trailer. "It records the activity at the gate near the security-code box."

"Did you know people were living in your units?"

Neither owner would meet Jackson's eyes. "We suspected," Sally finally said, "but we don't watch the security video unless something happens."

"We'll need to see the last few days. Can you save the file to a flash drive for me?"

"Of course."

"How well do you know Todd Sheppard?" Jackson had his notebook in hand but had little hope of getting answers.

"We don't know any of our customers." Ezra sounded a little defensive. "We see them when they sign up to rent a unit, then not usually again. They mail a check or use PayPal. Only a few stop in and pay in person, but they don't stay and chat."

"Do you have any idea who would want to kill Craig Cooper?"

"None." Ezra shook his head. "We haven't spoken to him since he rented the unit early last month."

"Any unusual activity around here? Or signs of stolen goods?"

"Nothing recently." Sally hugged herself against the cold. "But we don't monitor what people bring in here. How could we?"

Jackson handed her a business card. "I may have more questions after I talk to the suspect."

"We'll wait in the car."

It had started to rain again and Jackson didn't blame them. He hated to make the old couple stay out here, but this was a homicide investigation and they'd survive the inconvenience.

Inside the twenty-foot trailer, Evans paced behind the desk, and Todd Sheppard sat in the chair next to the door. Or Jackson assumed there was a chair. He couldn't actually see it. Todd's body completely covered whatever was under him. Cramped, cluttered, and illuminated only by an overhead lightbulb, the space was still better than the interrogation room at headquarters. Eventually, Jackson would take Sheppard downtown to make a formal statement, but he wanted to question him here and now, before the suspect got intimidated by the thought of incarceration. Jackson also didn't want to leave the big man unattended in the interrogation room while they verified his story. The last time he'd done that, the suspect had had a seizure.

"Want me to record this?" Evans asked. "I have a camcorder with me." From her shoulder bag, she dug out a little white device the size of a cell phone, only a little thicker. Jackson held back a smile. Evans was prepared for everything.

"Good idea." He turned to their suspect. "We're going to record your statement, all right?"

Sheppard blinked, still looking sleepy. "Okay, but I told you, I didn't do anything."

"Let's start at the beginning." Jackson took a second metal chair and turned it to face his suspect. "Where were you earlier tonight?"

"The library, then I had dinner at the free restaurant on Eighth Street."

"Did you see Craig?"

"No." Sheppard looked puzzled. "Craig works at the gas station."

"Which station?"

"Four Corners. Right down the road."

"Do you have a job?"

Sheppard shook his head. "I'm disabled."

The suspect seemed fine, but that didn't mean anything. "How are you disabled?"

"I have a brain injury from football. I forget things."

Like killing someone? Jackson wondered. "How do you pay for the space here?"

"With my disability check."

Jackson wanted to know where Sheppard collected his mail, but it wasn't important at the moment. "When did you arrive here tonight, at your storage unit?" He couldn't call it a *home.*

"I'm not sure, but it was after dark."

"When did you encounter Craig?"

"I saw someone on the ground in front of his unit, so I went over there." Sheppard's forehead creased with the memory. "Craig was dead. Someone stabbed him."

The blood on Sheppard's face had dried, but it reminded Jackson that this man was probably a killer. "Who stabbed him, Todd? Was that you? Were you mad at Craig?"

"No. I liked Craig." The suspect's face held no malice, no dishonesty.

Had he forgotten the fight or was he just a bystander . . . who happened to get a bloody nose later? "How long had you known Craig?"

"Since he moved in."

"When was that?"

"I'm not sure. A month? He was saving for an apartment."

"What did you do when you saw Craig's body?"

"I cried."

The simplicity and compassion threw Jackson off his game for a moment. This man was either a brilliant psychopath or a gentle giant. "Have you ever hurt anyone, Todd?"

"Not since I played football. And even then, I didn't mean to."

"What did you do next? After you cried for Craig?"

"I tried to help him, but he was dead. So I went to the tavern and called 911."

"You called 911 and came back here and went to sleep?"

"Yes. My brain just shuts down sometimes."

"Why didn't you give your name?"

"I didn't want any trouble."

For the moment, Jackson believed him. "Can I take a sample of the blood on your face?"

"Why?"

"I want to make sure it's not Craig's."

"It's not. I had a nosebleed."

Jackson didn't know if that was actual permission, but he dug in his carryall for a DNA swab. "I'm just going to get a little bit of the blood on the end of this stick, okay?" He moved slowly toward the man, but Sheppard didn't flinch. Still, Jackson planned to leave him handcuffed.

After he bagged the swab, he glanced at Evans. "Did you check his record?" She always had her little computer tablet with her and was quick with database searches.

Evans nodded. "No violence. Just a theft one charge long ago and a more recent public drunkenness charge."

"I wasn't drunk." Sheppard sounded upset for the first time. "They gave me the wrong medication."

"I believe you." Jackson wanted to keep him calm. "I can't let you go back into your sleeping space tonight because we still need to check out things in there. So we have two choices: jail or the Mission."

The suspect's massive body tensed. "They won't let me into the Mission this late."

"They will if we take you."

"I don't want to go to their church in the morning."

"You can leave then and come back here. We'll be done."

Sheppard scowled. "All right."

Relieved, Jackson stood. He was anxious to leave the claustrophobic trailer and felt glad he didn't have to book Sheppard into jail, a time-consuming, pointless process unless they filed homicide charges. The underfunded facility released almost everyone, so the booking process was mostly a paper trail and a place to hold the suspect for short while.

Evans clicked off her video recorder. "Do you want me to take him?"

"No. I'll send a uniform." Jackson turned to Sheppard. "Will you stay here tomorrow in case I need to talk to you again?"

"I don't like to stay inside during the day." The big man still looked upset. "But you can find me at the library or the Catholic Services Center."

"Good." Jackson gestured for him to get up and turn around. He caught himself holding his breath as he took the cuffs off. But Sheppard just shook out his hands and rubbed his wrists. The cuffs had been snug on his thick arms.

They stepped outside into the rain. The first patrol officer stoically waited for further instructions. If there had been any homes nearby, Jackson would have sent him out to pound on doors looking for witnesses who might have seen or heard something. But this wasn't a residential area and it was nearing midnight.

"I need you to take Mr. Sheppard to the Mission for the night, then go home after that."

"You sure?"

"Yes. Thanks."

"Don't forget the Goldsteins are still in their car."

The officer looked Sheppard up and down. He was probably trying to guess the suspect's weight.

Jackson turned to Evans. "Let the owners know the office is clear and they can download the security video for us. I'm going back to see what the ME has."

The report was disappointing. All Gunderson would say was that Cooper had likely been killed between six and seven, just prior to sunset, and that the stab wound appeared to have been made by someone most likely right-handed.

"There isn't much blood," the ME added. "It'll be interesting to see what his toxicology report says."

"You think he was intoxicated?"

"Maybe. Or he went into shock and died almost instantly."

Jackson remembered the ink. "What do you think of the tattoo on his left hand? Do you recognize it?"

Gunderson, on his knees next to the corpse, lifted the hand. "I think it's a prison tattoo. The clover or club represents bad luck."

Jackson wanted to search the criminal database, but he'd left his new tablet computer in the car. He'd get to it soon enough. He stood from his squat and realized his legs were tired and his hands were cold. A cup of hot coffee was imperative because this night was far from over. He looked around at the nearby businesses. Except for the tavern, they were dark. But there was a doughnut shop down the road. He would send Evans for coffee. She'd roll her eyes, then be glad for the caffeine.

"Let's wrap him up, Joe." Gunderson nodded at the evidence tech, who trotted to the van and came back with a black plastic body bag and gurney. They worked the corpse into the bag, while Jackson took a moment to strategize the next steps of the investigation. "Help us get him loaded," Gunderson said.

The three men lifted the dead man onto the gurney and slid him into the van. Jackson didn't mind assisting, but it was a little weird. Before the recession, five detectives would have been at the scene, along with three people from the crime lab, and three or four uniformed officers. He hadn't liked coordinating with that many people, but this other extreme was worse.

As the ME's van pulled away, Jackson and Joe stepped back into unit C13. They hadn't finished searching or fingerprinting before Todd Sheppard's cries had distracted them. Jackson spotted a laptop propped against the wall behind the folding chair. He picked it up and flipped it open.

Joe looked over. "What's a homeless guy doing with a laptop?"

"Entertaining himself in this dark box he called home." Jackson tried not to assume the device was stolen. "Todd Sheppard, the big guy who found the body, said Cooper had a job and was saving for an apartment."

Jackson slipped down into the camping chair, relieved to be off his feet. The laptop screen glowed in the shadows that fell outside the tripod lights. He opened a browser to see what websites the victim had visited.

The top four were Facebook. Jackson clicked open a bookmark and saw that Craig Cooper had his own page. The victim didn't have a home or a car, but he had a Facebook page. Jackson still marveled at how social networking had changed the culture and often made his job easier. With only fifteen friends, Cooper's information was easy to scan through. None of the names meant anything to him except Jane Niven, Cooper's sister. Jackson needed to contact her and let her know her brother was dead and to find out what she knew. He looked at his watch: *12:42.* Could anything be gained by waking the sister at this hour? He decided to wait until morning. As he was about to close the computer, thinking he would search more thoroughly later, Jackson changed his mind and opened the message icon.

The top text was from Jane and it had been sent two days before: *I've done everything I can do. I don't know where he is. Leave me alone about it.*

What the hell did that mean? No signature, but it was Facebook, which provided a picture of the sender. Jackson slipped out Cooper's wallet and compared photos. She was the same woman, twenty years apart. Had Cooper's sister killed him? Should he head over there now?

Instinct told him it wasn't necessary, but he knew it was more likely his exhausted bones complaining. Jackson decided to grab a couple hours of sleep and see Jane first thing in the morning. On his walk to the car, he questioned his decision. Was he willing to wait because Cooper was a homeless man who'd likely been in prison recently? If the victim had been an innocent young girl, would he be sucking down coffee and knocking on doors?

He didn't know, but it made him think about Katie being locked in the Serbu detention center instead of being home in her bed. Anguish washed over his exhausted frame.

He climbed into his car and sent Katie a text: *I love you. I'll see you at your hearing tomorrow.* A moment later, he realized they'd probably taken her phone when they booked her in.

In the morning, he would call the juvenile court and find out the time of the proceeding. For now, he texted Evans: *Let's meet back at the crime scene at nine and look at everything in the daylight.*

CHAPTER 4

Jamie Dallas smiled at the man next to her, trying to decide if she would hook up with him. The upside was the potential to find out about his involvement in an eco-terrorist attack and, more important, maybe learn what the group planned next. The downside? If they busted him and he told her supervisors they'd had sex, she might get fired. She couldn't let that happen. Being an FBI agent suited her restless, needy personality like no other job could. She loved being Agent Dallas, or just Dallas, as her coworkers called her.

"Want another beer?" Adam Greene ran his fingers through hers in a provocative way.

Her body responded with a surge of pleasure, making the decision harder. She didn't want any emotional attachment to someone she might have to arrest and send to prison. And that was why she was here, in Tony's Tavern, drinking with this man.

"Sure." Dallas massaged Adam's fingers in an equally sexy way. She needed to get inside his home for a look around, even if they didn't end up having sex. With his curly hair and thin frame, Adam wasn't her usual type, but he was open, charming, and funny in a refreshing way. "No, make that a shot of tequila." A little more social lubricant seemed appropriate. But not enough to get drunk. A fine line.

"It's going to be that kind of night?" Adam raised his eyebrows. "Why not?"

When Dallas had joined the FBI four years ago, she'd never envisioned herself in this position. But undercover work was the ultimate adrenaline high, and it had become her specialty. When she'd read the memo asking for a young, single agent willing to transfer, her whole body had responded with anticipation. The only downer had been the location: Eugene, Oregon. But the quest—infiltrate an eco-terrorist group—had been too compelling to ignore. She'd beat out three other agents who wanted the assignment. Dallas knew her gender, long hair, and good looks had given her an edge, but she still had to deliver.

After the bartender brought their drinks, Adam asked, "What are you doing this weekend, Fiona?"

Fiona B. Ingram. She loved her alias. "Nothing special. There's not much happening until April."

"We could hike the butte."

"It'll be muddy." Dallas gave him a seductive smile. "But that could be fun."

He leaned forward and whispered in her ear. "I like a woman who isn't afraid to get dirty."

She racked her brain for a comeback, and a man tapped Adam on the shoulder. "Let's go."

The man had shaggy ash-blond hair, sharp features, and was in his late twenties. Dallas recognized him from the profile photos. His name was Chris Noonaz, but everyone called him Cricket. He was the leader of an environmental group called Love the Earth. He'd been her original target, but he had a girlfriend and was harder to approach.

Adam kissed her cheek. "I've gotta talk to some people for a while, but I'll be back."

"Don't make me wait too long." Dallas poured on the charm, coming short of licking her lips.

As soon as Adam's back was turned, she pulled out her smartphone, keeping it hidden in her palm, and clicked into camera mode. She glanced up to see Adam and Cricket sit down at a table in the corner with two other guys. One was thirty or so, a big guy with a full beard and collar-length hair, and the other looked fresh out of high school. If not for his short mohawk and unshaved face, he would have seemed too young for someone plotting an act of vandalism, sabotage, or arson.

Dallas slid off the barstool and headed across the tavern. When she passed their table, she snapped a couple of pictures without turning her head, hoping her aim was accurate. The noise of the bar chatter drowned out the faint click of the camera. She would have loved to be sitting close enough to eavesdrop, but she had to be careful and move slowly to earn their trust. Cricket had seemed wary of her when she first talked to him at a Love the Earth meeting at Cozmic Pizza last month, so she'd focused on Adam instead.

She'd overheard that the group's inner core met at Tony's Tavern, so Dallas had started hanging out there. The place was old and funky, a renovated turn-of-the-century house, gutted to become a tavern with a kitchen. But in Oregon, all establishments that served alcohol were required to serve food. Another quirky little law, like the one that didn't allow people to pump their own gas. But overall, Eugene wasn't a bad place to hang out if you liked earthy people and microbrew beer. As long as she had her Kindle Fire and a connection to the internet, Dallas could be content almost anywhere . . . for a while.

In the bathroom, Dallas checked herself in the mirror, with mixed feelings. Who wouldn't want to have watermelon-pink lips, bright blue eyes, and blond hair? But she had dyed her long tresses for other assignments and discovered that people took her more seriously as a brunette. She wondered if her cheerleader looks kept her from getting certain UC jobs, and she considered cutting her hair. But she would wait until she saw the next undercover posting and found out what the role required.

The activist meeting lasted twenty minutes, and at one point Cricket and Adam argued loudly. Even if Dallas had been a lip-reader, with people milling around the conversation would have been difficult to follow. Finally, Dallas went out for a walk to stimulate her system and keep from getting too inebriated.

The central Eugene neighborhood was dark, damp, and quiet except for the rock music at Sam Bond's Garage down the street. Dallas was tempted to step in and dance for a while, but that seemed a little off task. Despite the alcohol and potential intimate encounter, she was working, as she had been for six weeks—and would continue to be for another couple of months, or longer, if needed.

When she came back into the bar, her stool was taken, but Adam was standing nearby, looking disappointed. His face brightened when he saw her. "Hey, gorgeous. Thanks for waiting."

"I almost didn't. That looked like a pretty serious meeting."

"Not really. We're just making plans for Earth Day, which is coming up next month."

"A celebration?"

"Of sorts. Let's get out of here."

"Ready." Dallas hoped he would tell her more later. She'd done her homework and knew enough about Earth Day and other environmental events to sound like an activist rather than just an average citizen who recycled and drove a fuel-efficient car and thought that was enough.

The sight of the dark parking lot gave her second thoughts. Would he want to take one car? What if he got aggressive with her when she said no at the last minute? Dallas turned toward her car. "Maybe I'd better go home."

He pushed her up against her leased Prius, grabbed her by the back of her head, and kissed her hard. His intensity set off little fireworks in her torso and she was back in. Who knew the Earth-loving hippie types had it in them? After a make-out session that left her looking around to see if anyone had reported them for public indecency, Dallas agreed to follow him to his place.

On the drive over, Dallas changed her mind again, hating the prospect of lying to her supervisors if asked about her relationship with Adam. So when they got to his place, she made a trip to the bathroom, then told him she'd started her period and couldn't have sex. He had smoked a bowl while she was out of the room and seemed disappointed but okay with her change of heart. She considered giving him a hand job, but worried the bureau would still consider that sex. Should she ask Agent River what was allowed, or was it better to just not talk about it? This was her third undercover assignment but the first time the issue of sex had come up. Hopefully, it wouldn't be the last. She loved undercover work and felt perfectly suited to it.

As a child, she'd lived out of an overnight bag, staying with her grandmother for a couple nights, then off to her aunt's house for a while, then back to her worthless drug-and-alcohol-abusing parents. After a week of watching them drink and fight, she'd call one of her relatives, pack her bag, and they'd come pick her up. She'd learned to love being anywhere but home and always looked forward to her next excursion. Sweet Aunt Lynn had enrolled her in dance classes, piano lessons, summer day camps, and eventually acting lessons, which she'd loved most of all. Dallas knew, even then, that the point had been to keep her busy and happy, so she didn't think about her crappy home life, but all of those skills had prepared her for undercover work. She could become anybody and fake her way through anything.

She and Adam talked about LTE's goal of getting plastic bags banned in Eugene, then Adam smoked another bowl while she nursed a beer. Twenty minutes later, Adam passed out in the middle of a sentence. At first Dallas was pissed that she'd made out with a stranger who didn't wear deodorant without earning a chance to probe for more information. Dallas reminded herself that undercover work took months or sometimes years, and she had to be patient.

She got up to leave, then thought, *To hell with that.* The eco-terrorists' first act had been sabotage, damage to equipment and property, but no lives at risk. What was next? And how many people might be hurt?

Dallas tiptoed into the bathroom. She planned to search Adam's personal documents as much as she could, but first she needed aspirin. The tequila would give her a headache in the morning if she didn't take something.

She looked through the medicine cabinet above the sink, surprised at how clean everything was. Why would a person who kept his bathroom this clean not wash his hair every day? She chuckled at her hypocrisy. Why would an FBI agent who had dedicated her life to her country almost hook up with a man who might be plotting to burn down a manufacturer? Everyone had their own set of contradictions.

Not finding aspirin—or anything incriminating—in the bathroom, Dallas crossed the hall into the kitchen. The small house, heated with only a woodstove, sat on the back lot of a larger piece of property. She suspected an LTE member owned the bigger house up front, and she'd made note of the address when she'd driven in. Dallas found aspirin in a cupboard, downed two, and hurried into the adjacent living room.

A coffee table crafted from a tree stump caught her eye. Beside it on the floor was a silver laptop. Did she dare? She had to. That was the goal of Downdraft, as this case had been nicknamed—to catch the perps in the act. She needed to discover what they had planned next.

She stepped back into the alcove-like hall and peeked into the bedroom. Adam was sleeping, making soft little snoring sounds. Dallas darted to the laptop, flipped it open, and powered it up. Heart hammering with anxiety, she sat on the coffee table and did a quick search for files labeled Earth Day. When Adam had said that was the topic of the meeting, she'd thought it was just a convenient cover story. But what if they were really planning something for Earth Day? Terror groups couldn't resist symbolism.

They were also prone to violence. What would Adam do if he caught her spying? Try to kill her? He and his co-conspirators faced a decade or more in federal prison if they were convicted of arson or sabotage. Judges had handed down harsh sentences to earlier eco-terrorists, so the group understood the risks, and so did she. Dallas grabbed her purse from the floor and set it on the couch next to her, so her pepper spray and small handgun would be in reach. Normally, she wore her Glock on her side, but undercover work required sacrifices, and the big semiautomatic was in her rented condo. She had a palm-size Kel-Tec in a secret compartment in the bottom of her bag, but it wasn't quick to get to. If Adam or anyone were to discover she carried a weapon, it would be a major tip-off.

The Earth Day search produced no files or folders in the dialogue box, and Dallas regretted wasting her time. The computer's desktop was clear except for the hard drive icon, so she opened the documents folder and quickly scanned labels: Photos, Games, Letters, Bills, Herbs, and a dozen more that sounded equally benign. She glanced up at the hallway. What if Adam caught her? What would she say? *I'm a compulsive snoop; it doesn't mean anything.* What would the group do if they figured out she was with the FBI? Were they any less dangerous than a drug cartel or biker gang?

Unable to stop herself, Dallas opened the Herbs folder on the chance that it might be code for environmental remedies, but it contained mostly PDFs with herbal research. She remembered the seminar on codes from her training and began keying in possibilities: *Christmas, Easter, fireworks, birthday.* Nothing. Dallas keyed in all the months and got nowhere. Think! Love the Earth was modeling its activities on a previous group, the Earth Liberation Front, so maybe Adam had used something connected to its role model. She tried *ELF, elves, magic, second chance, repeat,* then finally, *replay.*

Yes!

The dialogue box began loading with documents. She spotted the name JB Pharma, but before she had a chance to open it, a cell phone rang in the bedroom. *Oh fuck!* Her heart slammed into her rib cage as Dallas closed the dialogue box and held down the power-off button. The next time Adam turned it on, the computer might announce that it hadn't been shut down properly, but she didn't have time to go through the steps. Dallas snapped the lid closed, set the laptop on the floor where she'd found it, and hustled toward the bedroom.

She stepped in just as Adam groped for his pants and pulled the phone from a pocket. He put the cell to his ear and said hello without looking up. Dallas slipped back out just as quickly. A late-night call could be anything, but she might as well listen, in case it was important.

After a moment, she heard Adam say, "What the fuck?"

A pause, then, "I'm home, of course."

A brief silence, followed by, "Why? You think I did it? Acting on my own?" Adam sounded hurt and angry.

What the hell was going down?

"I'll send you a fucking picture of me sitting here naked, and I've got company who'll vouch for me."

Time to move. Dallas slipped into the kitchen and turned on the water, so he could hear it, then drank another glass before heading toward the bedroom. She paused in the open door and waited for him to look up. Her pulse was still throbbing in her ears, but she smiled. "Do you need more privacy?"

He nodded, so she went back to the living room and picked up her purse. Inside it, her *Fiona* phone buzzed with a text message. Dallas dug it out and stared at the caller ID: *Aunt Carla.* Code name for Agent River, her lead on this case. What the hell had gone down tonight? Dallas shouldered her purse and hurried for the bathroom, locking it behind her.

The text said: *Breakfast tomorrow?* That meant they needed to meet first thing in the morning. Dallas took three long, slow breaths and willed herself to feel calm. She would kiss Adam good-bye and simply say she had to go.

He was off the phone when she came back in. Seeing the tense look on his face, she decided to keep her distance. "It's a good thing your phone woke me; I really need to go home."

"That's cool. I've got to go help a friend."

So he was going somewhere. As she walked out, Dallas plotted where she would park her car and wait for him to leave. Wherever he was headed, she would follow and find out.

CHAPTER 5

Carla River finished reading the chapter out loud and closed the book. "That's it for tonight." Reluctant to leave, she added, "What do you think? Do you like this one as much as the first book?" Recently, she'd read most of *The Hunger Games* to this trio of homeless teenagers, and now they were reading *Catching Fire*.

"Sort of." June, a plump girl with a shaved head, sat up, looking serious. "I don't like the violence, and I'm not sure we should be reading it."

"Why not?" Saul argued. "It's better than watching violent movies or playing video games." A lanky boy of sixteen, Saul sat on the floor by the narrow bed. June had earned her own space in the shelter, partitioned by heavy sliding curtains, which gave them some privacy. Saul was still a drifter, who didn't stay at the facility every night, so he had to sleep on a cot in the big room.

"I agree with Saul," Molly added. "Reading about violence doesn't make anyone more dangerous. In fact, I think stories like these teach us a better way to live." Molly, the third teenager in their group, wanted to be a writer and was working on an urban fantasy story. River was glad the girl had never asked her to read it.

They all looked at her to voice an opinion.

"I'm inclined to think Saul is right, in that reading is better than watching, which can make you desensitized to violence and cruelty." River struggled to find the best way to phrase her thoughts. These kids were so impressionable, and she didn't want to turn them off reading. "As long as you're aware of how you're reacting to what you read, then its ability to influence your behavior is minimal. But good books should make you think."

"What about people who aren't aware?" June argued. "Millions of kids have read this. How many are discussing the sick premise and what it means?"

"I think a lot of them are." River smiled at June. She loved the girl's sense of worry about the world. "But we can switch to another book if the others agree." After River's father went to prison for killing thirteen women, and her mother committed suicide, River had lived on the streets as a teenager, and her survival had cost her dearly. She knew what teenagers had to do just to eat and sleep out of the weather. Once River had settled into her life as an FBI agent, she'd started volunteering to mentor teens in homeless shelters. She couldn't be as consistent as she wanted, but she did what she could.

As the other two kids voiced their objection to switching stories, River's work phone rang. She kept its ringtone distinctive from her personal cell, which rarely received calls. Sliding the phone from her jacket pocket, she looked at the caller ID: *Denise Lammers*. "Excuse me," she said and stepped out of the curtained space. The noise from the rec room forced her down the hall to the bathroom, a gender-neutral facility with a shower in the corner. Coming here always gave her flashbacks to her teenage homeless days.

She popped in her earpiece and clicked receive. "Agent Rivers."

"It's Sergeant Lammers. We had a firebomb at the Rock Spring bottling company tonight. It's probably an eco-terrorist, so I thought the FBI should take the lead."

River's pulse quickened. *Their perps were escalating!* "Was anyone hurt?" The group had sabotaged a pharmaceutical company two months before without any violence.

"I don't know yet," Lammers said. "I sent out two detectives, Schak and Quince, but it's only been a few minutes. I called you right away."

"Thanks. I'll head out there." River started to click off, then asked, "You said firebomb. Is the factory burning?" River wondered how much evidence would be left to work with.

"Dispatch didn't report it one way or another."

"The business is off Laurel Hill Drive, correct?" River was still learning her way around Eugene.

"Yes. Take the freeway to the Glenwood exit."

"I'll be in touch." River hung up, stopped in and said good night to the teens, then jogged for her car. Excitement pulsed in her veins, a feeling she loved and had come to live for. Turning it off had become the problem. She'd thought the transfer from Portland to Eugene would settle down her career and give her more of a nine-to-five job, but that hadn't been the case. In the six months she'd been in town, she'd already handled a ransom kidnapping and had a shootout with a man wanted on sex trafficking charges. Now she and an undercover agent were tracking an eco-terrorist, and if they didn't stop him soon, people would get hurt.

The bottling plant nestled into the side of a hill at the edge of the city limits. River had heard that springwater flowed freely on the property, and the company pumped it to the surface, poured it into plastic bottles, and sold it for a premium. She didn't understand why an eco-terrorist would target the company, but the saboteur had probably let the owner know what his grievance was. River spotted the parking lot filled with first-responder vehicles—police cars, fire trucks, and an ambulance—and knew she was in the right place. She also noticed a box-shaped reinforced vehicle and figured it had to be the police department's Explosive Disposal Unit.

Relieved that she didn't see flames, River parked along the arterial road and walked toward the chaos. Cops and firemen stood around, but there wasn't much activity. She was likely the first federal agent on the scene. The giant overhead door was open, and a fire hose snaked into the building. River approached a cluster of men near a small door at the end of the building, recognizing the barrel-shaped body of Detective Rob Schakowski. The male domination in law enforcement never intimidated her. Until recently, she'd been one of them. Now she was a tall, broad-shouldered woman with a strong-featured face.

The men turned at the sound of her footsteps. The halide lights from the top of the building cast shadows that made their faces seem tense and creepy. Schak said, "Agent River. Good to have you. I figured this was a federal case. I'm not even sure this property is within city limits."

River noticed the gorgeous Detective Quince and nodded at him too. "What are the details?" She clicked on the recorder in her pocket, not wanting to take notes in the dark, wet parking lot.

"The night watchman, Jerry Bromwell"—Schak gestured to the civilian across from him—"heard someone in the building, confronted him, then escaped just before the firebomb went off."

"You're calling it a firebomb. Has someone identified the device?" River would get to the witness in a minute.

"We did." The big man next to Quince reached out to shake her hand. "Sergeant Bruckner, EPD SWAT commander. We found the remnants of an incendiary device. Its primary purpose was to start a fire, but it didn't do much damage, because most of the building is metal."

"I'm familiar with the mode. A similar device was used as a distraction at a protest outside Pan Pacific Oil in Portland last year." River stopped herself from saying more. She'd been working the local case for six weeks now, and she wasn't authorized to talk about the investigation. "I'd like to take the evidence back to the federal building."

"ATF will want it," the firefighter captain said. River hadn't caught his name. "They've got someone coming down from Portland."

"ATF can get it from us. Our bomb tech needs to see it first." These investigations involved so many departments, it was confusing and counterproductive. River wished they would consolidate all the federal law-enforcement agencies into a single department the way countries like Germany and Japan did.

"You work it out then. "Sergeant Bruckner shrugged. "The evidence is in the truck. I'll get it for you."

"Thanks. I'd need to go in and see the location now."

"Not yet. The explosives unit is still searching for more devices. It should be clear soon." Bruckner turned and strode toward the reinforced vehicle.

River looked at Quince and Schak. "Who owns this company?"

"Ted Rockman. He's a state senator, and this is just one of his businesses."

"Is he here?"

"No one has been able to reach him."

"Do you have his number?"

"I'll text it to you." Quince completed the task while River talked.

"Do you have any insights or observations I should know about?"

"You have to consider the possibility of an inside job," Schak said. "The perp came in through a supposedly locked door."

"That one?" River pointed at the standard-size door nearby.

"Yes." Jerry Bromwell, the night watchman, spoke up. He was in his late thirties, with a face that had been attractive before he lost his back teeth. "The overhead door didn't open, and that's the only other way in."

River was ready to question him at length, but it had started to rain and she wasn't dressed for it. "Let's go sit in my car while you answer some questions."

Bromwell's eyes flashed wide, and she wondered why that worried him. River turned to the detectives. How to put this diplomatically? "We're already tracking a local group we think might be responsible. There's no need for the Eugene Police Department to spend its scarce resources on this case."

Schak grinned. "You're telling us to go home?"

River smiled back. "I'm suggesting that you can."

"Then I'm out of here." Schak fist-bumped Quince's shoulder. "You should go too."

Quince didn't move. "I worked a bombing at the Planned Parenthood a few years ago with Agent Fouts, so if you need me, I'd like to be on the task force."

"I appreciate that. I'll set up a meeting for tomorrow and let you know when."

They all headed for their cars, but River stopped and signed for the transfer of the bomb evidence. The parts now fit into a small plastic bag that she tucked into her briefcase. "Thanks, Bruckner. I'm setting up a task force meeting tomorrow, if you want to be there. Your experience could be helpful."

"I'll check with my supervisor."

Next to her, coatless and hatless, Jerry Bromwell shivered in the rain.

"I'll be in touch." River nodded at the sergeant, then grabbed the witness' elbow. "Let's go."

On the way, he mumbled, "I already gave my statement to the detective."

"That's fine. We'll do it again. We often get more information with each session."

In the car, she started the engine and cranked up the heater for Bromwell. River pulled off her coat, knowing she'd be sweating in a moment. She twisted sideways in her seat to face her witness and started a new recording. "How long have you worked for Rock Spring?" If the bomber had inside help, the night watchman was a good candidate.

"Two years. Why?"

"I'm going to ask a lot of questions. They're all important. Please just answer them."

"Fine."

"Where were you when you heard the intruder?"

"In the office. It's upstairs in the back of the factory."

"Were you alone?"

He blinked rapidly. "Of course. Why?"

River pulled in a breath of patience. "First, I think you just lied to me. And second, do not ask me *why* again. I want to know everything. It's how I do my job."

She stared at him until he finally mumbled, "It's an old habit. My wife is nosy."

"Who was with you in the office?"

How does she know?

Bromwell's lips didn't move, but River heard the question anyway—a panicked cry that crossed the space between them without being uttered out loud.

"Who is she?"

Bromwell blinked and stammered. "No one. I told you. The second shift leaves at seven thirty, and I'm alone until the day shift comes in at five."

River let it go for now. She would circle back when he was feeling less guarded. "How did the intruder get into the building?"

He squirmed in his seat. "I don't know. He couldn't have used the overhead door because I would have heard it open. And the man-door is always locked and you need the code to open it."

"Do you know the code?"

"Of course."

"Who else does?"

"The owner and the shift leaders. There could be more, but I don't know."

"There's no other entry?"

"There's an emergency exit in the back, but it's a one-way door with no handle on the outside."

River made a mental note to examine it for pry marks. "Where did the sound of the intruder come from?"

"Downstairs, but that's all I could tell. At first I thought it was the foreman coming back for something, so I headed down."

"What happened next?"

"I called 911 as soon as I saw him."

"Where was he?"

"In the little hallway leading to the break room."

"What was he wearing?"

"All black, with a black ski mask."

It was the first time anyone had seen the potential eco-terror-ist, and River was disappointed not to get a description "Did he notice you?" She had some concern for Bromwell's safety.

"Yeah. He tried to run past me and I grabbed him." Bromwell gestured with a clenched hand. "I tried to cuff him with the plas-tic slip cuffs they issued me, but the prick hit me and ran off." Bromwell paused.

River sensed he wanted praise. "That was brave, but maybe not a good idea."

The night watchman's face fell. "I didn't go after him because I saw the bomb, and I wasn't sure what to do."

"What did you do?"

A slight pause. "I ran from the building."

His story didn't sit right with her, and River returned to the idea that he had someone with him. But she needed physical details first. "Tell me about the guy in the ski mask. How tall was he?"

"Big guy. Maybe six-two and muscular. He had forty pounds on me and I weigh two hundred."

Here we go, River thought. The watchman wanted to make himself feel better about running away. "This is critical," she said. "Without a description of his face or ethnicity, we need to know his exact size and shape."

Bromwell bristled. "I told you. He's at least six-two and two-forty. And strong."

River studied the witness' face. No bruises or red marks. Was he exaggerating? "Where did the attacker hit you?"

He patted his chest. "Right here."

"So he ran out, and you looked at the bomb. Where was it?"

"On the floor in the hallway."

"You recognized it?"

"Oh yeah. It was obvious."

"What did it look like?"

"A shiny metal thing attached to a stick of dynamite."

The metal cylinder had likely held a flammable liquid that burned when the dynamite exploded. Sweat began to roll down her chest into her bra. Time to switch gears. "Have you heard of the group Love the Earth?"

Bromwell shrugged. "I think I've seen the name in the paper."

"Do you know any of its members?"

"No. Why?"

She let that one go. "What are your environmental politics?"

He narrowed his eyes in irritation, but worry lines appeared on his forehead. "I don't know what you mean. I recycle at home, but I'm not a nutcase about it."

"What else can you tell me? Any sign that the perp had been here before?"

He thought for a moment. "I don't think so."

"Any threats? Letters, e-mails, or texts complaining about the company?"

"We had some protestors last year, but that's all I know about. The owner recently added the night watch shift, so he must have been worried."

"When did that shift start?"

"Two weeks ago."

"Do you know the owner?"

"I see him at the Christmas banquets. Nice guy."

"Okay, Jerry. We'll wrap this up. But as soon as the building is cleared, I'm going in there to look around. And if you had company tonight, I'll find evidence of that. And tomorrow, I'll arrest you for obstruction of justice." She patted his arm. "Anything you want to tell me now?"

A long pause. "No."

River stuffed the bomb evidence under her seat, they climbed out, and she locked the car.

"Can I go home?"

"Yes, but I'll want to talk again tomorrow."

The rain had let up, and River felt strangely energized. This was the kind of case she loved. Tracking a perpetrator who kept hitting new targets and taking more risks until they caught him. It was usually a bank robber, but she would enjoy this challenge. She had worked a similar eco-terrorist case in Portland, which was why her new boss had assigned this one to her.

River called the owner, Ted Rockman, left him an urgent message, then jogged back toward the building, ready to take a look inside. But first she had to examine the entry door and see just how secure it was.

The man-sized door had an electronic lock, operated by a key code. Anyone who knew the code could enter. She pulled out her recorder and made a verbal note to ask the owner for a list of everyone who knew the code and how often it was changed. The idea of an insider intrigued her. River was reminded of the animal-rights activists who went to work for the poultry or pork companies to secretly record what they considered to be atrocious conditions. She admired their dedication to their cause. But she still didn't understand the hostility toward the bottled water company.

Had anyone dusted the entry for prints? River had called one of the bureau's evidence technicians on the way over and left a message, but she hadn't heard back or seen him yet. River took pictures of the door and key code, and headed toward the open overhead door in the middle of the building. She nearly bumped into a tall Asian woman wearing a long black raincoat and carrying a large dark case.

"Excuse me. I'm Agent River."

"Jasmine Parker, with EPD crime lab."

"Sergeant Lammers called you out?"

"She called everyone." Jasmine's face was expressionless, but her eyes held mirth.

River smiled. "I appreciate you working tonight. Someone from our evidence response team should be here soon too. Please coordinate with him and let me know what you find." River handed her a business card.

"I will." The tall woman stepped under the door's awning to get out of the rain. "Good luck."

"Thanks." River never counted on luck to solve her cases, but every law enforcement officer knew that serendipity often played a role in their outcomes.

The fire trucks left the parking lot as River approached the overhead door. Bruckner gave her the signal that she could enter the building. The stench of burned wood and metal made her eyes water, but at first glance she didn't see any damage. The bottling lines were intact, and she wouldn't be surprised to hear they were back in operation soon.

Past the conveyor belts, she spotted the burned area near a short hallway. Unlike the high-ceilinged metal exterior, the interior rooms had been constructed of wood and drywall, and the perp had placed the device strategically to start a fire. Two men stood at the edge of the blackened area, pointing and talking. River introduced herself, then learned that the older man was the fire chief and the stout guy with the sideburns was a police sergeant with specialized training in explosive devices.

"What have we got?" she asked.

"An incendiary device set off by a homemade detonator," the fire chief said. "A crude but effective firebomb."

"The night watchman saw a metal cylinder attached to a stick of dynamite. Have you seen anything like it used here locally before?"

"No."

The bomb expert added, "We haven't had any eco-terrorism in Eugene since the feds convicted most of the Earth Liberation Front. But your office would know more about that."

"The key word there is *most*," River said. "We believe three members left the country and are still at large. It wouldn't surprise me to discover they'd come home." The international organization had contained a subgroup that lived mostly in and around Eugene, but they had damaged lumber mills, ranger stations, and other targets all over Oregon and Washington. In Eugene, they'd burned a car lot full of gas-guzzling SUVs.

"Bastards." The fire chief almost spit the word.

"What else can you tell me?"

"Not much until we analyze the evidence and see what liquid was used."

The bureau would do that at Quantico. "Show me the fire's point of origin."

The fire chief led her across the blackened floor and down the short hallway. "I believe the perp placed the incendiary device about here."

A chunk of wall was completely burned out, leaving only the metal trusses on the concrete floor.

"He chose this spot because of the wood and drywall, I assume." River was looking for confirmation.

"Looks like it. I don't think he expected the whole place to burn, just to do some damage."

"He may not have expected anyone to be here," River added. "The watchman said he's only been on shift overnight for two weeks."

"So the owner was expecting trouble."

"Could be." River was ready to move on. "I think I'll look at the emergency exit, then head up to the office."

She located the back door by the glow of the red sign in an otherwise dark area stacked with boxes. They'd left a path to the door, but just barely. River stopped five feet out, got on her knees, and shined a flashlight on the cement in front of the door. No footprints. Even if they had dried in the last hour or two, the dirt outlines would have still been there. She took photos of the floor, then pushed open the door and braced for an alarm.

None sounded. She would have to ask if there actually was an alarm and, if so, who had disabled it. A small light above the door gave her some illumination, but she ran her flashlight along the seal. There were no signs of the emergency exit having been pried open from the outside.

As she climbed the stairs to the office, River felt weary for the first time that evening. It was a good sign and she hoped she would sleep well when she finally got home. The rectangular room had a long window overlooking the factory floor but otherwise was utilitarian with dirty white paint, fluorescent lights, and cheap desks. Only the couch gave it a comfortable touch, and the first thing River noticed was a pair of men's underwear stuffed between the cushions.

So she'd been right. Jerry Bromwell had company when the intruder broke in. Who was she and why had he lied?

CHAPTER 6

Craig Cooper's sister lived in central Eugene, a few blocks from the library, in one of the few adobe houses in town. Even in the predawn darkness, thanks to the shift from daylight saving time, Jackson noticed the smooth exterior, curved-edged windows, and peculiar roofline. He stopped to read the sign at the edge of the walkway: *Jane Niven, Spiritual Guide.*

Oh crap. Woo-woo types drove him crazy. Whenever the department asked for the public's help, they always got calls from the genuine crazies and a few from the borderline types who thought they communicated with the dead. He prayed Jane Niven was neither.

At the door, he squared his shoulders and took a deep breath before knocking. The tall cup of Italian coffee he'd drank on the way over hadn't kicked in yet, and the three hours of sleep he'd managed to get hadn't done much except remind him that he was tired. He waited a few minutes, then pounded again. A single-seat electric car was in the driveway, so he assumed someone was home.

Finally, he called out, "Eugene Police."

Two minutes later, a long-haired woman in a lime-green bathrobe opened the door. "What's wrong? What the hell time is it? Let me see your badge." The words came at him quickly yet had a sleepy, surreal tone.

"Jane Niven?"

"Yes." She flipped on the porch light, and he could see that she had the same narrow nose and mouth as her brother.

"Detective Jackson, Eugene Police. I'm here about your brother, Craig Cooper. May I come in?"

Her rounded shoulders sagged even lower. "Damn. I thought he was going to make it this time."

Jane walked away but didn't close the door, so Jackson followed her inside. She moved into a galley kitchen and turned on more lights. "It's not even seven. No wonder I'm half asleep." She turned to face him. "I'm making coffee. Whatever you want to know about Craig will have to wait until I can at least smell it."

When she had a pot brewing, they sat at a small round table with a flowered fabric cover.

"What is it this time? Did he relapse?" Jane's brow creased. "I've seen no signs that he was using."

Jackson didn't know how to ease into it. "Ms. Niven, I'm sorry to inform you that Craig is dead."

She tightened her robe and crossed her arms. Her eyes teared up but she didn't cry. After a minute, the sister said, "Long ago, when he was a homeless meth user, I braced myself for this. I promised myself I would never cry for him again."

Jane jumped up and lurched to the coffeepot. With a shaking hand, she poured two cups and set them on the table.

Jackson wanted to focus on something positive to put her at ease, but he reminded himself that she was a primary suspect. "You asked if Craig had relapsed. Does that mean he got clean for a while?"

"Prison will do that for you." She closed her eyes and gulped coffee as if it were a religious experience. "How did he die? An overdose?"

"He was stabbed, but we don't know who did it yet. I'm hoping you can help us." Jackson usually didn't drink out of open containers offered by witnesses or suspects, but he'd watched her make the coffee. It smelled incredible, and his body craved caffeine. He took a sip and waited to see what information Jane would offer, but she was focused on her coffee.

"What did Craig go to prison for?" Jackson had learned the basics from a database search late the night before, but it was always interesting to hear personal versions.

"Armed robbery." Jane shook her head. "It was the meth. The drug changed him. Craig wasn't a violent man."

"When did he get out?" Jackson remembered the tattoo on the victim's hand.

"A couple months ago." A stray tear escaped her brimming eyes. "I thought he was doing fine. He had a job, he was checking in with his parole officer and saving for an apartment."

"When did you see him last?"

"Thursday. He was here for dinner."

"How did he seem and what did he talk about?"

"He was fine. He talked about wanting a new job because the smell of gas gave him headaches, but he seemed upbeat."

Time to get to the heart of it. "Who was he looking for?"

She blinked and took a sip of coffee. "What do you mean?"

Jackson slipped Cooper's laptop out of his carryall. "You sent Craig a message saying you couldn't find someone and to leave you alone. What was that about?" Jackson opened the saved Facebook page. He didn't want Jane to waste time denying knowledge of the issue, whatever it was.

"Craig wanted me to contact Danny Brennan, one of the men he committed the robbery with."

"He wasn't apprehended?"

"Danny was caught before Craig." Jane sighed and rubbed her face. "I don't want to talk about this. It's too painful."

"I sympathize, but it could be connected to Craig's death."

"That seems unlikely."

Time for a little pressure. "Where were you last night between six and seven?"

"Seriously? You think I could have killed my brother?"

"Where were you?"

"I had dinner out with a friend, then I came home."

"What time did you leave the restaurant?"

"About eight." Jane stood and poured herself more coffee. "This is a waste of time."

"Then let's move through it quickly. Show me what you were wearing last night."

She shuddered, but headed out of the kitchen and down a hallway. Jackson followed, noticing that her living room had thick carpet and lots of pillows on the floor around a central low table. Did she conduct séances?

Jane turned into a bedroom, flipped open a laundry basket, and pulled out a skirt and sweater. She shoved them at Jackson. "See? No blood. I had no reason to kill my brother."

The pink sweater and gray wool skirt smelled like incense, but held no stains. That also didn't prove anything. She could have thrown away yesterday's clothes, but Jackson didn't have enough reason to start looking in neighborhood trash cans. Not with

Todd Sheppard, who lived a hundred feet away from the victim, having blood on his face. "Let me see your hands."

Jane held them out. Her bony fingers were covered with rings—oversize silver and copper creations—and the backs of her hands were freckled and scarred. A bandage covered her right pinkie, but otherwise she had no visible wounds.

"What happened there?" Jackson gestured at the bandage.

"I cut myself opening a can of soup yesterday."

"Let's sit back down. I need you to tell me about Danny Brennan and why your brother wanted to contact him." At the table, he took out his recorder.

She crossed her arms and leaned back. "I don't expect this to go well."

Jackson suppressed his irritation. "Just tell me."

A long moment. "Danny Brennan is dead, but Craig thought we could find out where the money is."

The two concepts clashed in Jackson's head, then he remembered Jane was a woo-woo. *Oh boy.* "You were trying to contact Danny's spirit to ask him where he stashed the robbery money?" Jackson tried to remember the old case. He didn't usually work robberies, and there had been so many over the years.

"Yes," Jane said, "and I failed. Danny's been dead for nine years, so I wasn't optimistic. And if a spirit doesn't want to communicate, there's nothing I can do." She folded her hands together in earnest.

Jackson couldn't believe he was having this conversation. He was glad Evans wasn't there. She would have snorted coffee on the woman. "But Craig wanted you to keep trying? How much money was it?"

"A hundred and twenty-five thousand. Craig said he wanted to find it and turn it in to the bank."

Jackson suppressed a scoffing sound. If he unraveled this thread far enough, he might find the killer and the cash. "Tell me what happened. How did Danny die?"

"I wasn't there, but Craig said Danny was carrying the money when they left the bank, then Danny ditched Craig almost immediately." Jane twisted a strand of long hair. "The police caught Danny soon after and killed him. But the money was never recovered."

Now Jackson remembered more about the case. Detective Dragoo had shot the perp when he'd pulled a gun. They'd searched Brennan's apartment—and everywhere—but the cash had never turned up. The next day, detectives had arrested Craig Cooper and questioned a third man. *Oh yeah. Danny's brother.* "What happened to Danny's brother?"

Jane shook her head. "I don't know. I haven't seen Patrick since Craig's trial. Patrick always claimed the police took the money."

Typical lowlife bullshit, Jackson thought. Patrick had probably been involved in the robbery and kept the money himself. "Do you know where Patrick is?"

She looked upset. "Why would I? They were Craig's drug buddies and partners in crime. I had nothing to do with them."

"But you spent time with your brother after he was released?"

"Craig had started a new life. He was clean and working a job." After a long sip of coffee and what looked like an internal conversation with herself, Jane finally said, "But I didn't let him stay here. I felt guilty about him living in that storage unit, but I had to make sure he wasn't going to relapse and cause me trouble."

"That's understandable."

"I did give him my old laptop, so he could play games and surf the internet when he could piggyback on someone's wireless.

I helped him set up a Facebook page so we could chat sometimes. I was the only real friend he had." Jane burst into tears.

As uncomfortable as her grief made him, Jackson was relieved to see she still cared about her brother. He'd recently reconnected with his own brother after a ten-year estrangement, and it had deepened his appreciation for long-term family ties.

He gave Jane a moment and stepped into the living room. The walls were covered in a creamy, textured paper, and bamboo plants were everywhere. Combined with the floor seating, the overall effect seemed Japanese. Except the art prints, which portrayed benevolent spirits. To each his own.

When her sobs subsided, Jackson went back to the table. "Was Craig trying to find Patrick too? Had he contacted him?"

"I don't know. Patrick always denied any part in the robbery, but nobody believed him."

"Did Craig ever implicate him?"

"No."

Jackson thought it was a good possibility that either Patrick had come looking for Craig after he got out of prison, or that Craig had gone looking for Patrick. One of them had the money, and they both wanted their share. Jackson would have to dig up the old files and talk to the detectives who'd handled the case. It would be nice to solve this murder and pin it on a man who'd skirted the justice system for too long. They might even recover some of the money. Time to wrap up this interview. "Do you know anyone else who might have wanted to kill your brother?"

"His ex-wife hates him, but that was long ago."

"What's her name?"

"Dora Cooper. Or it was. I don't know anything about her life now."

"Do you know how to contact her?" Jackson clicked off his recorder.

Jane stood. "I have an old phone number, but I doubt it's good anymore. Everyone has a cell phone now, and I haven't been in touch with Dora in ages."

Jackson followed her to a small back office, where Jane dug through a desk drawer. She produced an old address book with a phone number, then dug around some more. She turned and handed him a red envelope. "Here's a Christmas card Dora sent me a few years ago. It has a return address."

Jackson thanked her, expressed his condolences for her loss, and headed out. In his car, he called the juvenile justice court clerk. "This is Wade Jackson. I'm calling about my daughter, Katie Jackson. Does she have a hearing today?" Words he never thought he'd have to say.

"Just a moment." The clerk took her time. "It's at one thirty."

"Thank you." He clicked off and sat for a moment, willing the anxiety to leave his body. Katie would get through this. She just needed a treatment program and some intensive counseling. He'd taken her to a grief counselor, but after one session she'd refused to go back, calling it "pointless." Then Katie had started drinking and staying out late with people he didn't know. He'd tried to keep her busy with movies, shopping, and board games at home, but it had driven them both crazy. They weren't used to that much time together, and the more time Jackson had spent with her, the angrier she'd become. Katie blamed him for her mother's death, and he couldn't argue the point. He'd mistakenly shot his ex-wife while trying to rescue her from a kidnapper.

Jackson pushed all of it from his mind. Thinking and worrying and planning hadn't done any good. He would ask for the court's help today. For now, he had to check in with his boss before meeting Evans back at the crime scene for a daylight view.

CHAPTER 7

Wednesday, March 13, 6:30 a.m.

River turned off the radio and forced herself to sit up. Three hours of sleep was not enough and never would be, no matter how many times she'd gotten by on it. She skipped her morning yoga and headed straight for the shower. The family room where she normally did her yoga routine was being remodeled and currently didn't have flooring. The thought reminded her that she'd seen her contractor's van in a pullout just down the road from her house—at three in the morning when she'd finally made it home. What was that about? Had Jared been too tired to drive home?

She dressed in dark slacks and a peachskin jacket that hid her somewhat androgynous body, made a strong cup of tea, and warmed up leftover chicken marsala for breakfast. While eating, she checked her work phone for messages. Jamie Dallas, her undercover agent on the Downdraft case, had texted her at 2:27

a.m., and she'd missed it. The text said simply: *I have Cricket's address!*

River texted back: *Meet at Glenwood Cafe on Will. at 10.*

The young woman was making fast progress. Dallas had only been in town six weeks, but she'd already earned the attention and trust of Adam Greene, a prominent LTE member. River was eager to meet with Dallas this morning and find out if she knew anything about the firebomb incident.

The doorbell rang, and River reflexively checked her weapon. It had to be Jared Koberman, the handyman she'd hired to remodel her entire house. River headed for the front door.

She'd only been in Eugene six months, after transferring from the Portland office where she'd worked for years. Her transition from Carl to Carla had been liberating—like taking off an ill-fitting disguise she'd been wearing her whole life—but it had also made her a target of coworker harassment. Even though only a few agents had given her a hard time, River had decided that a new location to go with her new identity would give her a clean start. The heart attack that had triggered her lifestyle change turned out to be a blessing.

She glanced at the camera monitor, saw that it was Jared, and pulled open the door. "Good morning."

He smiled, and her core temperature rose. She loved Jared's weary but honest blue eyes, his trim mustache—which law enforcement men never wore—and his strong jaw line. His wrinkles didn't matter.

"Good morning, River." He stepped in carrying a toolbox, a leather tool belt, and a thermos. "What's wrong?" he asked a second later.

"Nothing. Just not enough sleep." She gestured toward the kitchen. "Can I talk to you for a minute?" River made another cup of tea but didn't offer Jared any. He had coffee in his thermos and would say no thanks, as always.

He looked worried as he sat down. "Did I leave too much dust yesterday after I pulled out the old carpet?"

"No. Your work here is great. I'm just wondering why I saw your van beside the road late last night."

Jared looked down, shifted in his chair, then finally met her eyes. "I told you I was losing my house?" He said it like a question.

"I remember." He'd also told her his business had almost gone under during the recession.

"They finally evicted me. A place I had lined up fell through, so I put my stuff in storage, and I'm sleeping in my van for now."

Now River understood why he'd been working late every night and seemed reluctant to leave. "I'm sorry to hear that."

"It should be temporary."

"You don't have any family you can stay with for a few weeks?"

"Not really. My sister is here in town, but she's already got a full house."

River's impulse was to invite him to stay with her in the interim, but her law enforcement brain kicked in and said, *Are you crazy?*

He stood. "I should get to work. I won't park out there if it bothers you, but I hate to waste my time and gas money driving back and forth."

"It doesn't bother me. In fact, you can park right in the drive-way." She'd only known him for a month, but she trusted Jared. She'd run a background check before hiring him, then eventually, she'd let him work in her house even when she wasn't home. It was the only way the entire remodel would ever get done. The only possessions she really cared about were her Glock, her

Honda Element, and her computers—all of which she took with her every day.

"Thank you." Jared's voice had a little catch in it. "I appreciate that. I should have a new place soon."

River stood to leave. "I'll see you this evening." She knew her colleagues would find it unsettling that she trusted this guy, but River had learned to rely on her instincts about people. The only person she'd ever been wrong about was her father, Gabriel Barstow, who turned out to be a serial killer. Though even as a child, she'd known something was off about him. Like the way he never hugged her or looked directly in her eyes. As a young boy, she'd thought it was mostly her father's discomfort with people of his own gender, but then the FBI had shown up to search their basement and she'd realized the terrible truth.

As she grabbed her briefcase and headed out, River remembered the warning her father had sent from prison six weeks earlier. An inmate he'd pissed off had threatened to "ruin her" as a way of retaliating against the old man. The inmate's name had seemed familiar, and River had looked up Darien Ozlo and discovered she'd been on the FBI team that had sent him to prison for extortion and assault. For weeks after receiving her father's letter, River had been on guard, keeping an eye out for lurking strangers or cars following her home, but so far, the threat hadn't materialized. She'd made a few calls and found out Ozlo had checked in with his parole officer after being released, so River was inclined to think his threat had been hot air and posturing. Or maybe her father had made it up just to get her attention after River had ignored him for a decade.

In her office, River prepped for the task force meeting later that morning. She pulled all her case notes together, then listened to her interview with Jerry Bromwell, the night watchman at Rock

Spring. Despite his denial, her priority was to find who he'd gotten naked with in the office and figure out whether that person had left the exterior door open for the bomber to enter the factory. She also had to check Bromwell's connections to see if he knew anyone in Love the Earth, or ELF Lite, as the FBI jokingly called it. The group seemed to be modeling itself after the Earth Liberation Front, a radical wing of environmentalists that had done millions in damage in the mid-nineties. Until recently, LTE had limited itself to protesting, tree sitting, and other obnoxious but harmless activities. Then, in January, a pipe carrying waste sludge from JB Pharma's manufacturing plant had been sabotaged. Love the Earth hadn't publicly taken responsibility for it, but the bureau had reason to suspect the group and had established Downdraft, with River heading the investigation. Her first step had been to put out a nationwide memo asking for a young agent willing to do undercover work in Eugene.

River's desk phone rang and she picked up. Their front office person said, "Ted Rockman is here to see you."

"Send him in."

River stepped out of her office so he would see her from the front area. Tall and lean, Rockman came toward her with long strides and stiff-shouldered confidence. He wore his dyed-black hair short, emphasizing his long forehead and prominent nose, and his charcoal-gray suit looked tailor made. River introduced herself and they shook hands, his grip lingering as he sized her up. She was still not used to men looking at her like that. Sometimes it repulsed her, and sometimes it made her cheeks flush. Today, she was too focused to care.

"Thanks for coming in so early." River rounded her desk and sat. "I tried to reach you last night."

"I was in Salem. The legislature is in session, and I have an apartment there during the week. I drove down as soon as I got your message." He sat on the edge of the guest chair, as if he didn't plan to stay long.

River wondered about his political aspirations. Was he headed for Washington next? Some men got bored with money and sought power too. "Did you stop by the factory?"

"Yes. It's not badly damaged. We'll be up and running tomorrow." Rockman clenched his fists. "I'm not letting that bastard dictate how I run my life or my company."

River understood the rage of being threatened. "We have a task force meeting today, and any information you can give me will be helpful."

Rockman pulled a folded letter from a slim leather binder and handed it to her. "I received this letter in the mail a few weeks ago. I didn't take it too seriously, but I did add a night watchman at the plant. Now I wish I'd installed a perimeter fence."

River noted the letter was on white lined paper that had been ripped from a binder. She read it slowly.

Dear Mr. Rockman,

Much has changed since I first protested in front of your company. I know a lot more about myself and about you. I'm prepared to reveal what I know to the public, unless you stop selling bottled water. Don't you realize how evil your business is? You put water—a free resource with no pollutants and no carbon footprint—into plastic bottles that end up in landfills. Do you know how many plastic bottles end up in landfills each year? 36 billion. Each year. Do you know how many end up in our rivers and oceans? No one does, but there's a beach at the southern tip of California that has more plastic particles than sand. Most people have access to recycling facilities and they don't use them. You have a moral obligation to shut down your business. I know you don't need the money. Do the right thing.

—A citizen of the Earth

All River could think was, 36 billion a year? It had to be an exaggeration. "When did you receive this?"

"On February twenty-fifth." He handed her the envelope. "It came to my office downtown, but I didn't see it for a few days because I was in Salem. As I said, I didn't take it seriously at the time because there wasn't a direct threat. As a legislator, I get e-mails and phone messages from environmentalists all the time."

"Any idea who this letter is from?"

"No." His eyes expressed disappointment. "I was hoping you would."

"We're watching a group called Love the Earth, and we're starting to get names and data." River came back to the odd part of the letter. "It's peculiar where the writer says he or she will reveal what they know about you. That sounds personal. Any idea what they're talking about?"

"It struck me as odd too, but I'm mystified by it. I wish I'd taken the letter more seriously. I'm just glad no one was hurt last night."

"According to the night watchman, he was the only person in the building." River paused to see if Rockman would jump in. When he didn't, she continued. "But I think someone was with him. There was a pair of men's briefs stuffed in the couch, and something Bromwell said made me think he was lying about being alone."

"You're saying he had sex on the job?" The owner looked outraged.

"Most likely. Any idea who Bromwell would bring in?"

"No. But if he did, he's done working for me."

"I'd like to see his application file. What if the person he had a tryst with left the door open for the arsonist?"

"An inside job?" Rockman rubbed his face. He probably hadn't had much sleep either.

"It's always a possibility." River softened her voice, hoping he would cooperate. "I'd like to see the personnel files for all your employees."

"I'll have someone in my office send the PDFs. I trust the information will never be abused?"

"I'll keep strict confidence." Time to probe a little. "Do you own the company outright?"

"My wife and I are joint owners, but we have a profit-sharing plan with our employees."

"Your office isn't on the factory site?"

"No. I have a building downtown." He shifted as if preparing to leave. "Part of my office is used for the Rock Spring operations and another company I own, and I use the back portion for my political headquarters."

"What other business?"

"Rockman Real Estate."

He apparently liked the sound of his own name. "Do you have any disgruntled ex-employees?"

"Only one that I know of. She quit after she claimed Jerry Bromwell sexually harassed her. I thought she had fabricated the incident so she could collect unemployment. Now I'm rethinking it."

"Her name?"

"Angie Turnbull. You'll get her file along with the others, and everyone who's worked for me in the last year."

River jotted down the woman's name. "Will you flag all the employees who've been fired?"

"There are only a few. Most quit because they're bored." Rockman stood to leave.

River stood too, nearly as tall. "Thanks for coming in." She handed him a card and hoped he wouldn't grab her hand again. "Call me if you remember any significant incidents."

Rockman nodded and strode out, buttoning his jacket as he moved. A confident man who hated the uncertainty his life and business had been thrown into.

River checked her watch: *9:52.* She had to get moving. Her meeting with Dallas was in eight minutes.

She parked in front of the Glenwood Cafe, lamented that she didn't have time for eggs Benedict, and texted Dallas: *Bring me out a mint tea and we'll go for a ride.*

It was best for her undercover agent not to be seen with anyone from the bureau or come anywhere near the federal building. Dallas had an apartment about a half mile away, so River had chosen this location to be convenient for both of them. It was also nowhere near the Whiteaker, downtown, or campus areas where LTE members often hung out.

Dallas came out moments later and didn't make eye contact as she approached River's charcoal SUV. Dressed in jeans and a green sweater and looking twenty-two, Dallas could have been a University of Oregon student. Instead, Dallas was a four-year federal agent with a track record of successful undercover work. River admired her. Long ago, River had made a similar decision to serve her country, particularly because of an agent named Joe Palmer. He'd led the investigation into her father's murders and given her his business card, saying she could call if she ever needed anything. Years later, after her mother had killed herself and River had been homeless and desperate, she'd called Joe and he'd taken her in and given her direction. As a young male, River had modeled her future after the man who'd profoundly affected her life twice.

River started her vehicle as Dallas slipped in. "Sorry for the late-night text, but there was another attack and the task force is meeting today." She headed out of the parking lot.

"What happened?"

"Someone set off a firebomb at the Rock Spring bottled water factory. It could be the same perp who sabotaged JB Pharma."

"So that's what they were talking about." Dallas gestured for River to get into the right lane. "We're headed for the campus area. I want to show you where I think Cricket lives. I followed Adam to his house last night."

A rush of adrenaline charged up River's spine. Dallas had sent a picture of Cricket the week before, and they'd found him in the database with arrests for vandalism and failing to comply with a police officer. Now they had a current address. "How did you get the location? Were you there?"

"This is kind of wild." Dallas turned to her, eyes blazing. "I hung out with Adam again at Tony's Tavern. He and three other guys talked intently at a corner table for half an hour. I took pictures, which I sent you, but they're probably crap without enhancement." Dallas' voice held the same excitement River felt. They would bust these guys soon. Maybe even catch them in the act.

Dallas continued. "We left the tavern and went back to Adam's place. After he fell asleep, I opened his laptop and started poking around. I found a file called *Replay* and a bunch of documents came up. One said *JB Pharma*, but before I could open it, Adam's cell phone rang. I had to slam the laptop closed and get the hell away from it before he caught me."

"Was he suspicious of you?" River noticed Dallas hadn't mentioned having sex with Adam, but if he'd fallen asleep, that meant she probably had. It was Dallas' choice, and River wouldn't ask about it.

"No. He was upset about the phone call." Dallas reached into her shoulder bag for her computer tablet. "Later, when I was in my car, I keyed in what he said." She read from her notes. "*What the fuck? I'm home, of course. You think I acted on my own? I'll send you a fucking picture of me with someone who'll vouch for me.*"

"This was after the Rock Spring fire?" River tried to quickly process the information.

"It was around midnight, so it had to be."

"Maybe someone accused him of doing an independent act of sabotage," River speculated. "We might have a copycat or someone in ELF Lite who's hitting his own targets."

"I think someone in the group went rogue," Dallas said. "The meeting I witnessed last night seemed argumentative and loud at times. But I didn't hear anything specific."

River turned left on Amazon Parkway and headed toward downtown. "When do you see Adam again?"

"Tomorrow night. We're going to a potluck party."

"Will Cricket and the other guys from the meeting be there? Should you wear a wire?"

"I don't know who'll be there, but I'm not wearing a wire." Dallas was adamant. "I can keep my digital recorder in my pocket for some situations. I transfer files off it to my tablet all the time. I leave an interview I did for a grant-writing gig on it in case anyone is ever suspicious of the recorder."

"Be careful. Getting too close to your target can be dangerous."

After a long moment, Dallas said, "Don't worry, I haven't slept with him and I don't plan to."

"Good." Everyone in the bureau understood that some agents made such personal choices to accomplish their goals, but it was against policy, so no one talked about it. River had never done it, but then, she had worked a lot of financial stings in her early years and had lived a mostly celibate life. "We'll make a move on them as soon as you have something solid."

"I'd rather wait. I think they have something big planned for Earth Day. Let me see what I can find out."

As they neared the University of Oregon campus, Dallas directed River to go east on Eighteenth Avenue, then turn again on Onyx. "I don't want to drive by the house," she said, "but when we stop at the nearby corner, I'll point it out to you."

The gray sky and leafless trees didn't diminish the charm of the neighborhoods south of campus. Many of the homes were stately and more than a century old, but even the cottages were well kept with tidy yards and full-grown shrubbery. The farther they drove from the campus, the more the homes began to look like student rentals.

As they approached Emerald Alley, Dallas pointed to the third house down on the left, the least-valuable property in sight. "I sat here on the corner and watched him go in, but it was dark and I was too far away to see the house number."

"We'll find it on Google Maps or in the county building if we have to." River was trying to envision how agents would stage a raid on the place. Access to the home was from a narrow alley. It might be difficult to surprise Noonaz, but they could certainly box him in if he tried to run.

River drove Dallas back to her own neighborhood and dropped her off at the market across from the cafe. "Send me intel as it comes in. If we're dealing with a copycat or rogue activist, he may not wait long to hit his next target."

"You got it."

"Be safe."

They both laughed. Nobody joined the bureau looking for a safe job.

CHAPTER 8

Wednesday, March 13, 11:35 a.m.

Jackson ordered enough pizza for five people, then finished typing up his case notes to share with the task force. When he'd updated his boss, Sergeant Lammers, she'd told him Schak would be joining the investigation. Jackson had also contacted the detective who'd worked the original bank robbery and the district attorney, Victor Slonecker. He expected Dragoo to be there, but Slonecker would probably send an assistant DA or wait until they developed a lead to get involved. For the detectives, every homicide got their full dedication, but for the media and the upper law-enforcement people whose careers could be damaged by public outrage, some murders got more attention. An ex-con who lived in a storage unit wasn't someone the public would get worked up over—even if he was trying to start a new life.

A few minutes before noon, Jackson headed into the conference room, a windowless space with a narrow table and folding metal chairs that made his butt numb if he sat too long. He realized this might be one of the last cases he worked on in this claustrophobic space. The city had purchased and renovated a new building with more space and natural daylight, and they would soon make the move.

"Hey, Jackson." Evans strode in and took a seat across from him. She looked remarkably fresh for someone who'd also had just a few hours of sleep. They'd met earlier to canvass the crime scene in the daylight, and Evans had mentioned doing a quick workout that morning. He envied her energy. She reached across the table and put down a cup of coffee in front of him. "You look like you could use some caffeine."

"Thanks. I think."

Rob Schakowski came in, looking as puffy-eyed as Jackson felt. The veteran detective's blue jacket strained against its buttons and his buzz cut was going gray. But he was diligent and dedicated, and Jackson was relieved to have him on the task force. "Hey, Schak. Good to have you."

"The feds didn't need me on the firebombing, for which I'm grateful. What a clusterfuck." He grinned and sat next to Evans. "Agent River has the lead, but she has to coordinate with the fire department, ATF arson investigators, and our bomb squad."

"And Quince," Jackson added for laughs.

"River indicated it wasn't an isolated incident, so there's probably more shit coming down." Schak pulled a notepad from his carryall. "What have we got with this case?"

"A dead ex-con and almost no forensic evidence." Jackson stood and rolled the dry-erase board into place. He wrote *Craig Cooper* at the top. "The victim lived in the storage unit next to where he was killed."

"No shit?" Schak scowled. "Those places don't have heat or electricity, do they?"

"Nope," Evans said. "Some newer units are heated, but they're more expensive and there aren't many."

The desk officer stepped in with two pizza boxes. "These are for you, I assume."

"Grab a piece if you're hungry," Jackson said.

"I'm good." The uniformed officer set down the pizzas and left.

Schak opened the larger box and helped himself. "Thank God you still eat meat."

Was that a reference to Jackson's health-conscious girlfriend? "Hell yes I do."

While they ate, they talked about the upcoming move to the new headquarters. Five minutes in, Jim Trang, an assistant DA, showed up.

"My subpoena man," Jackson joked.

Trang put his briefcase on the floor and grabbed a slice. "Whatever I can do to help."

Evans finished first, headed for the board, and started filling in what she knew. In the left column, she wrote *ex-con, employed at 4-Corner Gas, sister: Jane Niven.* In the right column, she listed their suspect: *Todd Sheppard, neighbor, found the body.*

Schak raised his hand in mock deference. "How does a guy who lives in a storage space have a neighbor?"

"Sheppard lives in a unit too," Evans said. "And he looks like he's been there a while."

"Two homeless guys?" Schak's tone was skeptical. "Why don't we have Sheppard in custody?"

Feeling a little defensive, Jackson explained. "Sheppard has a brain injury, and without a car or money, I don't see him being a flight risk. If the evidence implicates him, we know where to find him."

"And he weighs three-hundred-plus pounds," Evans added. "The director at the Mission didn't look too happy to see us last night when I dropped Sheppard off. Which reminds me—" She turned and wrote on the board: *blood on his face/DNA?* "It'll be interesting to see what that reveals."

Jackson had sent the swab with the crime scene technician the night before. Joe would test some of the sample for easy identifiers like blood type and send the rest to the state lab for DNA analysis. With any luck, they'd have some results by tomorrow and a DNA report in a week. Sometimes it took longer.

"Any other evidence at the scene?" Schak asked.

"Very little." Jackson looked at his notes. "The victim seems to have died from a stab wound to the throat, but we didn't find a weapon. Cooper's storage unit was kind of Spartan, but he did have a laptop. I haven't searched it thoroughly yet."

The door opened again, and Detective Dragoo came in. He was in his forties, but he wore his hair slicked back in a retro style and walked with a subtle limp. "Sorry I'm late, but I'm on my way to court and I only have a few minutes."

Schak and Evans both looked surprised as Dragoo sat down.

"We have another suspect," Jackson announced. "Cooper was involved in a robbery nine years ago. His partner, Danny Brennan, was shot while being apprehended, and the money was never found. Danny's brother, Patrick Brennan, was questioned but never charged. The missing money seems like a good motive for murder, so Dragoo will tell us about the old robbery case."

"How much money?" Schak wanted to know.

"A hundred and twenty-five grand and change," Dragoo said. "We thought Danny either stashed it before we confronted him or he handed it off to his brother, Patrick. But despite thorough searches of all three homes and vehicles, the cash never turned up."

"How did you track the robbery to Danny Brennan and Craig Cooper?"

"We had an anonymous tip."

Interesting, Jackson thought. "Maybe Patrick turned them in to get Danny to panic and hand over the money."

"It's possible," Dragoo said.

"Where did you confront Danny?" Jackson was careful not to say *kill*. He knew what it felt like to be in that position.

"At his home." Dragoo seemed pained by the memory. "We tore the place apart looking for the cash, but it never turned up. We also didn't find any safe deposit keys, and it wasn't in his bank account."

"Who worked the case with you?" Jackson asked. Jane Niven's allegation that the police had taken the money was fresh in his mind, but he wouldn't bring it up with Dragoo in the room.

"John Iverson. He retired about six months after we closed the case." Dragoo sat forward. "I know the perps' families think one of us took the money, but it's bullshit. I hope you find it so we can put that rumor to rest."

"Do you know where we can locate Patrick?" Jackson asked.

"I don't think he went far. He and Danny have family here in Lane County." Dragoo tapped the folder he'd laid on the table. "You'll find them all in here." He got to his feet. "I have to be in court, but if you need more information, let me know."

After Dragoo left, Schak said, "This is definitely more interesting than a homeless-on-homeless killing."

"We need to find out exactly when Cooper was released," Jackson said. "His sister says it's been a couple of months, so the old robbery and missing money may not be connected."

"You want me on that?" Schak asked.

"Sure. Then see if you can track down Patrick Brennan or his wife or whoever else might know where he is. I'd like to bring Patrick in for questioning."

"Does Cooper have a widow?" Evans voiced the detail Jackson had forgotten to mention.

"According to my source, he has an ex-wife." Jackson had to look at his notes for her name. "Dora Cooper. Jane Niven gave me a phone number and address, but they could be outdated." He handed the information to Evans. "Would you track her down, please?"

"I'm on it." She wrote the wives' names on the board, then stared at the data. "We're missing Danny's family. I'll see if I can find his widow too." Evans added the detectives' names from the old robbery. "So Iverson retired after the hundred thousand went missing. What you do think?"

Jackson didn't blame her for asking. Still, he said, "Iverson put in his twenty years. Let's not make any assumptions."

"I worked with him," Schak added. "I never saw anything out of line."

That wasn't the same as saying Iverson was a good man. "I have a personal matter this afternoon," Jackson said. "Then I'll dig into Cooper's laptop and check in with the lab. We'll meet back here at six." He hated passing the witness work to his team, but he didn't have a choice. Katie's future was on the line today.

Across the boulevard from the towering Autzen Stadium, home of Duck football, was the John Serbu Youth Campus. It housed the juvenile justice court, incarceration facilities for young offenders, and a treatment center. Jackson had come here as a police officer on a few occasions, but he'd never been here as a parent. Walking across the parking lot filled him with a strange grief, a sense that his family life as he'd known it was gone. Katie, who he loved more than anyone, was here somewhere, feeling abandoned, angry, and lonely for a mother who wasn't coming back.

The other two women in Jackson's life were waiting in the lobby of the juvenile justice building—a high-ceilinged room with plenty of windows, but with tables and benches made of metal. Indestructible material that was painted over every six months or so. Today, it was a sunny yellow.

Kera, his girlfriend, kissed him on the check. Just the sight of her filled the hole in his heart. Tall and athletic, Kera fit nicely into his frame as he hugged her to him. He breathed in the tropical scent of her hair and wished he could stay like this long enough to heal his grief and guilt.

"Where's Micah?" he asked, pulling back. Kera's toddler grandson was the product of a brief relationship her son had engaged in before being deployed to and killed in Iraq. Both Micah and the baby's mother lived with Kera—the only reason Jackson didn't.

"He's with Danette. She's on spring break this week."

Jackson turned to Katie's aunt, the woman who'd filled in the gaps of his parenting. "Thanks for coming, Jan. It'll be good for Katie to know you're here." Jan was his ex-wife's sister, but they looked nothing alike. Jan was blond and plump and generous with her smiles. She gave him one now, and he had a flash of guilt. When he'd shot Renee, Jan not only hadn't blamed him, she'd offered him comfort.

"Let's go in." Jackson trudged up the wide steps. The late-night work felt heavy in his legs, and his troubled child weighed heavy in his heart.

Inside the small courtroom, Jackson was relieved to see a female judge behind the bench. Katie was seated in the first row with a woman on either side. Kera and Jan took their seats, while

Jackson rounded the first bench and stopped in front of the trio. "Hi Katie."

His daughter slumped with relief, but didn't smile or greet him. She'd been angry for a while now and he was a little numb to it. When she'd first started expressing her hostility, it had been like a knife to his heart. But the counselor he'd been to as a job requirement had helped him accept that it would pass. Only it hadn't.

"I'm Wade Jackson," he said to the woman in the pantsuit.

She stood and shook his hand. "Wanda Parsons, Katie's court-appointed attorney. And this is Debbie Myers, a caseworker with Children and Family Services."

Hearing the state agency's name brought a fresh wave of guilt. He had failed as a parent, and the state thought his family needed monitoring. He shook the caseworker's hand and managed to squeeze a greeting past the lump in his throat.

"Today's hearing is an informal opportunity for all of us to talk about what's best for Katie." The caseworker smiled warmly.

Jackson tried not to hate her. He'd known the state would get involved when he'd asked the officer to arrest Katie the night before. Now he had second thoughts. *What if they put her in foster care?* He told the attorney, "I'd like her to go through a treatment program. I think she needs to understand alcoholism."

"You'll have a chance to say that to the judge in a few minutes." The lawyer didn't smile, but Jackson didn't sense any animosity.

He took a seat next to Kera and she reached for his hand. She held it gently until the courtroom aide announced the case details, then let go. She knew him well.

Judge Holt, a stout woman with scalp-short white hair, asked everyone to introduce themselves, then summarized the situation. This was Katie's second charge of minor in possession of alcohol. The first had netted no punitive action, only a recommendation for counseling. A second offense a month later meant new ramifications. Focused on what he would say, Jackson barely heard the words. The judge called on him immediately afterward. He didn't know if he was supposed to stand, but it seemed right, so he did.

"Katie recently lost her mother in a tragic accidental shooting." Jackson hoped he would not have to explain. "She's grieving and angry. In addition, her mother was an alcoholic, so she's prone to the disease. I would like her to begin a treatment program that educates her about alcohol and addiction. I also plan to take her to a grief counselor."

"Thank you." The judge nodded. "I need to know if the shooting happened at home."

"No, your honor. Katie's mother, Renee, was kidnapped."

Katie called out, "I don't want to talk about this."

The court was quiet for a moment. The judge looked at her. "Katie, I can't help you if I don't know what I'm dealing with. We'll keep it brief." She turned back to Jackson. "Your wife was killed by her abductor?"

"Yes and no." Jackson drew in a painful breath. "The assailant engineered the situation, but I shot her accidentally." Emotions overwhelmed him and he had to pause. Silence filled the room, as if everyone had stopped breathing. Finally, Jackson found a solid voice. "I acted according to my training, and any other officer would have done the same. I thought Katie had forgiven me, but now I realize that may take a lot of time."

"I'm sorry for your loss." The judge's voice was soft and stunned.

Jackson hadn't wanted to deal with this today, yet in his heart, he knew it was important that everyone understand what Katie was really going through.

The caseworker stood. "I agree that Katie needs treatment and counseling. The question is whether outpatient treatment will be effective or whether she needs a more-specialized inpatient treatment. Considering her family circumstances, I'm inclined to suggest inpatient treatment."

Jackson cringed. He hated the thought of Katie being gone from his home for a month, but he wanted her to get the help she needed.

The caseworker sat down, and the lawyer took a turn. "I think we should let Katie speak before any more recommendations are offered."

The judge nodded. "Katie?"

She didn't stand. "I want to go home. I'll go see a therapist every week, but I want a different one. Please don't lock me in here."

The judge looked back at Jackson. "You're a police officer and a single father. Can you supervise your daughter adequately?"

Jackson tensed, then slumped with guilt. He'd been struggling with this issue for a long time. Even when he and Renee had still been married, Renee's alcoholism had kept her from being a dependable parent. When he felt under control, he stood again. "Katie has other people in her life to help me. Her aunt Jan has been a care provider all along, and Katie is bonded to my partner, Kera. Katie is usually at one of their homes whenever I have to work late." Jackson gestured at the women sitting with him, feeling grateful and humiliated at the same time. *Please let this be over soon.*

The caseworker spoke up. "I'm concerned about Katie's anger toward her father. Maybe removing her from his home for a while will help her work through it."

Jackson resisted the urge to argue.

After a long moment, Judge Holt said, "We just learned that our inpatient treatment program lost its funding, so I'll honor Katie's desire to go home. But I want her in daily alcohol treatment sessions and weekly grief counseling. Please make the necessary arrangements and submit the paperwork to me by the end of the day Friday. If there's another incident, I'll have no choice but to recommend incarceration."

Tension flowed out of Jackson's shoulders. Katie was coming home. He'd thought he wanted to force her into a treatment program that would contain her and remove her from his responsibility for a while. But after one night of knowing she was behind locked doors, he'd changed his mind. He tried to gauge Katie's reaction, but he couldn't see her well enough from the side to tell.

He turned to Jan and Kera. "Thank you for being here. Now I need to find Katie a new counselor."

The caseworker walked over. "We'll process some paperwork, then Katie will be released into your custody in twenty minutes or so." The social worker didn't look happy, but she dug into her purse and handed Jackson a business card. "This therapist is terrific with troubled teenagers. I'll give her a call. I think she's even in the building today."

Jackson took the card, said thank you, and headed out to wait in the bright light of the lobby. He wanted this to be the last time he set foot in this building, but he knew it wouldn't be. Now that he had a homicide case to work, he would have to depend on Kera and Jan to keep his daughter out of trouble while he sought justice for a man who'd robbed a bank. On the surface, it seemed wrong, yet Jackson couldn't—or wouldn't—change who he was or how he lived his life.

Kera stepped up next to him, and he realized the one change he could make was to move in with Kera. Maybe it would be good for Katie to be around Kera, Danette, and the baby. It might give her a new sense of family.

While they waited for Katie, a woman approached him and held out her hand. "Wade Jackson?" She was in her forties, well groomed, and very overweight.

"Yes?" He shook her hand, feeling a little reluctant.

"I'm Charlotte Diebold, a therapist who specializes in counseling teenagers."

Jackson looked at the card in his hand. Same woman. "It's good to meet you. The social worker gave me your card."

"Yes, she called me. I do a lot of work with kids who come through this courtroom, and I'd love to help with your daughter."

Jackson decided to trust the caseworker's recommendation. "How soon can you see Katie? She needs an intervention."

"I'll check for an opening this week and get back to you."

"Thanks." Jackson nodded and started toward the door. He was ready to get the hell out.

CHAPTER 9

True to his word, Ted Rockman had sent personnel files immediately, and River's in-box was flooded with PDFs when she
returned from her meeting with Dallas. While they printed, she
skimmed through the documents looking for a woman with a
connection to Jerry Bromwell, the night watchman, or someone
with a history of volunteer work that suggested an environmental
empathy. Eventually, River and/or Agent Fouts would read the
files of every single male under thirty as well, in the off chance
that the firebomb had been an inside job.

For now, she had to focus on the woman who'd had a late-
night booty call with Bromwell. It was not likely a coincidence
that she'd come into the building around the same time as the
arsonist. She might not be an employee, River reminded herself.
And it might not even be a woman. Jerry may have had a male
guest. She picked up the files from the printer, found Bromwell's,

and noted his address. It was seven minutes away on Mallory Lane.

River drove over and parked in front of the house next to Bromwell's. The night watchman's Ford Mustang was in his driveway and his front curtain was open. River dialed his number, and his greeting had a nervous quality that encouraged her. "Mr. Bromwell? This is Agent River."

"Yes?"

"I'd like to come over and ask you some questions."

"When?"

"Right now."

"I'm not home," he stammered. "I had to help my mother with something."

River slipped out of her vehicle and headed for his walkway. "Then I'll come pick you up and we'll talk at the bureau."

"I told you everything. I've got to go." The little shit hung up on her.

River knocked on his door and called out, "FedEx."

A moment later, the door opened and Bromwell stood there, openmouthed.

"Step outside and turn around." River pulled out her handcuffs. "You're under arrest for obstruction of justice. We don't like to be lied to."

"I'm sorry," he pleaded. "I just don't want my wife to find out." His face crumpled with grief and fear. "Let's just talk here. There's no need to arrest me."

River gave him her best hard stare. "It's twelve hours after the fact. I should have had this information last night. The eco-terrorist could be preparing for another attack today."

"I'm sorry. I was scared. If the affair gets out, I could lose my job too."

"Come with me and make a statement, and I'll do my best to keep from informing your wife."

Bromwell ran a nervous hand through his thinning hair. "Let me grab a coat."

The booking area in the FBI headquarters served as an interrogation room but also contained an all-in-one machine that took digital fingerprints and processed them into the system. But there was no camera. The FBI preferred not to document their techniques—clips that could be shown later to juries. Instead, they had suspects and witnesses sign a statement of their testimony.

River put Bromwell through all the motions but didn't intend to turn him over to the federal marshal for arrest. She was curious to see if his fingerprints would come up in the database, or if he'd ever been arrested for trespassing or vandalism. The witness/suspect sat at the table fidgeting while she scanned the monitor. No print matches surfaced.

River sat and opened her bottled water. The threatening letter to Rockman echoed in her mind—thirty-six billion plastic bottles a year—and she had a flash of guilt. But she always recycled, so she assumed she wasn't part of the problem. "Let's start at the beginning. Who came into the factory to see you and what time did he or she arrive?"

"Candy Morrison. And it was just before eight."

The last name seemed familiar, as if River had seen it recently when looking at employee files. "Does Candy work at Rock Spring?" River made notes as she talked.

"Yes, she works in the sorting room."

"What's the nature of your relationship?"

His face flushed pink. "We're just friends."

River gave him a look. "I found a pair of your underwear in the office couch."

"Okay, we had sex."

"Why did you lie and not tell me about her presence in the factory at the time of the arson?"

Bromwell's mouth twitched when she said *lie*.

"We're both married, and Candy's husband is the plant foreman. I was afraid we'd both get fired and probably end up divorced too."

She tried to empathize with him but couldn't. "Does Candy have the code to the door or did you let her in?"

"She has the code."

"Did you give it to her?"

"Her husband has it too, so she already knew it."

River began to doubt her theory that Candy might be working with LTE. "How often did Candy visit you?"

"I've only been on the night watch for two weeks, but she comes on Tuesday."

So it wasn't a one-time thing. "Why Tuesday?"

"Her husband plays poker that night."

"Did anyone else know about Candy's visits to you?"

He shuddered. "Of course not."

"Would Candy have told anyone?"

"I doubt that."

River shifted gears. "When did you start working at Rock Spring?"

"Five years ago."

"Do you know anyone in the Love the Earth environmental group?"

Bromwell pulled back, visibly disturbed. "No. Why do you ask? You think I was involved?"

"I'm trying to find out how the arsonist entered the building."

"I don't know. Maybe Candy didn't close the door properly."

River thought someone might have been watching the property and discovered Candy's visits, then took advantage of the opportunity. Still, she would question Candy. "Tell me what happened when you became aware that someone was in the building."

"It's pretty much like I said before. I went downstairs and I confronted the guy, then when I saw that he'd left a bomb, I went back for Candy and we ran outside."

"Then what?"

"Candy took off and I called 911."

"I'd like you to write out and sign the revised statement you just made." River handed him a tablet of lined paper with FBI letterhead. "I'll be back in a few minutes."

The task force meeting would start in an hour, so she headed to the conference room and set up the whiteboard and the projector screen. River hoped ATF would be content to analyze the evidence and lend support, but not take the lead from her. This case wasn't just about arson. If Love the Earth followed the lead of the Earth Liberation Front, more vandalism and sabotage were on the agenda as well. And the perp's willingness to set off a firebomb—even a small one—with people in the building meant he or they had stepped up their game. Who knew what was next or how many people would be hurt?

After escorting Bromwell out of the building, River went back to her office and uploaded the images Dallas had sent from the LTE meeting in the tavern. Using in-house software, she separated out the four faces, all somewhat dark and blurry, into distinct files, enhanced them, and forwarded them to everyone on the task force.

Thanks to Dallas, they had already identified two of the men: Chris Noonaz (aka Cricket) and Adam Greene. But according to the phone call Dallas had overheard, both men were surprised by the attack on Rock Spring, so it was unlikely that either had conducted it. The priority was to identify the other two suspects and start surveillance, if they could get more people down from Portland. In the few minutes she had left, River uploaded the two unknowns and ran a quick search for matching features. She got one hit that pulled up a man in Colorado who was still in prison. River gathered her documents, grabbed her laptop, and headed for the conference room.

Agent Fouts and Detective Quince were already present and discussing the firebombing. They wore similar gray jackets and both turned when she came in, but Fouts was older, thinner, and crankier, while Quince was handsome, sturdy, and serene.

"What's your take?" Fouts asked. "Is the whole ELF Lite group a front for the terrorist activities, or is there a core internal group that's acting independently?"

"I think it's a few individuals." River set her laptop on the table. "Four, to be precise. With maybe an unpredictable fifth. But I'll get to that when everyone arrives." She connected the computer to the projector and opened her digital folder.

A big man she didn't recognize came into the room. "Darrell Shoemaker, Special Agent in Charge, ATF." He had coffee-colored skin, military-short hair, and a deadpan delivery.

"Agent River." She shook his hand, hoping he would be pleasant to work with.

Behind him was Agent Mason Roberts, a bomb expert in the Eugene FBI headquarters. River had given him the remnants from the bomb first thing this morning and he'd met with the ATF.

Agent Roberts took a seat but Shoemaker remained standing.

So did River. She suspected Shoemaker thought he was going to run the meeting, but this was her case. "I think we're still expecting someone from the fire department, but I'd like to get started."

"No, we're handling the fire investigation, and I spent hours at the site this morning." Shoemaker nodded at her to sit.

River remained on her feet. "Some of you may not know this yet, but the bureau considers the arson at the Rock Spring plant to be part of a larger investigation."

"You've had other arsons? And didn't call us?" Shoemaker bristled with a below-the-surface irritation looking for a place to erupt.

"No." River turned to address him directly. "The first incident was a protest at Rock Spring fourteen months ago, during which several people were arrested. The group that staged the demonstration calls itself Love the Earth, and since that protest it has been peacefully working for its causes through petitions and legislative initiatives." River turned back to the men at the table. She wished Agent Jamie Dallas could be there, but the fewer people who knew about her undercover involvement the better.

River continued. "The second incident was an act of sabotage at JB Pharma on January thirteenth, about eight weeks ago. A pipe carrying sludge from JB Pharma's manufacturing plant was purposefully damaged, and toxic waste spilled out on the property. They shut down production for a week while they cleaned up. I was assigned the case, and recently became aware of a core group of individuals within LTE that are the likely perpetrators. I think they're modeling their eco-terrorism on the Earth Liberation Front, which means we can expect more attacks, but they may not be arson."

"I see." Shoemaker finally took a seat. "I'd like you to keep ATF in the loop."

River nodded. "This is a long-term investigation, and after the sabotage, we recruited an undercover agent and got her into place. I'm also looking for someone inside LTE who I can turn as an informant. We've identified two of the inner core, and we might be on the verge of a breakthrough."

"Excellent. Would you like my report?" Shoemaker said.

"Yes. Thank you." *Now he would report and run*, she thought.

"The origin of the fire was the hallway near the employee break room. It's the only internal area of the building constructed of flammable materials, except for the stairs and the office overhead. The arsonist used a crude incendiary device made of a metal cylinder most likely filled with a flammable liquid. It was attached to dynamite and set off with a simple timer, likely made from a watch. We only found small bits of the timer, so we can't compare it to other bombers' MOs, but a similar device was used in an incident in Utah. The perp, Jason Keller, is in prison for burning down his ex-wife's business." Shoemaker slid a stack of paper across the table to River. "This is your copy, but we still have to run some lab tests."

"Thank you." River slid the report into her briefcase. Arson evidence rarely led to an arrest. It was usually a witness or an informant that provided the critical information. She looked up at the group. "Our undercover agent reports that four members of LTE had a heated meeting last night at Tony's Tavern. The meeting took place between seven ten and seven thirty. Jerry Bromwell, the night watchman at Rock Spring, called in the fire at eight twenty-seven, giving one of them enough time to drive out to the Glenwood area to set off the firebomb."

River cued up the four images on the projector screen. "Top left is Chris Noonaz, aka Cricket, the founder of LTE. Top right is Adam Greene. He's been a member of LTE for five years and has been arrested twice during demonstrations for trespassing and vandalism. We know he didn't personally set the fire last night because our undercover agent was with him at the time."

"Did the UC get any audio of their discussion?" Fouts asked. He knew River was working with Agent Dallas but understood the need for discretion.

"No, but the UC took these photos." River tapped the bottom pictures with her pointer. "We need to identify these other two. I sent you digital files this morning. If we have to, we'll use the media to ask for public help, but I don't want the perps to go underground or run. That's why we're not bringing anyone in yet. Our UC says they're planning something big for Earth Day. I want to find out what it is and be there to stop it and arrest all of them at the same time."

"I have time to search the databases for these guys," Quince offered. "But the guy on the left with the mohawk looks really young. He may not have a record."

"Thanks." River looked at her agenda for the meeting. "Another thing I wanted to mention is that our UC was with Adam Greene after the meeting. Greene got a call about the arson and sounded defensive, as if the caller was accusing him of doing it on his own. The UC concluded that neither the caller, nor Greene, knew about the Rock Spring arson before it happened. Which could mean we're dealing with another group or individual, or a rogue member of LTE."

"Well, shit." Fouts shook his head.

"Any idea who the caller was?" Quince asked.

"Based on what we know about the hierarchy of the group, Greene was talking to someone with more authority, which means it was probably Noonaz."

"You said our UC reported that the meeting was heated?" Fouts asked.

"Yes. At times they seemed to be yelling."

"Then it's probably one of the four. Someone who wants to step things up, maybe hit harder or move faster." Fouts seemed to vibrate with tension. "So if it's a rogue operator, the next attack could come at any time."

"That's my concern as well. It's why I'm looking to turn an informant." River clicked off the images. "Our biggest unknown about these attacks is the access factor. How did the perp get into each of the two buildings? Or do they have insiders working at both JB Pharma and Rock Spring?"

"The door didn't look jimmied or scratched," Shoemaker said.

"I know. I examined it too. But here's the kicker." River glanced at her notes for the name. "The night watchman had a visitor, a woman who works at the factory who has the code and stopped in for a booty call. They're both married, which is why he didn't mention her presence last night. I just learned her name is Candy Morrison, and I plan to interrogate her next. She may be working with LTE."

"How often does she visit him?" Quince asked.

"Bromwell has only been on the night watch for two weeks, but she visited him on all three Tuesdays." She nodded at Detective Quince. "I know what you're thinking. Someone casing the building spotted the pattern, maybe discovered the code by watching her or checking the keypad after she entered."

"Or blackmailed her into giving it to him," Fouts added.

"Or she's complicit." River looked at her notes from the earlier sabotage. "JB Pharma has far better security than Rock Spring, so we assumed that was an inside job. But we were unable to link any of the employees to LTE in a significant way. It's disturbing to think they have people working at all their targets."

"What do you think they'll hit next?" Quince asked the million-dollar question.

River had pondered it, but she wanted to hear what everyone else thought first. "What is your best guess? Anyone?"

"What about the mining operation on Parvin Butte?" Fouts suggested. "The neighbors and tree huggers hate that."

"What's their complaint with the bottled water company?" Quince asked.

"I wasn't sure about that either," River said. "But I talked to Ted Rockman, the owner, this morning, and he showed me a threatening letter he received two weeks ago." She clicked her laptop and displayed the scanned letter. "The sender is hyper-concerned about plastic bottles in the landfills and seems to think he or she knows something that Rockman would want kept private. A vague blackmail threat."

"That seems more personal than just an eco-terrorist message." Quince stared at the screen. "Where was the letter sent to? His home or business?"

"Rockman's office. But he's a state senator and uses his office as his political base as well, so he's easy to reach there."

"So the letter writer could be the rogue operator," Fouts said. "Unless ELF Lite is focused on plastic bottles."

"They're working on an initiative to ban plastic bags," Quince offered. "I read that in the paper a few days ago."

"Any potential targets you can think of based on that?" After a moment of silence, River glanced at Agent Fouts. "I need you to analyze the Rock Spring employee files. Then look at possible connections with the JB Pharma employees. We have to find the insiders." She turned to the EPD detective. "Quince, you already offered to do what you can to identify the two other men. Don't forget to check social media sites like Facebook and Twitter. LTE has a Facebook page, but they have hundreds of followers, and I haven't had time yet to look at them all."

"I'll start there."

River added, "When we identify the other two members, I'll ask for surveillance people from the Portland bureau."

She wrapped up the meeting, passed off most of the Rock Spring employee files to Fouts, and headed back to her office. Her first priority was to find Candy Morrison, who might be an LTE sympathizer.

Candy's employee file listed two phone numbers and River called both, leaving a casual message, indicating Candy was just one of the many employees the FBI wanted to talk to. River jotted down her home address, then googled the woman to see if she was involved in social media. Her Facebook page came up at the top of the search. After a few minutes of clicking through Candy's list of friends, a familiar name popped up.

Chris Noonaz.

CHAPTER 10

Wednesday, March 13, 2:35 p.m.

Jackson was torn. He had a homicide to work, but he needed to be with Katie, at least for a while. He reached across the car seat and lightly touched her shoulder. "Do you want to go somewhere fun? Bowling or skating?" Why the hell had he said that?

The old Katie would have laughed at the thought of him on roller skates. The new Katie jerked her head toward him and stared openmouthed, as if he'd just suggested they get gang tattoos. "I'm really not in the mood."

Yeah, he got that. "Katie, I realize these are the worst months of your life, but you have to understand that they will pass. Your life will go on. Someday soon, you'll be twenty, and if you're lucky, you'll hit forty. You have to ask yourself: Do I want to be a forty-year-old woman with a drinking problem, a suspended driver's license, and a criminal record? Or do I want to be someone with a good job, a house, and a car?"

She was silent.

Jackson took that as a sign that she was considering what he'd said. "I love you. I can't bear the thought of losing you too." He never talked about it, but he grieved for Renee. She'd been the love of his life once, and being responsible for her death had crushed what little optimism he had left.

He drove toward home, thinking they would watch a movie together, then he would take Katie to Aunt Jan's. He would meet with his task force, then pick up Katie by eight. "Let's stop by your school, and I'll go in and get your assignments from today."

"Please don't. I can't face anyone I know right now."

"All right. We'll go home and watch a movie."

"Just take me to Aunt Jan's. I know you have to work."

"I can take a couple hours off. In fact, I want to." He tried to sound sincere.

"A movie won't change anything. I'd rather be at Aunt Jan's house."

It stung, but not as much as the first time he'd heard it. They would get through this. The phrase had become his peace of mind. "I found a new therapist for you. Your caseworker recommended her." Jackson tried to form his next words carefully. "The court says you have to get grief counseling, in addition to the treatment program. It's not optional. So I'll make an appointment and go with you."

"Whatever."

Jackson's phone rang, and he touched his earpiece automatically. "Jackson here."

"It's Schak. I found Patrick Brennan. But based on what his ex-wife tells me, I want you there when I pick him up."

Jackson glanced at Katie, who stared out the window. He pulled off into a parking lot. "Where is the suspect?"

"Up on Wolf Creek."

Not a quick trip. "Where are you now?"

"Heading back to the department."

"I'll meet you there. We'll drive out together."

He hung up and repeated his daughter's name until she turned to face him. "I love you. I'm never giving up. We'll always be a family."

"I know. I just don't want to be around you." Katie looked back out the window.

He dropped off his daughter, hugged his ex-sister-in-law, and drove downtown feeling uneasy. He should have been more assertive about spending time with Katie, and he should have told Schak to take Evans with him. But as skilled as she was, Evans just wasn't as intimidating to suspects. She'd proven she could kick ass if provoked, but Jackson preferred to keep suspects docile. And it wasn't just about gender, Jackson reasoned, it was about size and looks—because Sergeant Lammers scared everybody.

After a second brief call, Schak met him in the parking lot under City Hall and climbed in. In this scenario, it made sense to take one vehicle. It was an hour trip, and once they got back, they would question the suspect together.

They drove west out of town, then turned on Crow Road, which would take them directly to the Wolf Creek turnoff. On the way, Schak updated him. "I found Kathy Brennan, Patrick's ex-wife, when I read about the original robbery. Which happened on Saint Patrick's Day, by the way."

"Is that significant?"

"The Brennan family is Irish."

"Perps love symbolism too." Jackson wondered if the men had gotten drunk and done it on a stupid impulse. "What did she say about Patrick's involvement?"

"She's adamant that Patrick is innocent, and she says the cops ruined his life by implicating him. She says Danny was always the troublemaker."

"And the money?"

"She has no idea, and she doesn't live like someone who's had a windfall."

"It was nine years ago," Jackson reminded him. "It doesn't take long to burn through a hundred grand."

Schak laughed. "With a kid in college, I can do that in a year." His partner unbuttoned his jacket. "I think Danny hid the money, and it's just sitting somewhere untouched. It sure would be fun to find it."

"Until we had to hand it over to the bank."

Schak turned to face him. "If no one but us knew, would you be tempted to keep it?"

"I can see how the idea might flash through a person's brain, but no. Money won't solve my problems."

"Wait until Katie starts college." Schak shook his head.

"I'll feel lucky if she makes it to that point."

"Things still bad with her?"

"Yeah."

Jackson turned on Wolf Creek and they started the winding climb. If they stayed on the road long enough, they would pass the Forest Work Camp buildings, where they used to house inmates who served their time putting out forest fires and cleaning up state parks. The facility had been shuttered when the recession hit and tax revenue shrank. A shame. Men who spent their time at the camp had lower recidivism rates.

"I'll watch for the address," Schak added. "His ex-wife says it's only a mile from the turnoff."

"Why did she tell you where to find him?"

"Pure charm." Schak grinned. "But she says Patrick owns weapons, which is why you're here."

"Nice."

A minute later, his partner called out an address and announced they should take the next turnoff. Jackson almost missed it. The dirt driveway had weeds growing in the middle and overgrown blackberry bushes along the side.

Uneasiness crept into Jackson's gut. "What else do we know about this guy?"

"He did a stint in the army, then worked for Coyote Steel. Patrick's been collecting disability for the last ten years. Only two charges in his file: reckless driving in 2005 and possession of cocaine in 1993."

No violence. Jackson felt a little better. "What motive are we going to press?"

"That he killed Cooper in a rage when Cooper wouldn't tell him where the money was?"

"Or maybe that he confronted Cooper and they fought. We'll play it soft."

"We're not bringing him in?"

"I don't know yet. We don't have anything on this guy."

The cabin perched on the edge of a bluff, its wood siding weathered and gray. Under a cheap canvas awning sat a battered yellow Bronco. Jackson wrote the license plate number in his notepad. Behind the vehicle was a massive pile of split wood and, behind that, a forested hillside. A hound dog came around the Bronco and stood guard as they parked in the small clearing. *A damn dog.* Jackson had dealt with more than his share of dogs lately, and it hadn't warmed his heart toward them. The scar above his left eyebrow reminded him every day that the creatures couldn't be trusted.

As they stepped from the car, a burly man in a thick plaid jacket pushed out the door. He held a rifle at his side.

Jackson brought up his weapon and Schak did the same. "Put the gun down," Jackson called. "We're just here to ask a few questions."

"Who are you?" The man's voice was deep but ragged, as if his throat was scarred.

"Detective Jackson and Detective Schakowski, Eugene Police. Put the rifle down."

Jackson's mind flashed on the bed-and-breakfast in the south hills, and he saw Renee bleeding on the stone path. Dread filled his stomach. He never wanted to fire his weapon at a human again. Three weeks of leave hadn't changed that.

Schak stepped forward and took the lead. "We just want to ask you about Craig Cooper. Put down the rifle and step away from it."

Surprise registered on Patrick's face. After a hesitation, he squatted and carefully placed the rifle on a grassy spot instead of on the dirt under his feet. "I'd rather take the rifle inside. It's gonna rain again."

"It'll be fine. Let's go in the cabin." Schak moved quickly, his broad body forcing Patrick Brennan to turn and go into the house.

Jackson followed, relieved that they had avoided a showdown but disturbed by the weapons collection on the back wall. Three hunting rifles, a shotgun, a tomahawk, and a compound bow. Without a warrant, they couldn't even determine if the guns were registered.

Sacks, canned goods, and mail covered the kitchen table, so Schak gestured for Patrick to sit on the couch. From the stains and the dirty breakfast plate on the coffee table, it seemed obvious that Patrick ate most of his meals in front of the TV. The suspect sat down slowly, as if his back hurt, and Jackson wondered about his disability. Could he climb a fence like the one at the storage business? Maybe he hadn't had to.

Schak pulled a chair from the kitchen area, and Jackson sat on the coffee table next to the dirty plate. Out of habit, Jackson took the lead. "Where were you last night between six and eight?"

Patrick processed the question thoroughly, his expression changing from what seemed like resentment to concern. But his sagging cheeks and droopy eyelids made him hard to read. "You said this was about Craig Cooper. What happened?"

"We'll ask the questions. Where were you last night?" Jackson didn't want to give him time to come up with a story.

"I bought groceries in town, then I came home."

"What store and when did you leave the store?"

"Winco, right off Beltline. I think I left around six-thirty or seven. I'm not sure. It was still light out."

"Do you have your receipt?" Jackson glanced at the grocery bags.

"Probably." Patrick struggled to his feet, his big belly straining against his T-shirt. But his arms and legs were skinny, making him look like a caricature. The suspect searched the two sacks, then flipped through the stack of paper on the table. He finally checked the garbage. "Here it is." He walked over and handed the damp strip of paper to Jackson.

The time stamp near the top was calculated to the second: *18:29:47*. Patrick had checked out at six-thirty, leaving him time to drive the three miles to the storage unit and kill Craig before seven. Jackson jotted down the store and time. "May I keep this?"

"Does it clear me?" Patrick's lips pulled back, revealing his stained teeth.

The creepy smile gave Jackson a bad vibe. "No. Where did you go next?"

Patrick looked down and picked something off his shirt. "I came home."

Liar. Jackson slipped the receipt into his pocket. "Can you prove that?"

"I wish you'd tell me what this is about."

Schak, who'd read Patrick Brennan's file, asked, "How well did you know Craig Cooper?"

"He's an old friend. I get the feeling he may have died last night."

"He was murdered," Schak said. "When was the last time you saw him?"

Patrick's mouth tightened, but again, Jackson couldn't read him. Grief? Anger?

After a moment, the suspect leaned back on the couch, as if tired. "A couple weeks ago. Craig called and asked how I was doing. We met at the tavern for a beer and talked about old times."

"What tavern?" Jackson asked.

"Lucky Numbers."

"Do you know where Craig lived?"

"He said he had a place nearby."

"What did you talk about?"

"Like I said, old times." Patrick flinched in pain.

"Did you talk about the robbery?"

Patrick held his stomach. "I don't feel well. I need you to leave so I can lay down."

"We just need a few more minutes," Jackson pressed. "Tell us about the robbery."

"I wasn't involved and I'm not talking about it." Patrick scooted to the edge of the couch, then lumbered to his feet and headed for the short hallway.

"Where are you going?" Jackson and Schak were both on their feet.

"The toilet."

A noxious odor filled the room. Jackson and Schak glanced at each other. The bathroom door slammed closed.

"What now?" Jackson was a little stumped.

"I say we get the hell out of here before he lets loose with more of that." Schak's eyes went wide with mock horror.

"I think he's lying about coming straight home."

"I do too. We need to keep digging." His partner stepped toward the front door. "We'll show Patrick's picture around the storage unit and find out if anyone saw them together."

Jackson was inclined to agree. They didn't have anything to hold him on or charge him with yet, but they knew Patrick's address and vehicle information. He wouldn't get far if he tried to run, and he didn't seem like someone with the resources to buy a plane ticket to Mexico.

As Jackson moved to leave, a book on an end table caught his eye. Jackson pulled on gloves from his carryall before picking it up. But it wasn't really a book, just a front cover and a small chunk of pages. Embossed on the black surface were the words *Holy Bible*. In the lower left corner were the initials *DB*. Danny Brennan? The missing section of the torn Bible they'd found in Craig Cooper's storage unit.

CHAPTER 11

Wednesday, March 13, 4:45 p.m.

Schak's desk was six feet from Jackson's in a space crowded with several more desks and a half dozen filing cabinets. The odd vertical panels around the exterior of the building limited the natural light from the windows. But the violent crimes area was as familiar and comfortable as his own home.

"Should we make him wait?" Jackson asked. Earlier they'd waited twenty minutes for Patrick to finish in the bathroom before hauling the whining suspect into the precinct. Schak had taken the suspect into the interrogation room while Jackson picked up coffee.

"Make who wait?" Evans walked in, her hair damp and her forehead creased in irritation. She was still attractive.

"Patrick Brennan. He's in the interrogation room."

"Good." She gestured at their Full City cups. "Where is my coffee?"

"Sorry. I didn't know you were here." Jackson would have gladly traded his coffee for one of her little Provigil energy tablets, but he didn't dare ask in front of Schak.

Evans found an empty cup on her desk and held it out. "That's okay, you can share."

Jackson poured her some coffee and Schak grumbled and contributed too.

"Should I observe the interrogation?" Evans asked.

"Sure. But first, do you have anything new?"

"I learned Dora Cooper is dead, so the ex-wife didn't do it. I also found Danny Brennan's widow, and Maggie Brennan blames Craig Cooper for the robbery and for Danny's death."

"Interesting." Jackson sipped his coffee. "Cooper must have been quite a piece of work before prison stripped him of his mojo." He gestured with his head. "Let's step into the conference room and do a quick update on the board as we talk. I want to keep all these people straight."

Evans went first, grabbed the marker, and started a family tree. "This will be challenging with two of these men dead and two having the same last name." She listed Patrick and Danny next to each other, with Maggie under Danny's name. On the right of Danny, she listed Craig Cooper with Dora under his name, then made a line through it, with the word *deceased* above. Next Evans drew a box around Danny and Patrick and wrote *brothers*. Then she drew a box around Danny and Craig and wrote *bank robbers*. She turned to Schak. "Did you talk to Patrick's ex?"

"Her name's Kathy Brennan, and she doesn't seem to hate anyone. But she did tell me where to find Patrick, so she's not protecting him either."

Evans wrote *Kathy* on the board under *Patrick*, then picked up her coffee. "In case you're wondering," Evans said between sips, "the reason I didn't bring Maggie in for questioning is that she has an alibi. She was home with her daughter, watching a movie."

"How old is the kid?"

"Seventeen or so." Evans shrugged. "Her daughter could have lied to cover for the mom, but why would Maggie be blunt about hating Cooper if she killed him?" Evans wrote *Jenna, 17* under Danny and Maggie with family-tree lines drawn to her.

Schak asked, "Any other kids we know about?"

A moment of quiet.

"We may bring Maggie in yet," Jackson said. "And Kathy. Maybe play them off each other. See what they're willing to tell us about the robbery and the missing money."

"Sounds like fun." Evans looked at Jackson. "Should we grab something to eat?"

He glanced at his watch. "I just want to get this over with, but feel free to get something from the vending machine."

Schak stood. "Let's go talk to Grizzly Adams."

Evans raised a perfect eyebrow.

"Patrick Brennan lives on Wolf Creek in a cabin with a collection of hunting weapons," Schak explained.

Evans wrote it all on the board, her handwriting getting a little messy at the end. "You know that if we go far enough down this robbery path and waste enough time, our perp will turn out to be the brain-damaged giant who lives next door."

"But we could still find the money," Schak countered.

"We'll see."

On the way down the hall, his phone rang and Jackson looked at the ID: *Charlotte Diebold.* Not recognizing the name, he started to put his phone back, then remembered it was the therapist from court. "Wade Jackson here."

"It's Charlotte Diebold. I'm sorry for the late call, but I cleared a spot on my calendar for your daughter. Tomorrow at two."

"Thank you."

"Her name is Katie Jackson?"

"Yes. We'll see you then." Jackson hoped he could make good on that.

Under the harsh fluorescent lights, Patrick looked older than his forty-six years and he breathed with a wheeze. Jackson hoped he had his bowels under control. The windowless ten-foot-square room didn't leave any place for air to escape. It was fitted with a camera that displayed on a monitor in the conference room.

Schak sat on the inside with Jackson near the door. He needed to be ready to bolt. His claustrophobia was getting worse, and he couldn't wait to get into the new police building with its full-size conference and interrogation rooms. The money had come out of Eugene's "facilities construction" budget because the building they were in now wouldn't withstand an earthquake, and with all those patrol cars parked underneath, it was a potential worst-case scenario.

Jackson put his recorder on the table. He liked to have his own verbal copy for easy referral. "Patrick Brennan is here with detectives Wade Jackson and Rob Schakowski. Patrick has declined to call an attorney to be present." Jackson stated the time and date, then sipped his coffee. His stomach growled in protest. This could be a long one.

He went over the basic questions he'd already asked, such as where Patrick was Tuesday night at the time of Craig Cooper's death. Jackson hadn't mentioned the torn Bible when he'd cuffed Patrick, wanting to get the suspect on record lying about when and where he last saw the victim. That would give them leverage. Patrick repeated his earlier statement about seeing Craig in the tavern two weeks prior.

"Did you fight with him?" Jackson asked.

"No. We're friends." Patrick's facial skin hung so loosely he looked perpetually sad.

"Did you see Craig Cooper after that?"

A pause. "No."

"Were you ever in his storage unit?"

"No."

"Earlier you claimed you didn't know where Craig lived, yet you showed no surprise when I mentioned the storage unit."

"So? He just got out of prison. I didn't expect him to be at the Hilton."

Patrick was a wiseass. "Were you inside or outside Craig's storage unit when you fought over Danny Brennan's Bible and ripped it in half?" Jackson held out his phone and showed the photo he'd taken in Patrick's house. "The other half was in the murder victim's possession."

Surprise and shame flashed in Patrick's eyes. He finally stammered, "That happened in the tavern. I was surprised to see that he had my brother's Bible. It should have gone to me."

"Bullshit. One of our detectives talked to the bartender, and he doesn't remember the incident." That was fabrication, but they would verify it tomorrow. "You have to stop lying and digging yourself in deeper. Tell us where and why you fought over the Bible."

A long silence.

Schak prodded him with empathy. "Did Craig attack you? We understand if you tried to defend yourself."

"It wasn't like that." Patrick shook his head and his cheeks jiggled.

"Tell us what happened last night," Jackson pressed.

"I stopped by to see Craig after I bought groceries. I wanted to take him some beef jerky and some oranges. He loves 'em both and I knew he wasn't eating well." Patrick began to rock a little. "I felt bad for the way he was living."

Jackson and Schak both waited him out.

"I saw Danny's Bible when I was there and I asked him about it. Craig said he'd had it the whole time he was in prison. I told him I wanted it and he refused." Patrick looked down at his hands. "So I tried to take it from him and it ripped. I was so mad, I left. And the cover and a few pages were still in my hand."

"And Craig was dead on the ground, a knife wound in his neck." Jackson said it softly.

"No. He was alive and yelling at me."

"Did anyone see you leave? Or hear Craig yelling?"

"I doubt it. By then, it was after hours, and the owners had gone home."

Jackson was curious about his access. "How did you get in?"

"The gate was open."

"Fully open?"

"No, just unlocked and open a few inches."

"So you just walked in? What happened next?"

"I went to Craig's unit and we sat in the doorway and talked for a while. Then I saw a Bible and picked it up."

"Then what?"

"I told you. We argued for a minute, then he grabbed the Bible and tried to take it from me. It ripped in half, so I cussed at him and left."

"How loud was the argument?" Jackson hoped to find a witness, even if he had to call every customer at Safe and Secure Storage. Maybe there were more people living in the units.

"We kept it quiet. Craig didn't want the owners to know he was living there."

"Where was Craig when you walked away?"

"Standing in the doorway."

The door to Cooper's unit had been locked, with the bicycle outside. "Where was his bicycle?"

A puzzled look. "I think it was outside. And the door to his space was open, like he'd just got there."

"And open when you left?"

"Yes."

Jackson had found the torn Bible inside the storage unit. Had Cooper stepped out and locked the door, preparing to leave again? More likely Patrick was a liar. "Why did you wait to kill him until you were both outside?"

"I didn't do it. He was standing there, swearing at me, when I left."

"Did he mention going out somewhere?"

"No."

"Did you leave the gate open when you left?"

"Yeah."

Jackson had removed a knife from Patrick's belt when he'd taken him into custody earlier. He laid that knife on the table. "You were at the crime scene at the time of death, and Craig's blood is probably on this knife. Why not just tell us what happened? It will look better to the jury if you take responsibility for your actions."

"I didn't kill him."

Jackson mustered up some empathy. "We understand that it was self-defense. But we can't help you if you don't tell us what happened."

"I want my knife back. I'm done talking." Patrick's face twisted with a flash of pain. It was the same look he'd had earlier at the cabin.

Jackson stood. "We'll call the DA and see if he's willing to cut you a deal if you talk to us. Maybe manslaughter. Drink your coffee. We'll be back in a minute to talk about the bank robbery."

Patrick reached for the coffee, and Jackson noticed the suspect used his right hand . . . as the killer had. As they walked out, they heard Patrick groan.

"What do you think?" Jackson asked as they headed down the hall.

"I think that room is gonna be toxic when we get back."

"We'll have to ask him about the robbery money before we give him a bathroom break." Jackson stepped into the conference room.

Evans turned and scoffed. "You know he's lying. We need to look at the security video and see when he came and went. And I want to know why that Bible was so important to both him and Cooper. They don't seem like the sentimental type."

"Maybe it has a safe deposit number or some other clue to the money," Schak offered.

"We'll have to look it over." Jackson watched Patrick Brennan on the monitor. His face was pinched and he held his hands under his sagging gut. Jackson worried about holding him in the cell too long. But he was leery about taking Patrick to the county jail, where they released inmates as fast as they processed them. He turned to his task force. "Let's get the DA's office to write up paperwork ASAP. We need a weapons search and a DNA swab. Patrick needs to be either here or in jail until we have both."

"I'm on it." Evans started dialing and stepped to the back of the room to make her call.

Jackson didn't need to ask the DA about a deal. If Patrick confessed to killing Cooper in a fight, he'd get a plea bargain. Nobody wanted to waste a jury trial on an ex-con. A sad reality. On the off chance that Patrick was telling the truth, they'd have to keep digging. Jackson downed his coffee. "Let's go back in."

Their suspect looked relieved to see them so soon. "I need to use the toilet."

"You pulled that on us before," Schak said, his tone gruff. "You're going to answer some questions first."

"I have irritable bowel syndrome," Patrick whined. "And it's worse when I'm upset."

"Then let's get this over with." Schak leaned forward. "We know you were involved in a robbery in 2004. Even if you didn't go into the bank, you either drove the car or helped your brother and Craig plan it. You think Craig stashed the money, don't you?"

"I don't know. The cash never turned up."

"We're not going to press robbery charges," Jackson said. "We just want to know what happened to Craig. Right now it looks like you killed him over a Bible."

"No."

"You didn't go see him to deliver oranges either. There were none in his rental space. Tell us what you talked about."

Silence.

"A hundred and twenty-five thousand dollars is still missing, and everyone will assume you went to see him about it."

"I asked him about it. So what?" Patrick grimaced. "I'm sure his PO asked him about it too. And his sister."

"What did Craig say?"

The sour smell of diarrhea filled the room. Jackson tried to keep his face impassive.

"What he always said. That Danny was carrying the money and ditched him after they left the bank. Then someone ratted and they both were arrested."

"Did you turn them in?"

"Hell no." Patrick looked offended.

"Did you believe Craig when he said he didn't know where the money was?"

Patrick grimaced again. "I don't know."

Schak raised his voice. "If you didn't kill him, who did? Who would want to kill Craig Cooper—a lonely ex-con—except you?"

"I don't know."

Jackson's eyes watered from the stench. Schak made a gagging sound and lurched to his feet.

"Don't leave me here!" Patrick jumped up. "I have to use the toilet."

Schak jerked open the door, and Jackson motioned for Patrick to exit with them. In the hallway, they heard Evans laughing.

CHAPTER 12

Wednesday, March 13, 7:25 p.m.

Jackson pulled into Kera's familiar driveway at the top of the slope and felt his shoulders relax. She opened the door, and the sight of her striking face made his headache disappear. Kera's wide cheeks, full lips, and luminous copper hair caught people's attention, but it was her smile that made them want to know her. Jackson pulled her close, inhaling the scent of her warm skin. Kera tended to be in constant motion, except for these blissful moments.

"How's Katie?" she asked, as she led him into the house.

"Okay, I think. She's with her aunt, and she has a counseling appointment tomorrow."

Kera headed for the kitchen, and Jackson remembered the first time he'd come here to question her about a case. She'd fed him something healthy and made him laugh. He sat down at the table, the smell of meat roasting in the oven making him drool.

Kera poured him coffee. "I know you're going back to work and will drink it anyway."

"Thanks. It saves me a stop later. What is that incredible smell?"

"Italian-seasoned pork roast. But it can wait." Kera eased onto his lap and kissed him gently.

Her lips were full and soft, and Jackson wanted her. "You feel great," he murmured, pressing against her. But his body didn't respond. They hadn't had sex since Renee had died. Guilt, grief, and worry made him feel impotent.

Eventually, Kera pulled away. "I'm sorry. I'll wait until you're ready."

His jaw tightened. "I'm the one who's sorry. I just need more time."

"It's okay. You've been through a lot, and it's not over." She kissed his forehead and stood up. "You're just so sexy, I can't resist."

Jackson didn't know what to say. Their relationship had taken so many hits, he couldn't believe she still tried to make it work. Would they ever have a real life together?

"I love you," he finally choked out.

Over their meal, she asked about the case he was working, and he gave her a general description. "The victim's sister says he was trying to start fresh, but the hardest thing for ex-cons is to steer clear of old friends. Those contacts usually lead back to drugs, alcohol, or jail. This time, it may have cost him his life."

"That's sad, but it sounds like you'll get the killer." Kera reached over and touched the back of his hand. "You seem worried, but it's not about the case, is it?"

"No, it's Katie. She still doesn't want to be around me." Jackson put down his fork, no longer hungry. "I called her on the way over and she didn't answer."

"I'm so sorry. I'm sure the phase is temporary. She'll get tired of feeling lost and alone, and she'll realize you're her family, no matter what happened."

"I appreciate that. I'm hoping her new counselor will help." Jackson took his plate to the sink and checked his watch. He really had to get back to work. He hadn't talked to the victim's employer or retraced Cooper's steps from earlier in the day.

Kera hugged him from behind. "You're not going anywhere yet." As Jackson turned to kiss her, his phone rang. They both groaned.

Jackson looked at the ID. "It's Katie's aunt. I have to take it." He stepped away from Kera and said hello.

"Wade? Katie's gone. I'm so worried."

His meal turned to rocks in his stomach. "Gone where?"

"I don't know. I was fixing dinner and I heard her get a call. When I went to the guest bedroom to tell her it was time to eat, she wasn't there."

"No note or anything?" He knew better.

"No. I even walked to the little park to see if she'd just gone out for a minute, but she's not here anywhere." A pause. "And Wade?"

"Yes?"

"Katie took her laptop and all the clothes that she kept here."

Oh no! Where had she gone? "I'll see what I can do. Call me if you hear from her." He kept his tone casual as his heart tore open. "Thanks, Jan." Jackson clicked off, his mind scrambling.

"That was about Katie?" Kera's voice was gentle.

Jackson opened his eyes. "She ran off. She took the clothes she kept at Jan's house and disappeared without a word."

"Can you put out an alert or something?"

"No." In this situation, being a cop didn't help much. "She's fifteen and she left of her own free will. I can't force her to come home, so there's no point in getting patrol officers involved."

"We have to do something!"

This was why he loved Kera. She always wanted to be proactive. When Danette had disappeared, she'd gone looking herself. He nodded and said, "When Katie misses her first treatment session, she'll be in violation of her court order, so patrol cops can arrest her then." *If they find her.* Jackson hugged Kera and racked his brain for a plan. He would call all her friends, at least. Should he ask for another leave of absence? Would Lammers give him one or pressure him to retire?

"Can they put an ankle monitor on her?"

"Without personnel to track it, there's no point." Jackson grabbed his jacket from the chair. "I have an idea."

"Good. What is it and what can I do?"

"I'll hire Ed McCray to find her. He's bored and thinking of doing consulting work anyway."

Kera cocked her head. "And if he finds her?"

"We'll see. I just don't want Katie on the streets."

"Does she have a friend or boyfriend she might be staying with?"

Jackson grimaced. "I think she has a new boyfriend, but I've never met him and she won't talk to me." He stood in the kitchen and called the phone numbers he had for Katie's friends, leaving messages for two. The third girl claimed she hadn't seen Katie in weeks.

Jackson was anxious to leave. He needed to be on the move. Being out there, on the street driving, would feel less wrong than hanging out with his girlfriend while his teenage daughter was AWOL. "I have to go."

"Let me know if I can do anything." Kera kissed him, her forehead creased with worry.

If only he'd met her sixteen years ago, he thought for the dozenth time.

In the car, Jackson called McCray. While he sat in the driveway, Danette pulled in and unloaded the baby from his car seat. Jackson waved and looked back down, hoping the young woman wouldn't come over to chat.

McCray answered, "Hey, Jackson. What's going on? It's too wet and dark to golf, so I'm curious."

"I need your help." His least favorite words. But McCray had worked violent crimes with him for ten years before retiring, and somehow he didn't mind asking an old teammate.

"What can I do?"

"Find Katie for me. She ran off from her aunt's house. I'll pay you investigator fees, of course."

"Let's backtrack. What do you mean 'ran off'?"

Jackson had seen McCray once since Renee's funeral, and they'd talked briefly about Katie's troubles. McCray had raised twin girls but hadn't offered any advice except to "wait it out." Rain beat down on the roof and Jackson started the car. "I dropped her off with Jan this afternoon, so I could work a new homicide. Six hours later, Katie took all the clothes she keeps over at Jan's and left." Needing to keep moving, Jackson backed out of the driveway. "We went to court today, and the judge mandated a substance-abuse program. It's outpatient, but Katie apparently doesn't plan to go."

"That's a pisser. I hope she pulls through this soon. In the meantime, I'll do what I can."

They didn't talk about the money. Jackson fully intended to pay McCray, but he knew his friend would resist it until the end.

"I don't plan to interfere with Katie. I just want to know where she is. Unless she's on the street."

"And if she is?"

"Have a patrol officer take her to Serbu. I can't bear the thought of her sofa surfing with drug dealers and lowlifes."

"Any leads for me?"

Jackson was headed for the downtown area, where runaways gathered. "If Katie isn't in the obvious hangouts, then she might be with a new boyfriend. I'll e-mail you a current photo to show around."

"Do you want me to start now?"

Jackson heard his hesitation. Who the hell wanted to go out on a wet March night looking for a teenager who didn't want to be found? But how was he supposed to function, to sleep, not knowing where she was? "In the morning is fine. I'm checking the downtown area now. But I have an autopsy to attend in the morning and more people to interview for this case."

"She'll be all right, Jackson. Katie is smart and resourceful beyond her years."

Not when she's drunk. "I know. Thanks, pal. I'll let you know if I hear anything or come up with any leads."

"Keep your mind strong."

"Talk to you tomorrow."

Jackson cruised the core city blocks, past the bus depot and the library where the kids hung out during the day in small groups, often wearing trench coats and boots and sporting piercings and pink hair. But the teenagers were long gone, either home to the parents they defied by not going to school or home with friends to sleep on a couch in a tiny, filthy apartment . . . but not before getting drunk or high.

Jackson prayed Katie was smart enough to stay away from heroin or meth. But alcohol made people stupid, and Katie was hurt and confused. Should he have sent her somewhere? To a private school or camp? Unless she was locked in, no facility could keep her either. In a few short months, his daughter had morphed from a child he could control with a stern voice into a young adult who was beyond his reach. This was the point where counselors—and parents who had been through it—would encourage him to let go and accept the things he couldn't control or change.

He wasn't ready.

After a half hour downtown, he drove south to his own neighborhood, cruising past the home that he, Katie, and Renee had shared for most of Katie's fifteen years. He half expected to see his daughter sitting on the porch in front of the garage where the two of them had built his trike, a three-wheeled vehicle made from a Volkswagen bug and a Harley motorcycle.

Jackson circled back and parked across the street. He wouldn't have blamed her for wanting to come back here. It was her home. First he'd uprooted her so he could sell the house and get out from under the mortgage he shared with Renee, then Katie had been through the kidnapping and shooting death of her mother. Her life had been completely disrupted over the last six months. Jackson wished he could go back too. He would have given anything to have Renee hassling him about money again. If he had stayed in this house, would his ex-wife still be alive?

Shaking his head to throw off that line of thinking, Jackson eased back onto the street. Ten blocks away, he passed the home he lived in now, which was also the home he'd grown up in. The porch light was on, but the rest of the house was dark. His brother, Derrick, who had lived there all along, was on the road, driving a big truck twenty-five days of the month. Missing his only connection to his childhood family, Jackson pulled over and called Derrick.

His brother answered, sounding sleepy. "Jackson? What's wrong?"

Jackson wanted to chuckle and say *I must not call you very often.* But the words caught in his throat, and he blurted out, "Katie ran away."

"Oh no. Have you heard from her?"

"No. It just happened."

"Don't worry. She'll be back." Derrick chuckled. "Remember when I took off to go stay with Grandma when I was ten?"

"Of course. I went with you."

"No you didn't."

"What are you saying?" A weird distress wormed into Jackson's chest. "I remember packing a little blue backpack, the one with the flag decal sewn on."

Derrick laughed again. "Yeah, you packed all right, but you didn't go with me. You chickened out."

"No, I remember crossing the park with you and stopping to look at a dead bird."

"That was a different time, Jackson. We were older then. You didn't walk across town to Grandma's with me."

Stunned that his brain had co-opted his older brother's adventure somewhere along the way, Jackson changed the subject. "When will you be home?"

"Next Friday."

"Let's work on your trike that weekend."

"I'm ready."

"I've got to go. Katie is still out there."

"Take it easy."

Jackson hung up and kept moving. He had a missing daughter and work to do. Going home was not an option.

* * *

River stayed at her desk, reading through employee files on her monitor until she thought she'd go blind. The bottled water company had a high turnover and had hired twenty-eight people in the last twelve months, with twenty-two quitting and three being fired. None had any connection to LTE that she could find on Facebook, Twitter, or any other social media. She found her employee list from JB Pharma and scanned through it again, looking for overlap between the two companies.

A name popped out: Cory Shekel. A look at his termination/hire dates made it clear that he'd left Rock Spring to go work for JB Pharma, which paid a better starting wage. He'd been at the other company when each was attacked. River would pay him a visit—but only if nothing else broke open soon.

She scanned the JB list again and spotted a Samuel Greene. River's pulse quickened. Could Samuel be related to Adam Greene, the LTE member? Or maybe even an alias? River texted Dallas: *Does Adam have a brother? Or ever go by the name Sam?*

His employee file indicated he'd only worked at JB Pharma for three months, quitting two weeks after the sabotage incident. Mr. Greene was looking like a good possibility for the earlier vandalism. But Dallas had been with him at the time of the Rock Spring arson, so he wasn't the rogue operator. Should she ask the Portland bureau for a full-time surveillance team for Adam Greene? With Dallas already in the thick of it, and Greene not being their primary target, it seemed wasteful.

River's stomach growled again, so she shut off her computer, called in a to-go order from Papa Soul's, and headed out. The drive to the restaurant in the Whiteaker area only took her a few blocks out of her way, but it was worth it for deep-fried oysters and mouthwatering corn bread.

The delicious smell drove her crazy until she popped one of the oysters in her mouth as she crossed the overpass to River

Road. Once it hit her stomach, River relaxed. She became aware that very little traffic was on the road, but that a vehicle with high headlights was behind her. Had it been back there before she turned on Chambers?

River slowed, and the big vehicle slowed too, staying a set distance behind. Was it a tail? A prickly sensation ran up her spine. Who would be following her except someone who meant her harm? Someone like Darien Ozlo, the ex-con who'd threatened to ruin her?

A few blocks later, she pulled off into a 7-Eleven parking lot. In her rearview mirror, she saw a dark Suburban pass by with a man behind the wheel. River ate a few more oysters, checked her text messages, and pulled back onto the road. A vehicle in the distance ahead could have been the Suburban, but in the dark she couldn't tell. She checked side streets as she passed to see if he was waiting to get behind her again.

Nothing.

Her work phone rang and River answered with her earpiece. "Agent River."

"It's Dallas. I got your text, and I'll see what I can find out. Why do you ask?"

River told her about Samuel Greene's employment at JB Pharma and they discussed their next steps. As they talked, River glanced in her rearview mirror, but by now, she'd reached the Beltline intersection and more cars were on the road everywhere. In the dark drizzle, all she could see were glaring headlights. River shook off the earlier feeling as a little paranoia from being tired and hungry.

A few minutes later, she pulled down her driveway, and the sight of Jared's van gave her a rush of pleasure she hadn't experienced in a long time.

CHAPTER 13

Thursday, March 14, 5:30 a.m.

The alarm jolted Jackson awake, and he slammed the off button and pushed out of bed. He'd started to hate the damn beeping that forced him awake before he was ready. Typical for a homicide case, he'd stayed up late, working until he couldn't think straight, hoping he would pass out the minute he climbed into bed. But instead he'd lain there worrying about Katie, imagining her drunk and passed out in an alley. Or in some guy's apartment being sexually abused while she slept. How was he supposed to sleep, live, and function while his baby girl was out there, not in her right mind? Where had she gone?

He stumbled into the bathroom and took a shower, alternating hot and cold, until he shocked his brain and body into sharp focus. After gulping his prednisone, he dressed and strapped on his weapon, thinking of how Katie wouldn't hug him when he had it on.

Jackson made a pot of dark coffee and called the hospital, just to make sure Katie hadn't been admitted. Feeling relieved and disappointed, he sat down and glanced at the newspaper headlines while he ate some toast to soak up the acid in his stomach. The top story was the firebomb at the Rock Spring factory, but there was little real information. The reporter, Sophie Speranza— whom he'd grudgingly come to respect—had speculated that the same person or group had been responsible for the sabotage at JB Pharma. Jackson hoped the FBI caught the bastard before he hurt someone.

Where was Katie this morning? Was she warm and safe in bed somewhere? Or hungover and puking into a stranger's toilet? Not knowing ate at him like a toxic parasite, and Jackson feared he would go a little crazy if he didn't find her soon. What would he do to find someone else's daughter? Then it hit him. Phone records. Katie was on his cell phone plan, and he could access a list of her recent calls and texts online.

It took him ten minutes to log in and find his way around, but he finally had a printout of the numbers she'd texted in the last twenty-four hours. Without addresses, they weren't much use, but he would turn the list over to McCray, who could still access EPD's databases because of the cold-case work he did as an occasional volunteer.

Feeling like he'd had a breakthrough, Jackson pushed Katie out of his head. He had to focus on this case while the evidence was still fresh, and he hoped this morning's autopsy would give him more insight. Or at least provide some trace evidence that could be linked to the perp. He was pretty confident that Patrick Brennan was the right suspect, but without solid physical proof or a stronger motive, the district attorney might not get a conviction. Jackson made a mental note to ask Slonecker to their next task force meeting.

Grabbing a thermos of coffee, Jackson left early so he could cruise the downtown area on his way to McCray's to drop off the cell phone records. He knew the search would be pointless, but he had to do it anyway. He also had to go about his life, just like all the other parents whose kids had run away, disappeared, or become so addicted they were like strangers. He was grateful he had a job that kept his mind occupied.

The elevator ride down to the basement of the hospital filled Jackson with dread. The confining service elevator was unnerving enough, but the dark, narrow hallway was creepy. Jackson had to take a long breath before pushing through the door to Surgery 10, as the autopsy room was called. Looking nothing like the post-mortem venue in Portland, where he used to drive for autopsies, the space was shallow and not much bigger than his living room. Oversize stainless-steel drawers filled the right end, and a shiny counter lined the back wall. A tall wheeled table stuck out into the room, and Craig Cooper's body rested under a white covering. Rich Gunderson, the medical examiner, removed it as Jackson walked in.

"Hey, Jackson. Konrad's running late, but knowing him, that means he'll still be here before eight."

Rudolph Konrad, the pathologist, was a busy man who kept to a schedule and always commented when Jackson was a minute behind. "Good. I'm not ready for this anyway." He pulled on a protective mask and gloves and stayed near the door.

"We should give him a hard time," Gunderson said. "Maybe play a practical joke."

Jackson wasn't in the mood, and felt relieved when the pathologist walked in a moment later. Konrad's fleshy face and blond hair made him look twenty-five, but he had the personality of an uptight sixty-year-old. He was likely in the middle somewhere.

"Sorry to be late. We'll get started right away." Konrad moved to the sink to scrub his hands.

Jackson stayed back until Konrad was ready. He'd get plenty of corpse-staring time while the pathologist conducted a visual inch-by-inch search of Craig Cooper's skin. It was always interesting to see what people had hidden under their clothes—scars, tattoos, birthmarks, and piercings. They held surprises inside their corpses too, like tumors, shrapnel, or pregnancies.

Craig Cooper's body had gone soft and white in prison, obviously not an inmate who'd taken advantage of the weight machines or yard time. His lower legs were covered with thick black hair, and his arms were inked with tattoos. Only a couple of the images looked professionally crafted. The others had the crude black-ink-only look of prison tattoos created by people with limited skills and tools.

For the moment, Jackson focused on the victim's feet because they were closest. Cooper had a crooked little toe that looked like it had been broken and a nasty burn scar on the inside of his left ankle.

Konrad commented on both, then continued his search up the dead man's legs. Jackson mentally planned his day while he waited to hear something relevant. His next stop would be at the gas station where Cooper had worked, then he needed to update Lammers and check in with the lab. He hoped Joe would tell him they'd found blood on Patrick's knife and that the sample was on its way to the state lab. He would also check in to see if the DA's office had come through with a signed warrant for Patrick Brennan's cabin.

He heard Konrad mention a familiar name and tuned back in. The pathologist was examining a tattoo. "Do we know who Dora is?" Konrad looked over his glasses at Jackson.

"Dora Cooper. The victim's ex-wife. She's deceased too." Jackson leaned forward for a better look at the tattoo. A simple design with her name in cursive and the O in red ink in the shape of a heart. Another ink image below sported a green-and-black dragon. Jackson wondered if the dragon had been added later and if it also referred to the woman who'd eventually left him.

Konrad examined Cooper's shoulders and clavicles, then finally leaned over for a close-up look at the wound. He probed and used his magnifier and measuring tool. After a long couple of minutes that tested Jackson's patience, Konrad put the tools down.

"This is unusual. There are several entry points. The victim was stabbed several times, all in close proximity with a sharp, small blade. And the wound is very deep." The pathologist glanced at Jackson. "Multiple stab wounds usually indicate rage or a prolonged fight, but this victim has no defensive wounds, and the incisions are so close together they suggest a certain control or purposefulness."

Jackson tried to visualize Patrick standing next to Cooper, plunging a knife into the same area on his neck over and over. What did that mean? How did Patrick's height compare to Cooper's? "How tall is the victim?"

"Five-nine and a half." Konrad took a step back to look at the length of the corpse. "The stab wounds don't appear to have an angle, so the killer is probably around the same height."

Gunderson spoke up. "The wound is on the victim's left, so the killer is likely right-handed, which doesn't narrow it down much. But I also noted that there wasn't a lot of blood. Was the carotid artery severed?"

"Completely." Konrad made a small shrug. "Sometimes a wound like that sends the victim into shock and they die almost instantly. When the heart stops pumping, the blood flow eases." The information was meant for Jackson.

"What is this?" The pathologist grabbed a magnifier and used a tiny tool with his other hand to extract something from the wound.

Jackson waited while he examined it.

Finally, Konrad said, "It looks like a metal flake, but we'll have to send it to the lab for analysis." Jackson knew better than to ask him to guess. Konrad looked at Gunderson. "Let's turn him over."

Jackson glanced around the room, preferring not to witness the casual handling of a dead body. He was just glad it wasn't a female victim today.

The pathologist examined the back of the victim's neck. "Interesting." Konrad's usually deadpan voice sounded a little excited. He turned to the ME. "Let's get photos of this puncture before I cut into it."

"I already took them." Gunderson looked a little sheepish. "The red mark is in my report, but I thought it was just an insect bite." When he brought the bodies in, the medical examiner cleaned and photographed them, as well as collected trace evidence and blood samples. Konrad, the pathologist, performed the postmortem exam and determined the cause of death.

Konrad grabbed a scalpel and made two deep incisions. "As I thought. This is an exit wound. The weapon lightly punctured the skin on the back of his neck, but it didn't break all the way through."

Jackson tried to envision something long and sharp on the end. As it hit him, Konrad continued. "I believe this victim was shot with an arrow, then stabbed repeatedly with the same arrow."

CHAPTER 14

Thursday, March 14, 7:35 a.m.

River woke to the smell of frying bacon and sat up, confused and strangely eager. Was someone in her house? She grabbed her Glock, a split second away on her nightstand, then bolted out of bed. Except for the low hum of the heat pump, the house was silent. The lovely bacon smell drifted in through her bedroom window, which she always left slightly open when she slept. She remembered inviting Jared to park his van—his home on wheels—in her driveway. Was he cooking out there?

River glanced at the clock. *Damn*. She'd slept late after staying up until three, reading case notes and background history on Ted Rockman. She couldn't help it; her natural rhythm was to stay up late and sleep four or five hours. She was grateful she didn't need more.

Weapon still in hand, she hurried to the front room to look out the window. The curtains were half open—reflecting her need for both daylight and privacy—so she stopped at the edge of the area rug, not wanting Jared to see her in her purple silk pajamas. He had set up a gas camping stove on a sawhorse next to the van and was cooking breakfast. He wore black work pants and a faded denim jacket and looked happy. The early morning light cast a soft glow on the scene, and River wanted to be out there with him, sipping hot coffee in the cold air and sharing whatever it was that made him smile. She watched for a moment, imagining what it would be like to be intimate with such an unassuming and resourceful man.

Jared turned, as if sensing her stare, and River spun and fled down the hall. It wasn't a campground, she reminded herself, but her front yard. And he wasn't her boyfriend, just a nice, albeit homeless, remodeler who was working on her house. Still, she found herself smiling through her shower and thinking about waking up to Jared in her kitchen. If he liked to cook bacon in the morning, she could do worse for a roommate.

Once she was dressed, River stepped outside and invited him in.

"Thanks. I'd like to make some coffee in your kitchen if I can." He saw her checking out the camp stove. "Does it bother you? I should have asked first." He looked around. "I didn't see any nearby neighbors."

River smiled. "That's why I bought this place." An apple orchard bordered her property on the right, and a small oak grove gave her privacy on the left. "I liked waking to the smell of bacon, once I realized where it was coming from."

"I saved you some." Jared lifted the lid from the cast-iron frying pan.

River could have kissed him. "I'll have a piece." She picked up a greasy strip and ate it on her way into the house. Jared followed a moment later with coffee grounds in one hand and a tool pouch in the other. She made tea while he made coffee, and it pleased her to share her space with someone. She'd been alone for so long. With the exception of a three-week relationship with a woman she'd met on the job when she was new at the bureau—and still male—River had been on her own. The romance hadn't worked because the sexual chemistry had been nonexistent. For a long time, she'd believed she was asexual, a passionless person. But she felt some heat now and she liked it.

"I'll finish the family room floor today and maybe start on the bathroom," Jared said between sips. "That toilet has to go."

River couldn't help but laugh. The hall bath had pink fixtures from the fifties and didn't flush properly. She'd bought the property for the private Santa Clara location, its huge back garden, and fire-sale price. She'd viewed it as an opportunity to remodel and make the space her own. "I've got to get to work." She finished her tea and rose to leave. "You can call or text me if you have any questions."

"I'll be fine. Go make the world safe." Jared gave her a lopsided smile.

And he would be here when she returned, River thought on her way to her car.

Normally, she would have stopped at the bureau, checked her e-mail, and reported to her supervisor, but she was already running late, so she drove straight to the Rock Spring factory, where she hoped to find Candy Morrison at work. The woman's Facebook connection to Chris Noonaz, plus her entry into the building moments before the arsonist had arrived, probably wasn't coincidental. But this was Eugene, where people tended to be connected, even though it was a small city rather than a small town.

The full parking lot told her the factory was up and running again. River wondered if the arsonist realized that. Had he driven by to see the extent of the damage and been disappointed? She knew she shouldn't think of the suspect in only male terms, because it could be a woman, but the statistics didn't support that. Arsonists were almost exclusively men. And the night watchman had described the bomber as big and muscular.

As River strode across the parking lot, a security guard came out from a covered smokers' area and stopped her before she reached the building. River identified herself and showed her badge, glad to see Ted Rockman had beefed up his security. The guard called someone in the main office, then let her pass.

As she headed for the small man-door, the overhead door opened and a forklift carrying crates rumbled out. River scooted through the opening and made her way past the bottling lines. She looked for Candy, but didn't see her. The employees all wore hairnets, gloves, and jackets. The overhead heaters couldn't keep the building warm with the overhead door opening throughout the day.

River climbed the stairs, remembering the underwear she'd found in the couch when she'd investigated the night of the firebomb. But it wasn't Bromwell in the office. An older man, with mocha-toned skin and ink-black hair, stood and greeted her. "Ricardo Morrison, plant foreman. How can I help you?"

The name gave her pause. "Agent River, FBI. I'm looking for Candy Morrison. Is she related to you?"

"She's my wife. Why do you want to see her?"

"That's not your concern. Where is she?" River wondered if she should question Ricardo as well.

He didn't move or respond for a full ten seconds. "She's in the reject room. I'll take you there."

River followed him downstairs to the back of the plant. They passed through a door she hadn't seen when she'd been here Tuesday night and into a cramped room where two women sorted defective plastic bottles.

"Candy, this FBI agent wants to talk to you." Ricardo's tone was meant to be intimidating. He was clearly upset that he didn't have control of the situation.

A blonde woman looked up, startled. She looked to be in her late thirties but still two decades younger than her husband. She didn't wear a hairnet like the other employees, but her tight pony-tail wasn't flattering either. "Why me?" Her eyes flashed with fear.

"Good question, Candy." Ricardo crossed his arms. "Why does the FBI want to talk to you?"

"Let's go out to my car." River wanted to get the woman away from her husband. When Candy hesitated, River took hold of her arm and gave her a friendly smile. "Now, please."

Candy grabbed her jacket from the bench and didn't look at Ricardo as they walked out. River didn't let go until they were on the factory floor. The employees glanced up from their worksta-tions with worried eyes as they passed. The noise of the factory drowned out even the sound of their footsteps. River hoped they were all wearing earplugs.

The overhead door was still open and the wind blew into the building. Candy shivered.

Out in the parking lot, River turned to her suspect. "I won't tell your husband you were here with Jerry Bromwell Tuesday night, but I need the truth." As she spoke, River heard pounding footsteps and turned.

Right behind them, Ricardo yelled. "What the fuck did you say?"

Oh shit.

In the interrogation room, Candy Morrison picked at her finger-nails and tried to be defiant. River had ended up cuffing Candy's jackass husband to keep him from assaulting his cheating wife, then had left him in the back of a patrol car for EPD to handle. Her patience long gone, she didn't know how much rapport building she could stomach. But she tried.

"I'm an environmentalist too, Candy. Anyone who cares about the future of our species is." River leaned forward. "So I understand why you got involved with Love the Earth. But it's not worth doing ten years in a federal prison."

"I told you, I'm not involved." Candy chewed off a hangnail from her right thumb. "I don't even know Chris Noonaz. He's just a Facebook friend."

"Right now, a judge is issuing a warrant to search your home and computer." It would be true soon, but not quite yet. "Withholding information about an eco-terrorist who sets off bombs will not play well with a jury, even in Eugene."

"I don't know anything about the bomb, I swear." Candy was emphatic.

River didn't buy it. "The perpetrator came into the building shortly after you did. We think you left the door open for him."

"No." Candy shook her pretty blonde head. "I was just there to see Jerry, like I did last Tuesday and the week before."

"Did Jerry Bromwell give you the code or did your husband?"

"Jerry, but only recently."

"Who did you give the code to?"

"No one!" Candy's voice and eyes flared with passion. "Why would I let someone into the building to leave a bomb? I was in that building! We barely got out before it exploded."

Candy had a point, but people took all kinds of risks for their causes. And it hadn't been a high-powered explosive. An incendi-ary device was meant to start a fire, not blow things up. "Other people are in danger now too." River intensified her voice. "What if someone dies in the terrorist's next attack? How will you feel, knowing you didn't help us stop him?"

The suspect was quiet for a moment. "Okay, I do know Chris Noonaz. He's my cousin's boyfriend. And I know he's involved with Love the Earth. But I don't know anything about his plans, and I didn't leave the factory door open for him."

"What's your cousin's name?"

"Melody Light."

"Seriously?" River gave her a look.

"Yes. She hates her father. She had it legally changed."

River related to that. "Where can I find Melody?"

"She works part time at Hummingbird Wholesale."

Only in Eugene, River thought. "And her home address?"

Candy picked at her thumbnail again. "Melody may be a hippie, but she's not an eco-terrorist. And I don't think Cricket is either."

"Tell me where to find her."

Candy reluctantly gave her the location, a duplex near the fairgrounds, and River jotted it down. "Does Chris Noonaz live there too?"

"No. Melody has two kids. She and Cricket are just dating."

"Did you give Melody the code to the Rock Spring building?"

"No! I'm not involved with that group, and I only met Cricket once."

River realized Candy had admitted all she would. Time to make her uncomfortable again. "When and how did you get involved with Jerry Bromwell?"

"I don't know." Candy started to cry. "He flirted with me and it felt good. My husband is—" Her voice trailed off.

"Is what?"

Candy glared, and River heard her think *I hate you.* The thought hit her with an ugly force, taking her aback. River didn't hear thoughts often, but when she did, they were usually timid.

River shook it off. "Your husband is what?"

"Not the man he used to be."

Impotent is what she meant. River remembered Ricardo Morrison coming at her in a rage and had no sympathy for him. But she worried for Candy's safety. "Where will you go when I release you?"

"I don't know." The woman switched to chewing her other thumbnail.

"You need a plan. I want you to be safe. What about going to WomenSpace?"

"I'll stay with my brother until Ricardo cools down."

"Can I drop you off there?" River closed her notepad and stood, eager to question Melody Light, who dated an LTE leader. Maybe she would become an informant.

"Sure," Candy whined, "but I need to get some clothes from my house first."

River didn't have time for that. "I'll get a police officer to escort you."

CHAPTER 15

Thursday, March 14, 10:35 a.m.

The gas station where Cooper had worked was only a mile or so down the road from the storage unit where he'd lived and died. It was also right across from the new Sponsors apartments for recovering addicts, where Cooper had been on a waiting list. Jackson wondered how many of the station's employees were ex-cons. Bordered by empty lots on the left and back side, the station took up a chunk of real estate. Jackson parked off to the side and checked his notes. He'd talked to the owner after leaving the autopsy, and the man had agreed to meet him here. Jackson had arrived early so he could question employees as well.

As he climbed from his car, the sun broke out in an otherwise ugly sky, and for a moment the rain puddles glistened with a dark beauty. Jackson strode toward the attendant booth and the sunlight disappeared. A red truck left the forward pump, and the aging attendant turned and spotted him. Jackson saw the panic in his eyes from ten feet away.

"Are you Cleland Strep?"

"Yes." He swallowed hard.

"Detective Jackson, Eugene Police. Did you know Craig Cooper?" Jackson closed the space between them.

"He worked here and I saw him sometimes, but that's it. I heard he died." Strep shoved his hands in his jacket pockets, and Jackson tensed.

"Keep your hands where I can see them." When Strep complied, Jackson continued. "When did you see him last?"

"What's today? Thursday? I saw him Tuesday at the shift change."

"What time was that and what happened?" The gasoline smell intensified and Jackson wondered if gas pumpers ever got used to it. No wonder Cooper had been looking for a better job.

"Four in the afternoon. I worked the evening shift and got here ten minutes before start time. Craig had worked the midday shift and left about five minutes after four."

"Was he on his bike?"

"A woman picked him up. She was driving a little blue truck, and they put the bike in the back."

That caught Jackson's attention. "Do you know who it was? Had you seen the woman before?"

Strep shook his head. "She had messy light-brown hair and a tanned face, like somebody who's outside a lot. That's all I know. She didn't get out of the truck."

"What do you mean by messy?"

"You know, curly and frazzled."

A vehicle pulled in and Strep said, "I've got to get this."

Jackson had met Cooper's sister and the description didn't match. Who was the woman? A girlfriend? No one had mentioned her. Jackson filled out his notepad, then looked around for cameras and didn't see any.

A cherry-red 1977 Charger in perfect condition pulled in, and Jackson practically salivated in appreciation. The Charger was even more gorgeous than his midnight-blue 1969 Mustang. The muscle car pulled past the pumps and parked behind his city-issued Impala, which he was suddenly embarrassed to be driving. The owner strode toward him, an older man with a confidence that likely came from his cool-car factor.

"I'm Tom Peccanolo. You're the detective?"

"Wade Jackson." They shook hands, something Jackson didn't often do in his line of work. He reminded himself that the gas station owner was a suspect like everyone else.

"Shall we step into the booth?" Peccanolo gestured and zipped his leather jacket against the drizzle.

"We'll just move under the carport." Jackson hated small spaces. "When did you see Craig Cooper last?"

The owner laughed. "So I'm a suspect?"

"It's just routine."

"On Monday. I was here for a while in the afternoon and Craig was on shift."

"Was he a good employee?"

"My best. Always on time and polite with customers. I'm sorry to lose him. He was making a fresh start." Peccanolo was matter-of-fact.

"Do you know the woman who picked him up on Tuesday?"

"No. I wasn't here."

"Have you ever seen him with a woman who has curly, frizzy, light-brown hair and a tanned face?"

"I've never seen him with anyone." The gas station owner sounded clipped now.

Jackson pressed on. He felt like he still didn't know the victim, and the possibility of a girlfriend hinted at a new layer. "What do you know about Craig's personal life?"

Peccanolo shifted his shoulders, and Jackson couldn't read the gesture. Impatience? Remorse?

"In his interview, I asked Craig about his record, and he was up front about his past addiction and the crimes he'd committed. He seemed intent on staying clean and working to rebuild his life. But I didn't really get to know him."

"Did he mention a girlfriend?"

"No. He said he had a supportive sister who had stood by him during a rough childhood. I think he was in juvie for a while, maybe a foster home." The owner gave a gentle smile. "I have a soft spot for ex-cons, being one myself."

"How many of your employees have records?"

"All of them. No violence though, if that's what you're thinking. And I require random urine tests."

A cell phone rang in the station owner's pocket, and Peccanolo rushed his next thought. "I'm not saying one of my employees couldn't have killed Craig, but I highly doubt it." He took the call and stepped away.

Jackson decided he'd spent enough time at the gas station. He now needed to locate and question the woman who'd picked up Cooper from work hours before his death. What if she had been there when Patrick and Cooper fought over the Bible? Or maybe she'd come back to see Cooper afterward. She could be key to the investigation. Jackson headed for his car.

For a loner, Craig Cooper sure had a lot of company on the day he died. Jackson couldn't help but think it was still about the missing hundred-plus grand.

On the way to the department, Jackson called his ex-sister-in-law but she didn't pick up. Unusual for Jan. He left a message, asking if she'd heard from Katie, then called McCray, even though he'd promised himself he wouldn't bother the man with obsessive phone calls.

McCray answered on the third ring. "Hey, Jackson. I was just going to call you."

His heart lurched. "What have you learned?"

"I have an address for the number Katie was texting last night before she took off. I'm heading over there now."

"Where?"

"On Ferry Street." McCray read him the address.

"A house? Who owns it?"

"A property management company."

Not good. "So it's a rental?"

"Yeah. A couple blocks from her school." McCray kept his voice even. "What do you want me to do if I see her?"

"Just let me know she's okay, then keep an eye on her. I'll text and remind Katie that she has an appointment with a therapist at two." Jackson accepted that his daughter didn't want to see him. But someone probably had to take her. "If Katie wants a ride, will you drive her? She doesn't want to see me."

"Of course."

"If she doesn't go to the counselor or sign in for her treatment program by tomorrow, we'll have a patrol officer pick her up."

"Okay, pal. Don't sweat this. As long as she's still using her phone, we know she's okay."

"You're right." Jackson tried to be upbeat. But if Katie wanted him out of her life, she would ditch her phone as soon as she realized he was keeping track of her through it. "Thanks, McCray."

CHAPTER 16

Thursday, March 14, noon

At the department, Jackson forced himself to focus on his case. He ordered sandwiches for the upcoming task force meeting, then opened his Word doc and updated his case notes with the new information from the morning's autopsy and interviews. They had so little to work with. The victim didn't have a cell phone or a bank account, so there weren't any records to review. And Cooper's laptop had almost nothing on it. The sister had deleted all of her files before passing it on, and Cooper had only written a few e-mails. Jackson reminded himself they had Patrick Brennan, Cooper's old associate, in custody, and everything seemed to point to his guilt. So the task force would start to shift their focus to building a solid case against him. Unless the blood on Todd Sheppard's face turned out to be Cooper's. Jackson didn't want that to be true.

He met Schak and Evans in the conference room as the food was delivered. They ate quickly and talked about the firebomb case, which had made the front-page news.

"Quince says they think it might be a rogue operator," Evans reported. "He spent yesterday looking at mug shots trying to identify two guys from a photo taken in a dark tavern."

"Oh the glory." Schak smirked as he chewed. "I'm glad I didn't end up on that case. Doing Jackson's grunt work is tedious enough."

"I wish we had grunt work for this case," Jackson said. "It's weird not having phone or banking records to look at."

Evans pushed away her half-eaten sandwich. "Speaking of grunt work, has anyone looked at the video footage from the storage unit?'"

Crap. Jackson had almost lost track of it. "I gave it to Joe at the crime lab. But if he hasn't gotten to it yet, one of us needs to do it this afternoon."

"With any luck, it'll show Patrick Brennan leaving with blood on his hands." Schak finished his soda and looked at Jackson. "Should I take the board?"

"Sure." Schak's writing was awful, but Jackson couldn't make Evans do it every time. It was too sexist.

The board was already filled with the names of the bank robbers and their ex-wives and/or widows, plus Patrick, the brother who had probably known about the robbery, if not participated in it. Jackson had booked Patrick into the county jail on obstruction of justice charges and requested that he not be released. But sometimes it happened anyway. Without a history of violence, Patrick was a low-risk inmate.

Jackson got started. "A gas station employee saw Cooper leave work the day of his murder with a woman who has curly light-brown hair and a suntanned face."

Evans blinked in surprise. "That sounds like Maggie Brennan, Danny's widow. She told me she hadn't seen Cooper."

Lying bumped her up the list of suspects. "We'll go question her again right after this meeting."

"When did Cooper leave with her?" Schak asked.

"At four in the afternoon when his shift ended."

On the board, Schak added Maggie to the timeline of Cooper's death, and Jackson turned to Evans. "Didn't you say Danny's widow hated Cooper?"

"That's what she implied. She blamed him for getting Danny hooked on meth and involved in the bank robbery."

"Why would she pick him up from work, then lie about it?" Jackson mused.

"She wanted to ask him about the money." Evans said what everyone was thinking.

"But he'd been out of jail for six weeks," Jackson countered. "Why wait? Why did two people from his past both suddenly visit him the day he died? Something must have happened to trigger it."

"We'll bring Maggie in and ask her." Evans was ready to jump up and go.

"What else do we know?" Jackson looked at Schak.

"I canvassed the area around the storage business this morning but didn't find any witnesses or learn anything. No one seemed to know that people were living in the units."

"What if Maggie and Patrick were there at the same time?" Evans speculated. "They may have been working together to pressure Cooper to tell them where the money was."

"Possibly." Jackson remembered the autopsy. "Here's an odd detail. Cooper was most likely shot with an arrow. Then the assailant pulled it out and stabbed him in the same area three or four more times."

Schak sat up straight. "Patrick has a bow on his wall."

"But why stab him after shooting him with the arrow?" Evans' forehead furrowed. "Was Cooper still alive?"

"The pathologist thinks he died quickly."

"So the perp must have had hostility toward him," Evans said. "And shooting him with an arrow wasn't satisfying enough."

"That doesn't rule out either Maggie or Patrick." Jackson visualized the two rows of storage units and tried to imagine where the perp had stood. He or she had to have been close, because the daylight had been fading at the time of death.

"How close do you have to be to kill someone with an arrow?" Evans had taken the same mental path.

"I asked Konrad and he didn't know for sure. He's going to find an expert to help us out. But he thinks that piercing the heart or neck could be lethal even from a distance of thirty or forty feet."

"We need to round up Patrick's bow and arrows for comparison," Schak said.

"I'm waiting for the subpoena. But we can't forget Todd Sheppard, the neighbor," Jackson added. "He could have killed Cooper, then gone down the road to toss the weapon. Just because we didn't find it in the nearest dumpsters doesn't mean Sheppard is innocent."

"Patrick was also there in his storage unit and fighting with Cooper over the Bible." Schak scratched his buzzed head. "Did he walk away, then turn back and shoot him? He must have had the bow with him."

"The fact that he has a bow and was with the victim right before his death is probably enough to convict him." Evans sounded sure.

"I still want to know why Maggie Brennan picked up Cooper from work that day, then lied about not seeing him." Jackson looked at Evans. "Did you learn anything at the storage place this morning?"

"I've talked to almost all of the people who rented units in the same row as Craig Cooper and Todd Sheppard. Nobody even knew the men were there." Evans glanced at her computer tablet. "And Mary Akers, who has the unit across from Cooper's, was at the storage place Tuesday afternoon and didn't see anyone or anything unusual."

Jackson's phone rang and he looked at the ID: *Joe Berloni*. He answered and pressed the speaker button. "We're in a task force meeting. What have you got for us?"

"I found some prints on the victim's bicycle that belong to Patrick Brennan."

"Thanks, Joe. He admits to being at the scene, but we'll ask him about the bike. Have you looked at the video?"

"Sorry, but I haven't had time yet."

Jackson suppressed his irritation. They were all overworked. Schak got up. "I'll go view the footage now."

Jackson and Evans stood too. Time to get back to work.

Maggie Brennan lived in a single-wide in a mobile home park off Bailey Hill. She stepped outside just as Jackson and Evans parked on the narrow winding street. Maggie was slender with a mass of curly hair and carried a black apron.

Evans was already out of her car and hurried to block the path between the porch where Maggie stood and the blue Nissan truck she was about to get into.

"I can't talk right now. I'm on my way to work." Maggie's wary hazel eyes darted between Evans and Jackson, as if sizing up who was more of a threat.

"It's not optional," Jackson said. "Either answer our questions here and now or come with us to the department. I'll give you a minute to call your boss and let him know you'll be late." He moved toward her. "We might as well go inside." A steady drizzle had come down all morning.

"If my boss calls someone else in, I'll lose the shift. I can't afford to miss a night of tips." Her voice wavered with desperation.

Jackson couldn't let himself empathize with her. A man was dead, and Maggie had lied to them. She could be desperate for many reasons. Maggie pressed her lips together, grabbed her cell phone from her purse, and made the call. Jackson and Evans followed her into the house. A teenage girl sat on the couch reading a book. She looked up, startled. The young woman had Maggie's tall, slender build, but her flat nose and pinched-together eyes matched Danny Brennan's mug shot.

"Jenna, excuse yourself." Maggie gestured for the girl to leave.

Jackson remembered that Evans had said Maggie's daughter was seventeen. They would question her too, but not at the same time as her mother. He looked around the small home. Cluttered but clean and no signs of drug or alcohol consumption. The couch faced a large television and was the only place to sit in the living room.

"Let's do this at the table," Jackson said. The hard kitchen chairs and eye-to-eye level would be more conducive to questioning. Except for the cat sleeping in the middle of the wooden surface. Maggie nudged it until it fled. Jackson took back his *clean* assessment.

They sat down, with Evans next to him the way they would in the interrogation room. Jackson jumped right in. "Why did you pick up Craig Cooper from work on Tuesday?"

Maggie's lips trembled. "It was raining, so I gave him a ride home."

Evans snorted. "You just happened by?"

Silence.

Evans leaned forward. "Why did you lie to me and say you hadn't seen Craig Cooper?"

"It just seemed easier."

"Easier than what?"

More silence.

Impatience made Jackson bristle. "Tell us exactly what happened or I'll charge you with obstruction of justice and haul you to jail."

More trembling lips. "Craig called and said he wanted to see me. He said he wanted to make amends. I resisted at first."

"Why did you change your mind?" Jackson asked.

Maggie shrugged. "It seemed like the right thing to do."

Evans tapped her notepad. "You told me yesterday you hated him."

"I still do." Maggie's voice turned bitter. "He got Danny started on drugs, then talked him into that robbery. But I finally decided that if Craig was trying to make amends, I should hear what he had to say."

Yeah, right. "You thought he might offer you some of the cash. You hoped that was what he meant by *making amends.*"

She nodded, unashamed. "Why not find out? He owed me. And Jenna. It's his fault Danny's gone and we live like this. With me killing myself waiting tables at nearly fifty, and Jenna being so insecure and needing special help."

There was so much to ask, but Jackson had to stay focused. "What did Craig say when you saw him?"

"That he was sorry for everything. And that he would start giving me a little money every month as soon as he could."

"Did you ask him about the robbery cash?"

Another bitter twist of Maggie's mouth. "He said he hadn't seen the money since Danny ditched him after they did the job. I never believed that. Danny didn't cheat his friends."

No, just the bank. "What do you think happened to the money?"

"Craig probably stashed it and was living like a monk to fool us all into thinking he didn't have it. I'm surprised he didn't get the hell out of town."

Jackson wondered if Maggie had the money and was planning her own escape. "Where did your conversation with Craig take place?"

"In my car. I dropped him off at the storage unit he calls home and that was it."

"What time was that?"

She shrugged. "Four thirty or so. It was a short ride."

"Where did you go after that?"

"I stopped at Jasper's to buy a lottery ticket, then came home."

Jackson planned to show her photo at the deli/gaming center to verify her story. He didn't trust this woman.

Evans cut in. "That's not what you told me yesterday. You said you worked the lunch shift, then went home and watched a movie with your daughter."

"I did. I just didn't mention giving Craig a ride because I knew you would harass me about it."

"You know it's a crime to lie to a police officer."

"It's a crime to be poor too. And you're keeping me from earning a living."

Her defiance surprised Jackson. "I'd like to talk to your daughter."

Maggie's eyes narrowed. "Why?"

"Standard procedure." Jackson stood to summon the girl. She was seventeen and he didn't need her mother's permission.

Maggie squeezed her hands together. "Go easy on Jenna. She's fragile."

"I'll get her." Evans headed toward the short hallway.

"Second door on the right," Maggie called out.

"Why isn't she in school?" Jackson asked.

"She graduated early."

After a moment of knocking and calling Jenna's name, Evans opened the door and stepped into the room. A moment later, she came back into the kitchen. "Jenna's not in her room."

Jackson looked at Maggie. The trailer wasn't big enough to have many hiding places. The woman shrugged. "She probably left. She doesn't like cops."

"Why not?"

"She saw them kill her father."

Pangs of guilt and sympathy resonated. Jackson knew what a parent's death could do to a child. He had to push his concern aside. "We need to verify your alibi. So Jenna has to talk to us. Please call her and tell her to come back."

Maggie grabbed her apron. "I'll do what I can, but either way, I need to go to work. Money never comes easy to me."

Was that a veiled reference to the robbery money she'd never gotten her share of?

"She's probably next door. I'll go check." Maggie started to leave then turned back. "Jenna lacks social skills. Don't judge her by that."

Maggie went out back the way her daughter must have. Jackson followed, stood on the wooden landing, and watched as Maggie knocked on the trailer next door.

"What do you think?" Evans asked.

He glanced back. "Maggie is hiding something."

"Agreed. I think she's still pissed that she never got her hands on Danny's robbery haul."

After a few minutes, Maggie came back with Jenna. The shy dark-haired girl wouldn't meet his eyes. Jackson gave her a gentle smile. "Thanks for coming, Jenna. Let's sit down at the table."

She took a seat, and Maggie hovered behind her daughter, clutching her work apron. The mother clearly wanted to leave but didn't want to abandon her daughter.

Jackson glanced at Evans and she took the lead. "Did you know Craig Cooper?"

"Yes. He was my father's friend."

"When did you see him last?"

"I don't know. He used to babysit me when I was little but that was long ago. I called him Uncle Craig." Jenna seemed to look past Evans, not making eye contact.

"What about this last Tuesday, March twelfth?" Evans probed. "Where were you that afternoon?"

"I went to a movie with a friend and came home around five."

"What did you see?"

"*Mirror Mirror*. It was directed by Tarsem Singh."

The girl seemed socially awkward, yet she was intelligent enough to graduate from high school early . . . and retain odd details. Did she have a mental condition? He let Evans continue, thinking she might get better responses.

"Was your mother home when you got here?"

"No."

"When did she get home?"

Jenna paused, seeming to concentrate. "I don't know. I was reading. But it was before dinner."

"What time did you eat dinner?" Evans' tone was soft and patient, and Jackson was pleased.

"At six, I think. The news was on. I hate the news, but my mom watches it when she cooks."

"What did you do after dinner?"

"I cleaned my room. I was supposed to do it when Mom was at work." Jenna's facial expression and tone were oddly flat.

"Was your mother home?"

"Yes."

"What about after you cleaned your room?"

"We watched a movie." Before Evans could ask her, Jenna said, "*The Princess Bride*, by Rob Reiner. It's our favorite."

"You must like movies."

"I do, but I like novels better. Have you read *The Passage*? It's very good."

"I haven't." Evans smiled. "Did your mother leave the house after dinner?"

"No."

"Did you go anywhere?"

Jenna shook her head. "No. I lost my driving privilege for a few days."

"You have a license?" Evans sounded as surprised as Jackson was.

"Of course. I'm seventeen."

Evans glanced his way. Jackson could only think of one more thing to ask, and it was more personal curiosity than professional. "Why did you lose your driving privilege?"

"I didn't clean my room."

"Do you have your own car?"

"No. I drive my mother's truck sometimes when she's at work." Jenna's cheeks flushed. "I mean, she lets me. I drop her off and pick her up."

Jackson thanked Jenna and Maggie for their time and headed for the door. Outside, after Maggie drove off, he turned to Evans. "I have a personal errand. Will you check with the neighbors and see if you can verify Maggie's and Jenna's stories for Tuesday?"

"Sure." Evans cocked her head. "I think Jenna has Asperger's."

"That's what I was thinking."

"But I don't sense that she was lying for her mother. She's seems pretty guileless."

"I got that feeling too," Jackson said. "But I still think Maggie knows more than she's telling us. Maybe she threatened Cooper or stole the money from him."

"Maybe. See you back at the department."

CHAPTER 17

After Candy Morrison left, River went down the hall to Agent Fouts' office for an impromptu task force meeting. She was still waiting for the profiler at FBI headquarters to submit his report on their arsonist. They had one from the pharma company incident, but River was curious to see if the arson factor changed the profile of who they were looking for. Two of the four men they were focused on were still unknown, and she needed those names.

Fouts' door was open and he looked up when she stopped in the frame. "Come in." Fouts gestured, looking pleased with himself. "I think I've got the third man."

"Excellent. Who is he?"

"Rick Arbuckle. He was arrested at a logging protest in 2010 and did six months for vandalizing a truck. He's mostly clean-shaven in his mug shot, but that was two years ago. The identifying feature is his nose. Look." Fouts turned his monitor so she could see the side-by-side images. The one from Tony's Tavern was blurry and dark and showed a man with a full beard and shoulder-length hair. On the left was a well-lit image of a younger man with a small goatee and hair that came to his ears. At first, River didn't see the resemblance.

"Look at his nose, then look at his eyebrows." Fouts tapped his monitor, impatient.

River studied the mug shot first. The man's nose had a slight bend at the halfway point, as if it had been broken. The nose in the other image, although less clear, was the same. The thickness and arch of the eyebrows was identical too. "Good work. I might have missed this."

"I had help from facial recognition software."

River smiled. "What do we know about him?"

"Not much yet. Rick Arbuckle is an alias with no Social Security number and no known addresses. He never gave the police his real name, and he doesn't come up in the system anywhere else."

"Damn. Maybe Dallas can find something. But Arbuckle looks big, and the night watchman described the arsonist as big and burly. Unlike the kid with the mohawk, who looks like he has tapeworm." River felt like they were closing in. "We'll get a tail on Arbuckle as soon as we locate him." She remembered her late-night find. "A man named Samuel Greene worked at JB Pharma at the time of the sabotage. The Social Security number he gave is phony, and I think he's either connected to, or the same as, Adam Greene, which might also be an alias."

"I'm glad we've got Dallas on the inside." Fouts leaned back in his chair. "Who did you have in the interrogation room?"

"Candy Morrison. She was at Rock Spring at the time of the arson, and her cousin dates Chris Noonaz."

Fouts let out a low whistling noise. "You think she let our perp into the building?"

"She's adamant that she didn't, but I'm going to see her cousin, Melody Light, next. The good news is that Melody has fraud charges pending for some irregular banking activity. I'm going to try and turn her."

"Want me to come with you?"

"Thanks, but you should stay on Rick Arbuckle. And get me Mohawk's name."

Melody Light's duplex occupied a corner near a small health food store in central Eugene. River pulled up on the Tyler Street side and saw two toddlers playing in the front yard, unsupervised. In the rain. The little girl was still in diapers. River climbed from her car and said hello as she entered the toy-littered yard. The boy, about four, looked up and said hi. The little girl ignored her, intent on an object she'd just found in the grass.

As the girl stuck it in her mouth, River realized it was a cigarette butt. "No, sweetie." She ran to the girl and plucked the debris from her little teeth.

The toddler let out a yelp, then whined loudly.

"Sorry, but that's not good for you." River started to toss the butt into the street, then changed her mind.

A pretty woman stepped from the house and called, "Get away from my kids."

River held out her badge and strode toward the door. "Agent River, FBI."

The woman retreated into the house and slammed the door, the safety of her kids forgotten.

Mad as hell, River pounded on the door. "Open up now or I'm calling Family Services!" What the hell was wrong with this idiot? Was she taking a moment to hide her drugs? Or was Chris Noonaz sneaking out the back?

River pushed open the door but didn't enter. "I'm making the call!" She intended to report the incident, but later when she had more time.

Inside the house, she heard the woman rummaging around. River scanned the front room, a cluttered mess of toys, clothes, dirty dishes, empty food packages, and a corner overflowing with sewing projects. She listened for sounds in the backyard and watched the outside corner of the house to see if anyone was fleeing. River glanced back at the kids, who were both coming toward the house.

"Where's Mom?" The boy seemed curious but unconcerned.

"She's here. Come in out of the rain." River stepped aside to let them go through.

The woman rushed into the living room and bent to hug her kids, her long wavy hair nearly touching the floor. She wore a colorful collection of layered garments that didn't hide her shapely body.

"I'm coming in. We have to talk." Standing in the foyer, River tried to mitigate her anger. On the list of things you could do to damage your children, letting them play outside unsupervised for a few minutes didn't rate anywhere near the top, but she would use it to her full advantage. "Are you Melody Light?"

"Yes." The woman handed the boy a box of crackers. "Take Emmy and go to your room." A faint smell of pot wafted from the woman's hair.

"Have a seat," River commanded.

Melody complied, but River remained standing. "You're going to tell me everything you know about Chris Noonaz and his acts of eco-terrorism, or I will have Family Services take your children into state custody, while I take you into federal custody as an accomplice."

Melody burst into tears.

River was unmoved. "Where is Chris now?"

After a moment, Melody had control. "I don't know. We hang out sometimes, but we're not a couple."

"Tell me what you know about his activities or say good-bye to your children."

Melody glared. "They won't take my kids because I left them outside."

"I pulled this out of the little girl's mouth." River held out the cigarette butt, then slipped it back in her pocket. "And you smell like pot."

"I'm a good mother. I'm just having a bad morning."

River brought out the backup ammunition. "You have a court date next week for fraud charges. The FBI can either make those go away or make them worse. So you will lose your kids *and* go to jail."

She sighed. "You win. What exactly do you want to know?"

River decided to test her. "Where does Chris Noonaz live?"

Melody gave her the same location that Dallas, her UC, had supplied recently.

"Tell me what you know about the firebomb at Rock Spring."

"Nothing. Love the Earth didn't do that." Melody was emphatic.

"Have you and Chris talked about it?" River pulled out her recorder. "I'm going to record this, so don't lie to me."

"I haven't seen him since Sunday, but I called and asked Cricket and he said no. I wanted to know because I don't condone violence."

"But you thought he might have."

Melody swallowed hard. "I know that some LTE members have advocated for more drastic actions."

"What about the sabotage at JB Pharma? Who did that?"

"I don't know." The woman looked over River's shoulder and out the window.

"Save yourself a lot of grief and tell me what you know. As long as you're an informant, I guarantee you immunity from any federal charges regarding LTE."

Melody gulped in air. "I don't know anything for sure, but I heard Cricket talking to Adam Greene one night, and I got the impression Adam had done it. He worked there at the time."

So Adam and Samuel were the same person. "What exactly did they say?"

"I don't remember." Melody started to cry again. "I'm sorry. My uncle Craig was murdered recently. Even though I hadn't seen him in years, it's still upsetting and it's making me emotional. It's why I lost track of the kids for a minute."

River let herself feel a little sympathy, then moved on. "I'm sorry for your loss. But you must realize how important it is to find the arsonist. I'm trying to keep people from getting hurt."

Melody pulled a tissue from a large pocket in her purple tunic and wiped her nose. "Cricket swears it wasn't him or Adam. They think it might be a new guy in the group."

A rush of excitement filled River's belly. "What's his name?"

"I can't remember. It starts with an R though."

"Rick Arbuckle?"

"Maybe. I don't know."

Pot-smoking idiot. "Have you seen the guy or know what he looks like?"

"No. I'm not that involved with the group."

A yelp came from the bedroom. They both turned as the little girl came crying and running on stubby legs. Melody moved to comfort her. "What happened, sugar?"

The girl continued to cry. River didn't think the toddler was old enough to talk, but she didn't know a damn thing about babies. Eager to contact Dallas to see if she'd met Arbuckle or another guy whose name started with an R, River decided to wrap up. "I need you to make an official statement. Find a babysitter and come into the federal building on Monday. If you don't show, I know where to find you."

"I don't want Cricket to get in trouble."

"If he didn't set the firebomb, he has nothing to worry about." River handed her a card. "I want you to think about that name. Make some calls if you have to. Then get back to me. It's very important."

"Okay."

River touched the little girl's head. "And don't let your kids play outside unsupervised. There are too many nasty things out there."

CHAPTER 18

Thursday, March 14, 1:05 p.m.

The problem with an undercover assignment a thousand miles from home was the compulsion to work around the clock. Dallas tended to work too much anyway—everyone in law enforcement did—but without the distractions of either her dysfunctional family or good friend Stacie, she focused nonstop on her case. So instead of taking the afternoon off, knowing she would be shadowing Adam and his group later that evening, she was parked down the alley from Chris Noonaz's home, watching to see who came and went. So far, it was a bust. A Volkswagen van was in the driveway, so Dallas assumed someone was in the house. She'd texted the make, model, and license plate to River, but hadn't received confirmation that it was Cricket's vehicle. Normally, she would refer to suspects and targets by their last names as other agents did, but in undercover work she had to stay consistent in her head. She didn't want to slip and call Cricket Noonaz when she was talking to his friends. It might raise some suspicion.

The alley had only a few homes and was overgrown with blackberry and laurel. She was parked in a turnout next to a truck that had moss growing in the seams. Only one car had traveled the alley since she'd arrived. Dallas kept busy doing research on her computer and writing up a report of her activity. She couldn't imagine life without 24/7 access to the internet. She thought about all the money her aunt had invested sending her to college and felt guilty about how she now spent her time. But without the formal education, Dallas never would have gotten into the bureau. Or been able to afford years of therapy—most of it conducted via Skype—in her quest to figure out why she enjoyed sex with strangers and not with men she cared about.

About the time she was ready to drive off and look for a place to pee, the front door of the little blue house opened and Cricket walked out. Dallas recognized his shaggy ash-blond hair and ever-present denim jacket. The LTE leader sauntered to his van and climbed in.

Now what? One choice was to follow him and see where he went and/or who he connected with. Cricket could be on his way to buy bomb-making materials, and she would love to document that. Or he might be headed to Sundance Natural Foods to pick up some tofu, and that would annoy her greatly. There was a second choice. Take a quick peek inside his house while he was out and see what he had lying around. More risk, more potential reward.

Dallas bent down and waited for the van to pass, then made up her mind. She would search his house. If she could find out what the group had planned next, the bureau could put people in place. They could bust the eco-terrorists before they did more damage and possibly hurt someone. Dallas drove down the alley and parked where his van had been. Brazen was often the best approach. If Cricket came back early, it made more sense to say she was looking for him—as Fiona the LTE groupie—than to get caught being sneaky and blow her cover entirely.

She pulled a black bag from under her car seat and dug out thin gloves, a lock-picking tool, and a thumb drive. She realized that someone might be in the house, so she knocked on the front door and waited. When no one answered, Dallas trotted around to the side of the house, hopped over a short white fence, and made her way to the back porch. The wood was graying, and a giant outdoor grill took up half the space.

The lock gave easily, but the door didn't open. Dallas guessed it had a second sliding bolt. She checked a tall window next to the door: old-fashioned, with a catch on the wooden frames that met in the middle. She could see it wasn't fastened. With a hard push, the bottom window slid up and Dallas slipped in.

The kitchen was wall-to-wall cupboards, but she didn't bother looking in any of them. She had only a few minutes and had to prioritize. After a quick scan around the living room—ugly couch, dying plants, gaudy posters, but no computer or paperwork—she ran to a bedroom. A laptop sat open on the nightstand, its power pack plugged into the wall. Recoiling from the smell of sweaty sheets, Dallas sat on the edge of the bed, grabbed the computer, and hit the space key. The monitor lit up. Hot damn! He'd left it on and she wouldn't have to fuck around with passwords. A little warning flashed in her head, cautioning that if Cricket had left his computer on, he probably didn't plan to be gone long. She gave herself seven minutes.

His e-mail program was open and she clicked the top file, which had come in moments before. An e-mail from some-one named Melody who said the FBI had just been to see her about the firebomb. Melody claimed she'd convinced the agent that Cricket hadn't been involved. Dallas didn't get the sense that Melody believed Cricket was innocent. Melody referred to the agent as *she*, so Dallas assumed it was River. Her boss wouldn't be happy to know Melody had warned Cricket they were closing in.

Dallas opened the second e-mail, a note from the utility company urging him to pay his bill or they would terminate his service. Could they use that to their advantage? Two minutes gone. She scanned down the list of e-mails looking for headers indicating LTE meetings or plans. Nothing jumped out. But the members were probably smart enough not to communicate about anything illegal on traceable documents. The thought made her laugh. No one ever thought they'd get caught, and some very smart and powerful people had sent some very incriminating e-mails.

Four minutes left. She scanned his e-folders, clicked open one labeled Priorities, and quickly found a text document called Goals. As she double-clicked the icon, she heard a car in the alley. Her heart skipped a beat, then started to pound. *No! He couldn't be back yet.* She froze, listening for the sound of the engine. Was it slowing at all? She didn't think so, but Dallas put down the laptop and hurried into the hallway. She stopped and listened again. The car was right outside. She stood in the hall, willing herself to be calm, and waited.

The car passed by.

Dallas charged back to the laptop and stared at the open document. The goals were grouped into Legislative, Protests, and Targets. Under targets were JB Pharma, Ridgeline Plastics, and Cascade Lumber. She thought it odd that Rock Spring was not on the list. Dallas snapped a picture of the document with her phone, then shoved her thumb drive into the open USB port and copied the file. It took too long and she regretted the effort. She would probably never show it to anyone since she didn't have legal permission to be here. Just knowing now that Ridgeline Plastics was next had made this incursion worthwhile. She closed the document, put the laptop back exactly where she'd found it, and bolted from the room. She was over her time limit, but couldn't resist taking a quick look at the room on the other end of the short hallway. The door was open a crack and Dallas gave it a light push.

A woman slept on a mattress on the floor.

Oh fuck! Dallas spun and speed-walked across the kitchen, moving as quickly and quietly as she could. She climbed back out the window, closed it gently, and ran to her car. Once she was backing out into the alley, her brain kicked in and processed what had just happened. Her first thought was, *Idiot!* Then she burst out laughing. Sometimes the scariest things were the most fun.

CHAPTER 19

Thursday, March 14, 1:45 p.m.

Still parked in front of Maggie Brennan's house, Jackson called Katie. He'd texted his daughter the night before and earlier that morning, reminding her she had a counseling appointment. Katie hadn't responded to either message and she didn't pick up now. Every rejection was another blow to his battered heart. For a moment he couldn't think or breathe. Katie had to get help. She had to come to terms with her mother's death. And she had to forgive him. He couldn't live like this.

Jackson started the car and drove toward South Eugene and the address McCray had given him, which was a block from the school Katie attended. He just wanted to see her, even from a distance. It would give him some peace of mind. Was he being obsessive? Jackson wondered if he needed more counseling. Other parents lived in different states from their children and managed to function.

He stopped at a light and called McCray. His old partner didn't pick up. Worry vacillated with irritation. McCray was supposed to be watching Katie. What was he doing that he couldn't answer the phone? Or more likely, what was Katie up to?

Jackson forced himself to chill. Katie was fine, and McCray knew about the two o'clock appointment. Maybe he was talking to Katie and trying to convince her to go. Maybe Katie had gone to classes today and McCray was taking a nap in his car.

After a few minutes, Jackson turned on Ferry Street and spotted McCray's black jeep. Jackson parked two cars behind him but didn't see McCray in the vehicle. He climbed out for a better look at the house where Katie was staying. Small, white, and well maintained. No black paper or heavy curtains over the windows. Probably not a drug house. His shoulders relaxed a little.

No car was in the driveway. Where was everyone?

The front door opened, so Jackson slipped back into his car, feeling self-conscious, as if he were spying on Katie. Confused and frustrated, he watched McCray come out of the house, followed by his daughter. His heart lurched, a jumble of relief and anguish. Dressed in all black, Katie was thinner than he'd ever seen her. Her hair was pulled back in a tight knot and her mouth twisted down. But she walked with purpose, no drunk wobble. Jackson slouched a little, not wanting to be obvious, even if she did spot his car. If she and McCray were headed to the counseling appointment, it was best not to interfere. Jackson felt grateful she was going.

He couldn't resist texting McCray: *Are you headed to counseling apt?*

As soon as Jackson pressed send, he let out a laugh. His old partner probably didn't even know how to check for text messages, let alone respond. Feeling better, he decided to stop at the crime lab and see what Joe had for him, then go out to the therapist's office to arrange payments. He mostly wanted Charlotte Diebold to know that he was as involved as he could be in Katie's life and not willingly shirking his parental responsibility.

McCray called him a minute later. "I got your text. And yes, we're on our way."

"Thank you for this. Thank you for finding her." A rush of emotion caught in his voice.

"Nothing you wouldn't do for me. I gotta drive now."

"Call me back when you can talk." Jackson hung up. He had a dozen questions. For starters: Who was Katie staying with? He made quick calls to Jan and Kera to let them know his daughter was safe. Jan cried with relief, and Jackson was reminded that he wasn't in this alone.

The crime lab's gray-brick exterior, with no signs and no windows facing the street, had a secretive facade. Tucked into a low-rent, mostly industrial area with little street traffic, few members of the public even realized it existed.

Jackson rolled down his window, flashed his ID card at the camera, and waited for the arm to lift. The tall metal fence around the back lot reminded him of the storage business. He parked and hurried into the building.

He trotted upstairs, feeling a tug of pain with every step, and stuck his head into Jasmine Parker's office. "Hey, Parker. Just thought I would say hello. What are you working on?"

"Processing prints from your storage unit crime scene, so there's no need to schmooze me." The corner of her mouth ticked up, the closest she came to a smile. Parker didn't need fluffy hair or makeup to look good.

"Can't hurt anyway." He smiled back. "Got anything for me?"

"Nothing you don't already know. Patrick Brennan's finger-prints are on both sides of the torn Bible. But the only prints on the door handle and lock belonged to the victim, Craig Cooper."

"Thanks." Jackson gave a little wave and continued down the hall.

Joe wasn't in his office, so Jackson checked the lab, a compact space that contained high-powered microscopes, a refrigerator, a downdraft table, and superglue oven—the latter two used for fingerprints.

Joe had his eye pressed against a microscope and didn't look up. "Give me a second."

Jackson waited. Finally, Joe pulled away. He had a gleam in his eye that made Jackson hopeful.

"I was looking at the material Konrad found in the victim's wound. I have a few more tests to perform before I can be sure."

Jackson's hope plunged. "How long?"

"By tomorrow morning. But don't be too disappointed. I have another interesting report."

"Good. I need something."

"Remember the blood sample you submitted?"

Jackson had to think for moment. Then he recalled the swab he'd taken from Todd Sheppard, the brain-damaged ex-football player who'd discovered the body.

"It has two types of antigens, both A and O, which means it came from two different people."

What the hell? "What type is our victim?"

"Type O. I sent a sample from the victim and a sample from the suspect's swab to the state lab for DNA analysis, but that could take a week or so."

"So Todd Sheppard did have a nosebleed, but he had the vic-tim's blood on his face too?"

"Most likely. But it's not certain until we get the DNA reports."

It was enough to bring Sheppard in for more questioning. "Thanks, Joe. Let me know on the wound evidence as soon as you have it."

Jackson returned to his car, strangely disappointed to learn the homeless giant had likely killed his neighbor and friend. He'd felt sorry for Sheppard and believed he was too simpleminded to lie. But Jackson knew better than to think that way. Everyone lied, at least a little, when they talked to cops.

His phone beeped and he discovered he'd missed two calls. The first message was from Ed McCray: "Katie is staying with her boyfriend and his mother. She wouldn't give me names, but I looked at their mail, and the mother is Donna Shubert. I convinced Katie that seeing the counselor would keep her out of juvenile lockup. She seems depressed but otherwise all right. Do you want me to keep watching her? I can't do this 'round the clock."

Jackson's heart said yes, but his head knew it was ridiculous.

The second message was from Kera: "I love you, Wade. And so does Katie. Don't work too hard. Call me when you have time."

A little of the darkness cleared. He planned to return both calls on the drive across town. But first, he had to contact Schak. They had to go back out to the storage business and confront Todd Sheppard. Jackson remembered the suspect had said he spent his days at the library and only went home to his little enclosed space in the evening.

Jackson started the car, remembering he also had to call the DA's office and find out about the warrant to search Patrick's home. Some days he made as many as twenty or thirty calls. It wasn't what he'd envisioned when he'd taken the test to become a detective.

The therapist's office was in a small complex not far from the Serbu juvenile campus. Jackson parked and checked his watch: *2:45*.

Katie's session should be ending any moment. He looked around and spotted a black jeep. McCray was waiting for Katie and would probably give her a ride somewhere. Jealousy stabbed at his heart. The role of being a spectator—an unwanted nuisance—in Katie's life was disturbing. He wanted to pray for a quick resolution, but he never asked God for personal favors, so he prayed for Katie's safety and happiness instead, even if it meant she would be separate from him.

Katie came out of the office, looking grim, and glanced over at him. He nodded and she shook her head. His daughter turned away and ran toward McCray's vehicle. Jackson tried to feel numb.

After they'd left, he hurried into the building. A teenage boy of about fourteen sat in the lobby with his mother. The receptionist took Jackson's name and stepped into a second room. She was gone only a few seconds.

"Charlotte will see you for just a minute. She has a patient waiting."

Jackson only had a few minutes too. He strode through the open door.

The therapist stood to greet him and he was aware of the effort it took for her. He guessed her to be at least a hundred pounds overweight, and he had second thoughts about choosing her. Did she have issues of her own? Was she the best person to help his daughter? Jackson thought he might have made the decision too quickly.

Charlotte Diebold smiled and shook his hand. "Thank you for coming. I have the greatest respect for law enforcement officers."

Jackson felt a stab of shame. Her body size was irrelevant. She'd been recommended by Katie's social worker. She could be brilliant, for all he knew. "Thank you for making time for Katie. She's in crisis."

"I can't discuss her therapy with you. She's fifteen, and I recognize her as an adult with all the confidentiality that implies."

"I understand. I just wanted to make arrangements to pay for her sessions."

"Thank you. You can leave a check with my receptionist."

That was it. She expected him to simply leave. Jackson nodded and turned, glad to have a compelling case to keep him busy.

CHAPTER 20

Thursday, March 14, 2:30 p.m.

Sophie Speranza finished her news story about the firebomb, wishing she had more information. She'd made a ton of calls, but no one had called back and she had nothing so far. A trip to the factory with a photographer had netted some images for the story and a couple of bland quotes from the foreman, but she needed something that would make readers sit up and say, *What the hell?*

"Hey, Sophie. How's my favorite little redhead?" Carl Hoogstad, her editor, had tracked her to the corner area that served as a break room now that the newspaper leased its lower floor to an insurance company.

She tried not to cringe. He only called her that when he'd had a beer at lunch. "I'm good. What's up?"

"What have you got on the firebomb?"

"I have some quotes from the factory foreman, and Brian got shots of the burned area, so we'll have a story for tomorrow."

The TV stations would have a segment that evening, and it killed Sophie to always be a day behind. She should have gone into broadcast journalism.

"Any idea who's responsible?" Hoogstad moved closer. He was round and balding, with a strip of long gray hair on the back of his neck. Sophie never got used to looking at him.

"Not yet. I have a call in to a member of Love the Earth, but I don't expect them to take credit even if they did do it."

"Resurrect all the old Earth Liberation bullshit if you have to. That'll get readers fired up."

"I'll look at the coverage."

Her boss waddled away, and Sophie took her tea back to her desk. She opened the online archive of Willamette News articles and keyed in *Earth Liberation Front*. A dozen links displayed and they were all years old.

Her cell phone rang and it was Jasmine Parker. Seeing the name made Sophie smile. "Hey, Jaz. I hope this means you plan to spend time with me later." Her lover rarely called her at the newspaper.

"Sorry, but I can't. I'm working late. I sent the bomb scene fingerprints to Quantico, but Joe needs help with a homicide."

Sophie's interest piqued. "What homicide?"

Jasmine lowered her voice. "Some guy who lived in a storage unit. An ex-con who robbed a bank here long ago."

"His name?" It was greedy and wrong to ask, but Sophie couldn't help herself. She wanted to know everything.

"You have to call the department spokesperson. They haven't released anything yet, and I can't have a leak traced to me."

"I know. Thanks for the tip. I love you for it." Sophie said it casually, the way you would appreciate someone bringing you chocolate on a bad day, but it was the first time either of them had used the word *love*. Sophie hoped Jasmine didn't freak out. The last person Sophie had been this serious about was a man, and he'd dumped her when she mentioned love.

Jasmine laughed instead. "I know that's the main reason you date me. You're a whore for inside information."

"We all sell out for something. I'm just lucky that my source is so damn beautiful." Sophie cringed, realizing her voice was too loud and her cube neighbors were probably listening.

"I'll call you if I manage to get out of here before nine. Later."

Sophie hung up, feeling energized again. She called Jackie Matthews, the EPD spokesperson, and left a message, asking about the homicide victim, then called the FBI again. This time, the person who answered told her she needed to speak with Agent Carla River and gave her a cell phone number. Sophie called and left a message, feeling like she was at least a step closer.

On a roll, she called Ted Rockman again too.

His receptionist picked up this time. "R and L Enterprises."

"Hello, this is Sophie Speranza. I'm a reporter for the Willamette News. I'd love to set up an interview with Ted Rockman to talk about his campaign for the state senate." *And a few other things.*

"Yes. I got the message you left this morning. Mr. Rockman can meet with you tomorrow morning at ten."

Yes! "Thank you. Should I come to his office?"

"Please. We're near the corner of Mill and Fifteenth." A short pause. "Mr. Rockman doesn't want to talk about the arson at his bottled water business, but he did give me a statement you can use."

Sophie grabbed a pen. She didn't have her headphones on and couldn't type with one hand. "Thank you. I'm ready."

The receptionist cleared her throat, as if taking on a new role. "I will not let an individual's criminal actions endanger my business or my employees. Rock Spring will continue to produce a valuable product, and as its owner, I'll continue to look for ways to be sustainable and eco-friendly."

Sophie asked her to repeat it. She had to get this right if she wanted Rockman's interview. "Thanks. I'll see you Friday."

She read the quote again. Rockman was sending the bomber a message that he would not back down.

Stuck for her next move, she called ATF and Homeland Security, which turned out to be as productive as randomly dialing numbers.

Her thoughts returned to a local environmental group called Love the Earth that had staged a protest at Rock Spring the previous year. She keyed the group's name into the newspaper's archives and learned that some of its members had been arrested during protests. Sophie wanted to talk to a LTE member and see what they had to say about the Rock Spring incident.

She started calling friends and acquaintances and asking if they knew anyone involved with Love the Earth. After contacting several of the people they'd suggested, Sophie finally connected with a woman named Melody Light, who supposedly dated Cricket, aka Chris Noonaz, the LTE founder.

"Melody, this is Sophie Speranza of the Willamette News. Do you have a few minutes?" She knew better than to just jump in and ask about a federal investigation.

"Maybe. Why?" Melody sounded worried.

"I'd like to ask you about Love the Earth. Some people are speculating that the group is responsible for the firebomb at Rock Spring bottled water. But I was under the impression that LTE advocated nonviolent methods for political change."

"We are nonviolent. I don't know why the FBI is after Cricket."

Sophie's pulse quickened and she clicked on her recorder. "Has the bureau contacted you?"

"Agent River was just here asking about the firebomb. I told her Cricket wasn't involved." Melody suddenly yelled, "Put that down!" followed by a slapping sound and a little kid crying.

Sophie waited it out. She wanted an interview with Cricket, but would settle for a usable quote from his girlfriend. "Do you know who committed the Rock Spring arson?"

"No, but like I told the FBI woman, it might be a new member, a young guy."

"What's his name?"

"I think it's Russell something. He might have worked at Rock Spring for a while, but I'm not sure. I'm having a bad day."

Sophie wrote it down out of habit, but she'd never forget it now. "Tell me more about Love the Earth. Like how many members are there, and what are your political goals?"

"I'm not the right person to ask, but I think there's about twenty core members."

"Who should I talk to? Can you give me a name and phone number?"

"We have a website with basic information about our causes." Melody shifted into a less flaky tone. "Look, I really shouldn't be talking to you. And I'm waiting for Cricket to call me back."

"I'd love to talk to Cricket and get his side of the story. It's his chance to get some media exposure for his cause." Crusaders couldn't resist that. "Will you ask him to call me? Or just give me a time and place to meet him?"

"I'll give him the message, but he's laying low. He knows the feds are looking for him."

"But if he didn't commit the arson, this is his chance to win some public sympathy." Depending on how she wrote the story. But she would be open-minded, as always.

"I'll give him the message."

"Thank you." Sophie reluctantly hung up. Cricket would never call her. But she had some quotes and a first name now. If she ran a partial ID in the next story, someone might come forward.

Humming with renewed energy, she started crafting her story, one that she hoped would run on the front page. When she had the lead and a few bare bones paragraphs, she googled Rock Spring, found the website, and called the number listed. A recording thanked her for calling and asked her to leave a message. Instead, Sophie grabbed her red leather handbag and headed out. She would talk to employees at the factory until someone gave her Russell's last name or they kicked her out.

In the car, she called Detective Jackson. She wanted to run a story about the storage unit murder, but she didn't have a damn thing to go on.

Jackson surprised her by picking up. "Sophie, I'm busy. Can we talk later?"

"Just give me the name of the guy who was killed at the storage business."

"Tell me who your source is and I will." He sounded irritated.

She laughed softly. "You know I can't do that. But I can ask the public for help if you need it."

"I don't. We have a suspect."

"Great to hear." Sophie scrambled for an angle that Jackson wouldn't be able to resist. "I want to write about the issue of homeless people living in storage units. The public needs to know about this. It may help get a homeless camp funded."

A pause. "Craig Cooper. He was released from prison about six weeks ago and was trying to start a new life."

Yes! "Thanks, Jackson. Which storage business was he found in?"

"Safe and Secure." He made a funny sound. "The irony is a little much. I have to go now."

Delighted, Sophie jotted down the information. She loved exclusives. The TV stations had already stopped reporting on the murder because they didn't have anything new. She texted Jackson a capitalized *THANK YOU!*

Ex-prisoner, huh? She'd have to search the archives and see what crime Cooper had committed. Sophie changed her mind about going out to Rock Spring and decided to call the owners of Safe and Secure instead. She might even make a trip out there if she could find a photographer.

CHAPTER 21

After not finding Todd Sheppard at either the library or the Mission, Jackson met Kera for dinner at Sweet Basil downtown. She was already there when he walked in and she embraced him in a tight hug. His weary body seemed to draw vitality from hers. Jackson stayed in Kera's arms longer than he ever had in public. Damn, she was good for him. "Thanks. I needed that. Today was hard for me." They took seats across from each other.

"You must mean Katie. What happened?" Kera squeezed his hand.

"The good news is that she went to her counseling appointment. But McCray had to take her. She still doesn't want to be around me."

"I'm sorry. I know that hurts."

Jackson could see his pain reflected in her eyes. "I just hope the counseling helps her. I'm more worried about Katie's drinking

---

than anything else." Jackson hesitated, then finally told Kera about watching Katie at the rental and at the counselor's office. "Was that obsessive?"

"Of course not. You're just worried and not ready to let go of the idea that you can keep her safe."

"How do I let go?"

"You don't. It just happens gradually."

A young male server with pink hair that flopped over his eyes stopped and took their order. They hadn't even had to look at the menu.

"Where is Katie staying?" Kera asked.

"With her boyfriend and his mother."

His girlfriend winced. "Anyone you know?"

Jackson shook his head and a flash of anger surfaced. "What kind of mother lets her son's fifteen-year-old girlfriend move in with them? What is she thinking?"

Kera sipped her tea and took time answering. Her voice was gentle. "Maybe the mother reasons that it's better than having Katie on the streets. Or better than having both kids stay with someone else just so they can be together."

"The mother should have called me."

"That would have been the right thing to do."

Kera didn't ask him what he would have said if the boyfriend's mother had called. Jackson wasn't sure. But what he wanted to tell her was, *Don't let them have sex in your house. Don't condone their relationship and act like it doesn't matter.*

"You don't know that they're having sex," Kera said. "Not all teenagers in relationships do."

His girlfriend knew him well. But she also worked at Planned Parenthood and understood better than most people that trying to control teenage sexual behavior was impossible. She'd helped him understand that when two of her young clients had been murdered a few years back.

"I have to stop thinking about it."

"Good idea."

Kera talked about her volunteer work with injured veterans, then mentioned that Danette and her boyfriend seemed serious. "If Danette moves out, I'll miss Micah dearly. I can't imagine not having him with me." Kera's eyes brimmed with tears. She'd lost her son, Nathan—the baby's father—in the Iraq War.

"Danette will bring Micah over all the time for babysitting," Jackson reassured her. "And she hasn't gone anywhere yet."

Their food came, and while they ate Jackson talked about his case without mentioning names or critical details. "I have to interrogate a suspect again tonight, so I can't stay long."

"I know." She smiled and he knew they were okay. During his time off after Renee's death, he and Katie had spent a lot of time with Kera and her family. For a while, their companionship had masked the growing space between him and Katie.

Jackson's phone rang, and it was Schak. "Hey, partner. You ready to do this? I'm sitting outside the storage place, and Todd Sheppard just went inside his little hobbit hole."

"I'll be there in fifteen minutes. Should we call for some backup?"

"Hell yes." Schak laughed. "I'm not even sure a taser will take that guy down."

"I don't want to stun him. He has a brain injury already."

"I hear you, but I want to be ready for anything."

"Call for a uniform and get Evans too. She'll be annoyed if we leave her out. See you in a few."

A blue patrol car was parked on the street, and Schak's sedan was in front of the office. Schak and the officer stood next to the gate.

The moon peeked through the clouds and gave them a sliver of light. Jackson grabbed his taser and a flashlight and climbed from the car, aware that the steady downpour had finally stopped.

As he walked up, Schak said, "I called the owners for the code, but then I discovered the gate isn't latched properly." His partner gave it a push and it slid open.

"So anyone could have entered the night Cooper died." Jackson realized it hardly mattered. All three of their suspects admitted to being at the crime scene.

They heard another car pull up and turned. Detective Lara Evans jumped out and trotted up, carrying a sledgehammer.

"You brought a lock pick." Jackson envied her energy and foresight.

"I like to be prepared." She grinned, and Jackson remembered her bringing one from the storage office that night. She might finally get her chance to use it. "What's the plan?" Evans asked.

"We persuade Sheppard to come down to the department and make a statement. Once we have him in the interrogation room, we push for a confession." Jackson didn't say that the man's brain damage would probably make it easy to convince him to unburden himself, but they were all thinking it.

"What if he doesn't come willingly?" Evans asked.

"I have a recorder. We can take his statement here. If he confesses in any way, we take him to jail, even if we have to stun him. No batons."

"What if Sheppard doesn't confess?" Evans was forcing him to think it through. That's why Jackson always wanted her on his team.

"We leave him here and do our job until we have enough to convict him."

"You don't think he'll run?" Schak looked skeptical.

"It doesn't seem likely."

The wind gusted and Evans zipped her leather jacket against the cold. "I don't think he did it. My money is on Patrick Brennan."

"We'll search Patrick's place as soon as we have a warrant." Jackson turned to Schak. "Did you look at the video from the office camera?"

"A waste of time. The camera only catches people at the keypad, so once the gate is open, anyone can come and go without being recorded."

"Who do we have on the clip?"

"Craig Cooper. That's it."

Jackson hadn't put much faith in the camera, so his disappointment was minimal. "Let's pull your car up to his unit. No point in making work for ourselves." He pushed the gate fully open and started toward the third row of storage spaces. His nerves jangled and he had a bad feeling about this. Todd Sheppard was gigantic and unpredictable. And if the suspect felt threatened, he might go crazy on them. Stun guns worked best from ten feet away or more, so the two prongs would separate and lodge in different muscle groups. He would have to remember to step back before using his taser. Jackson turned to Evans, who walked at his side. "I want you to take the lead. You did a good job with Jenna Brennan today, and I think Sheppard might respond better to a woman as well."

"Sure. Thanks."

The patrol officer hung back two steps. His job was backup.

At unit D-7, they stopped and Evans called out, "Todd Sheppard? It's Detective Lara Evans. I need to ask you about something."

No response.

Schak drove up in the narrow space, left his lights on, and joined them in front of the overhead door.

Evans banged on the metal. "Todd, I'm with the Eugene police. We need to talk. Open the door!"

Except for the wind, the night was silent.

"Come out now or we're going to break the lock and open the door." Evans pounded again, then looked at Jackson.

He nodded. She had brought the sledgehammer, so he let her use it. Evans swung the heavy tool over her shoulder and brought it down on the lock with precision.

The noise shattered the night and Jackson flinched. The metal door dented but the lock was solid.

Evans swung the sledgehammer twice more. The second blow knocked loose the latch holding the lock, and the whole device fell to the ground. She dropped the big hammer and pulled her weapon. Jackson pushed open the door with his free hand. The headlights from Schak's cruiser cast a reflected glow on the cluttered interior.

Todd Sheppard's big body was sprawled on the floor.

CHAPTER 22

Thursday, March 14, 4:45 p.m.

Dallas hadn't heard from Adam all day and she started to get nervous. He'd invited her out this evening, but hadn't followed through with details. Just as she checked her Eugene phone again, a text message appeared from Adam: *Potluck is at 6. Should I pick you up?*

She texted back: *Let's meet there and see what happens. Should I bring something?* She had to keep her car with her in case the action changed and she needed to follow another target.

He responded: *Just your sexy self.*

The message made her smile—and start debating again about whether she would hook up with him. Only if it was the one way to get the information she needed. She texted back and asked for an address. Once she had it, Dallas found the address on Google Maps, then texted the location to River, hoping her boss would come back with the owner's name and some intel.

Feeling hyper and ready to get on with her assignment, Dallas changed into her Eugene clothes: faded jeans, a snug black sweater, and a pair of closed-toed Birkenstocks she'd bought for the UC assignment—shoes that were hideously ugly but weirdly comfortable. Her research had indicated that Birkenstocks were appropriate in Eugene, but so far none of the young women she'd met had been wearing them.

She grabbed her handbag, tucked a small Kel-Tec into a secret panel at the bottom, and threw in some pepper spray disguised as perfume. Her slim digital recorder went into a pocket of her sweater, and she slipped a switchblade into her jeans pocket. Dallas reluctantly left her Glock in the nightstand by the bed. She'd never fired a gun until joining the bureau, but she had a natural talent and was accumulating quite a collection. Her sniper gear was in a locked safe in her Phoenix condo, where she was based.

Dallas spotted the keys to her leased Prius on the bar counter. Tucking the keys into her front pocket, she glanced outside to check the weather. Even in the rain, she loved the view of the tree-covered hill from the living room window. But she didn't spend much time looking at it. She was here in Eugene on assignment, and when she wasn't out there making contacts, she was on her computer, learning everything she could about her targets, or beefing up her background. Fieldwork was like taking on an acting job and living the part 24/7. But not for a paycheck. For the safety and well-being of her country. What could be better?

Dallas grabbed her sunglasses, which she had no use for in Eugene, and headed out.

The home was in Glenwood, an ugly area between Eugene and Springfield that was home to pawnshops, trailer parks, and weird industrial businesses. Dallas had discovered the area two weeks ago when looking for a used camping backpack at a pawnshop.

Not wanting to be too early, she parked down a side street and watched the house for a while. It was larger than most of the funky little homes in the neighborhood, but moss covered the roof, the lawn was overgrown, and an old yellow school bus sat in the driveway. The bus didn't look as if it had moved in decades. If Dallas had to guess by appearance, she'd speculate that a pot-smoking slacker lived there, talking to his cat and making jewelry to pay his rent. She'd learned that the homes of bad guys tended to look like everyone else's.

Moments later, River proved her right with a text: *Amy Washburn, self-employed artist, drug possession and resisting arrest.* The information made Dallas smile. But she would have preferred to discover that the property belonged to one of the four core LTE guys. She waited until she saw Adam's car park in front of the house, then drove forward and parked behind him. She called to him as he headed up the walkway.

"Hey, Fiona." He kissed her cheek like an old friend.

His distance made her rethink the evening. Did he have plans for later that didn't involve her? Good. She would follow him again. Maybe do a little eavesdropping.

For an hour, she sampled potluck food and listened to people talk about their kids, liberal politics, and vegetarian recipes. Deadly dull. Dallas smiled and did her best, all the while keeping her eye on three of the four men who'd met at the tavern on Tuesday night. Based on the conversation she'd overheard between Adam and Cricket, she had to eliminate those two as the Rock Spring arsonist. She couldn't assume it was one of the other men, but they were a good place to focus. The older one with the beard hadn't shown up yet, and she was disappointed. River had texted his name that afternoon, Rick Arbuckle, and he seemed like the better bet. The young one with the mohawk, who looked fresh out of high school, was at the party but kept to himself. When she saw him step outside, Dallas decided to make his acquaintance.

On the covered porch, he lit a cigarette, its tip glowing in the dark. He turned when he heard the door open. Dallas smiled. "Hey, can I buy one of those off you?"

"You can have one." The pack was still in his hand, and he shook out a cigarette and lit it for her. Dallas inhaled a little. *Disgusting.* She didn't smoke, except when the job called for it. "Thanks. I'm Fiona Ingram."

"Russell Crowder." He had a narrow face with scraggly chin hair, and his eyes burned with the intensity of someone on stimulants.

Dallas tucked the name into her permanent memory. "We can hardly smoke in public anymore. Next, they'll start fining us." Whining about misguided government regulation was another popular theme with this crowd.

"No kidding." He shook his head. "Their priorities are really messed up sometimes."

"You mean government or voters? Oregon seems pretty progressive to me."

"We used to be progressive, but not anymore." Russell sized her up. "You're new here?"

"Just a couple months." Dallas took another small drag and tried not to cough. "What do you do for fun, Russell?"

He made a face and a scoffing sound. "Not enough. But I don't have time right now. I have some important things to accomplish."

A little shimmer ran up her spine. "Yeah? Like what?" She smiled, all charm.

"Personal stuff. Coming to terms with my past while making a difference in the world."

"Sounds good." She wanted to know more but didn't want to press too hard. "I'm a grant writer for charities and NGOs, so I like to think my time is well spent too."

"That's cool. Might as well spend taxpayer money on something besides war."

"Agreed. What are your priorities?"

His eyes shifted and Dallas worried she'd overstepped. But he responded, "I'm with a group that's trying to get plastic bags banned in the state, but I want to go after plastic bottles because they're more of a problem."

Now all her neurons were firing. "I know what you mean. I don't buy anything in plastic anymore."

Russell was suddenly agitated. "You know what's happening? Homeless people are buying loads of bottled water with food stamps, then dumping the water behind the store and turning in the bottles for the deposit cash."

The waste of taxpayer dollars pissed her off, but Dallas focused on the environmental issue. "At least the bottles are being recycled."

"I suppose." He took a long drag, then flicked his cigarette into the yard.

Hypocrite. Dallas looked around for a place to discard hers. "You're going back in?"

"No. I have to leave. I have to prepare for a big day tomorrow."

Dallas' brain kicked into processing mode. Should she try to tag along with him or tail him? Follow, she decided. He and Adam were friends, and it could blow her cover to get cozy with both. "Okay. See you around."

"Nice talking to you."

She watched him walk to a small car parked down the street. It looked like a Subaru, but it was too dark to tell. Maybe blue or dark green. Dallas pulled out her Eugene phone and keyed in a text to Adam: *Sorry. But I have to take off. The cramps are making me crazy. See you in a day or so?* She waited to push send and hoped she hadn't blown it with him. But Adam wasn't the arsonist, so she had to go with her gut. Russell was so young, if they busted him, he might turn on the group to cut a deal.

As soon as his car turned around in the street, Dallas trotted down the walkway and headed for her own car. Inside, she sent the text to Adam and took off. No other cars were moving around the quiet neighborhood, so she held back and hoped to spot Russell's car before he turned on the main drag. She popped in her earpiece and called Agent River on her work phone.

Her supervisor picked up. "What have you got, Dallas?"

"I just ID'd the young mohawk guy from Tony's Tavern. Russell Crowder."

"Good work. I'll see what I can dig up."

"Get back to me if you get intel on his car. I'm following him because he says he has a things to accomplish tomorrow." In the distance, Russell's car turned left at Franklin. He was headed for Eugene. "He's gung ho on banning plastic water bottles, so I think he might be our perp. And I think he has something planned."

"Can you get a sample of his writing? I'd like to have it compared to the letter Ted Rockman received."

"I'll do what I can."

"I can take a shift if you need relief following Crowder."

"I'll let you know.

"Be safe."

Dallas hung up and pulled out on the main road. She wished she knew the make and color of Russell's car. But traffic was light and she managed to stay with him until they were in downtown Eugene. At Pearl Street, he ran a yellow light, and she was too far back to make the same move. She pulled into a bank parking lot, gunned it across the empty side street into another parking lot, and got back on West Eleventh—a move that could have earned her a ticket. If Russell had been watching his rearview mirror, he might have seen it. Her best guess told her he wasn't that careful. He seemed like a preoccupied man.

She followed him to a large older home just west of downtown. Her first thought was that he still lived with his parents, then she worried that he shared the place with a posse of roommates. From across the street, she watched him head to the side of the house and disappear down a path into the backyard.

Dallas rummaged through the bag of extra clothes she kept in her car, grabbed a knit cap, and tucked her hair up into it. The jeans and black sweater would serve her well. She slipped out of her car and jogged across the street, glad to be wearing the ugly but silent shoes. Heart pounding, she ran along the grass next to the driveway, noting that Russell's vehicle was an old, dark green Subaru. She slipped behind a tree near the fence, then peeked around it and stared down the side of the house. A light at the far corner illuminated the area enough so she could see a small mother-in-law house in the backyard. Russell was just stepping inside.

Rounding the tree, Dallas kept her back to the fence and moved sideways in the dark until she came to another tree in the backyard. The light on the corner of the house was out of reach for her five-seven frame, or she would have unscrewed the bulb. Now what? She burned with the need to know what he had planned for the next day, but the idea of sneaking into his house while he slept seemed too risky. She couldn't think of a rational middle-of-the-night ruse to get him out of there. She didn't even know Russell's phone number. Nor did she have anything solid on his intentions. His "important stuff" could turn out to be laundry or a trip to the doctor. Until River got back to her, Dallas decided not to make any moves. She would sleep in her car and tail him again tomorrow.

The back door of the house banged open, startling her. Dallas spun toward the sound. A halide light came on over the deck as an older woman crossed it. *Fuck!* The woman was coming into the yard. Silently, Dallas stepped back against the fence and side-stepped her way to the front. She turned at the sidewalk and jogged down the street, in case the woman had seen her and followed. Dallas didn't want the woman to see her get into her car. No sounds came from behind her and no one called out.

After a jog around the block, Dallas made her way to her car and slipped into the backseat. She locked the doors and lay on her side so she wouldn't be seen. She texted River to update her, then read on her tablet until she got sleepy enough to nod off. As uncomfortable as she was, she wouldn't have traded this assignment for anything.

CHAPTER 23

Friday, March 15, 5:35 a.m.

She was driving down the highway, catching glimpses of a swollen river through the trees. Worried about reaching her destination on time, she pressed the gas. Out of nowhere, a semi smashed into her car, sending her through the guardrail. Frantic, River hit the brakes and glanced out the side window at the muddy water.

Suddenly awake, River sat up and stared out her bedroom window.

It was open.

River grabbed her weapon. Groggy, she swung the Glock toward the intruder—a dark shape in a dark room—but he was already right there and her hand slammed into his elbow. In a quick twist, he knocked her gun to the floor and grabbed her by the throat with a huge hand.

No! In her sitting position on the bed, she was almost helpless. All she could do was bring her hands up and try to dislodge the fingers crushing her windpipe. River heard the click of a switchblade open.

"A gift from Gabriel Barstow." His voice was soft and cruel.

No!

She sucked in her breath, then heaved herself sideways.

As she did, she heard a loud *thunk*. The fingers on her throat loosened and her attacker collapsed to the floor with a muted moan. River scrambled to find her weapon and turn on a lamp.

Jared stood there in his underwear, wielding a large cast-iron frying pan.

"He's not dead," her handyman said, his voice oddly calm. "I think we should truss him before we worry about what we're wearing."

Ninety minutes later, the last police officer and agent walked out her door, and River finally had a chance to sit at her kitchen table and decompress. A convict named Darien Ozlo had almost killed her, thanks to her fucked-up father. She touched her throat again. If not for Jared . . .

The handyman was looking in the refrigerator and turned to her. "You don't have much in here, but I can make eggs and toast."

"Thanks, but I can't eat right now." River stood and struggled to find the right words. "Saying thank you isn't enough. I'd like to offer you a place to stay, at least while you're working on the house. You can move into the guest room."

"You don't have to do that."

She stepped toward him. "I want to. I was thinking about it anyway."

"You're a good woman."

He opened his arms and she stepped in and hugged him. The joy of his warm body pressed against hers was almost overwhelming. How long had it been? River breathed in the smell of his flannel shirt and the light scent of sweat on the back of his neck. She remembered him standing in her bedroom in his underwear and she stepped back. She didn't want him to think the hug was anything other than mutual gratitude.

"I have to get to work." River realized she hadn't even checked her cell phone for messages yet.

"I think you're entitled to the day off."

"Not today. We have an arsonist to catch." She grabbed her briefcase and hurried from the house, experiencing a mix of emotions that made her thoughts jump from one thing to another. She glanced up her driveway and saw a tow truck getting ready to drive away with a black Suburban. The vehicle she'd seen following her the other night. Ozlo had parked at the end of the driveway and walked down. River planned to have Jared install a fan in the bedroom, because she might never sleep with her window open again.

Be master of mind rather than mastered by mind. River repeated one of her mantras until she felt focused. She climbed into her car and checked her phone. A text from Dallas from late last night: *I'm parked outside Crowder's house, 2040 W. 12. Will stay on him. I still think he's our guy. May need relief later.*

River texted back: *I'll ask for more people. Nothing on Crowder yet.*

She was still a little skeptical that someone so young had targeted the bottled water factory, both with a firebomb and a letter to its owner. Young men set fires all the time, but most were true arsonists who often stayed to watch the building burn. Their perp was passionate about environmentalism and resorted to criminal damage only as a means to further his cause.

River listened to her phone messages. The Quantico profiler wanted to know if he should e-mail his report or if she wanted to videoconference with him. River called and set up a conference at ten fifteen. On the drive into town, she called both Quince and Fouts and asked them to meet with her at ten. She was eager to see if the profile matched up with either Russell Crowder or Rick Arbuckle. River felt strangely disappointed to accept that Chris Noonaz hadn't been involved in either the sabotage at the pharma company or the firebomb at Rock Spring. She'd really wanted to bust him as the ringleader. River reminded herself that Noonaz's girlfriend, Melody, may have lied about the JB Pharma incident.

"River, I need to see you for a minute." Her supervisor called to her from the office next door.

Worry filled her stomach and she willed herself to be calm. She didn't want to be forced to take a leave of absence because of the attack. Not now. Maybe he just wanted to discuss the bureau bringing federal charges against Darien Ozlo.

River stepped out into the hall and through the open door next to hers. Ames Hartman, a heavyset man who hadn't been out in the field in years, looked up. "How are you? That must have been quite an ordeal."

"It happened so quickly, I didn't have time to be scared. And it's over now."

"I think you should take some time off."

"I'm fine. Really. This case I'm handling is coming to a head. The next few days are critical."

"Fouts can handle it."

"I have an undercover agent out there following an eco-terrorist. She texts me in the middle of the night, often needing intel. I can't just abandon her to another agent."

A long silence.

"Will you agree to see a counselor?"

"Sure." They both knew it was whitewash. Hartman could go on record as saying he'd ordered her to get counseling, but he'd never follow up. And neither would she.

"What's happening with the case?"

"My UC is tailing Russell Crowder, who she thinks might be planning something for today. We'll be ready to step in."

"Great."

"If nothing happens today, I may need more surveillance people. Can you request some?"

"I'll try. But the Portland bureau is dealing with a serial sniper, a rash of armed bank robberies, and two missing women."

"We'll do the best with what we have."

"Take some time off when it's over."

"I will."

River grabbed her casebook from her office and hurried down the hall to the conference room. Despite the calming mantra she'd been reciting all morning, a sense of dread had taken root in her system and was steadily growing. The attack on her life had kick-started the old anxiety and now it was in full bloom. When she got like this, wild scenarios played out in her head. Today's imagined drama featured an eco-terrorist setting off a bomb or poisonous gas in a very public place, after which River would have to call in a team of forensic pathologies to process the bodies.

No! Dallas had eyes on Russell Crowder, and they would locate Rick Arbuckle today. It had only been two and a half days since the firebomb. The perp hadn't had time to plan another attack, despite what Dallas thought. River took long, slow breaths as she updated the whiteboard.

Fouts came in, looking thinner than she remembered, but what caught her eye was his expression. He was missing his usual downturned mouth and worried eyes. River resisted the urge to ask him. If it was personal, he wouldn't share. If it was related to the case, he would bring it up after Detective Quince arrived.

"Hey, Fouts."

He shook his head. "You sleep with your bedroom window unlocked?"

The crap had started. "It's Eugene. And I live five miles from town. But I'm fine, thank you."

"Glad to see that. I'm starting to like you." A trace of a smile.

"Wish I could say the same," she joked in return.

"Seriously, what happened? Why did some California ex-con come after you?"

"I busted him when I was with the bureau in San Diego." It was a half-truth. She didn't talk about her father, ever.

Detective Quince strode in, and River was relieved. She liked looking at Quince's attractive face better than Fouts' pinched stare. "Hello, Quince. Let's get started."

River sat down. "We now have IDs on all four of the men who met at Tony's Tavern the night of the firebomb. Agent Fouts matched a mug shot of Rick Arbuckle to the older bearded man, and our undercover agent identified the younger mohawk guy as Russell Crowder." She looked at her printed notes. "I can't find Crowder in the system. But he's young, so I faxed a subpoena to a juvenile court judge to see if Crowder has a juvie record. Our UC is tailing him and thinks he may have something planned for today. It seems too soon after the firebomb, but we'll stay on alert. I may need someone to relieve the UC's surveillance duty later this evening."

"I'll do it," Quince offered.

"Thanks. I asked for more personnel, but the Portland office is dealing with its own problems and we may not get help." She looked at Fouts. "What can you tell us about Arbuckle?"

"He has a history of vandalism, so he fits the profile. More important, I checked with his PO and found his address and his employer. Bring Recycling. I'll try to get eyes on him today." Fouts looked pleased, and River realized that was the reason for his good mood. Fouts stood and added the details to the whiteboard.

"Excellent." River looked at the clock. It was almost time. She flipped on the big monitor at the end of the table. "A Quantico profiler is conferencing with us in a few minutes. Maybe we'll learn something that will help us prioritize our resources."

A moment later, Agent Moczary's craggy face filled the screen, and an overhead light shimmered on his endless forehead. Videoconferencing had not been designed with him in mind. "Good morning, Eugenians."

"Hey, Moczee." Fouts had known him a long time. "What have you got for us?"

"That depends. We've got two incidents: the sabotage to the pharmaceutical company and the firebomb at the bottled water plant. River tells me they may have been committed by members of the same group, but not necessarily the same guy." Moczary pushed back his nonexistent hair and grinned. "Let's start with the easy stuff. Either way, he's likely male, under thirty, and with the exception of the eco-group, he's most likely a loner."

River took notes, but this was Profiling 101, and everyone in the room could have come up with it.

Moczary continued. "The act of sabotage is more sophisticated, and that individual likely has above-average intelligence. He's also confident and probably worked for the company at one point."

River knew that too. "What about an alias?" she asked. "Would he change his last name to Greene to personalize his cause?"

"Excellent question." Agent Moczary pointed at her. "I've come across that in groups with superiority complexes."

River glanced at Fouts. "I'll see if my UC can find out Greene's real last name." She turned back to the monitor. "What about the firebomber?"

"He's harder to pin down. Of the five arsonist profiles, I'd say he best matches the Strategic Fire Starter." Moczary listed the attributes on his fingers as he spoke. "History of delinquent behavior, low self-esteem, membership in some kind of gang, and history of alcohol or drug use or abuse."

River didn't know enough about Crowder yet to properly assess the profile match. She'd only heard his name late last night, and this morning had been chaotic. "We'll know more about Russell Crowder soon, but I don't see anything that rules him out yet."

Quince jumped in with a question. "What about the pattern? One member committing an act of sabotage, then another member using a firebomb. Does that follow a profile?"

Fouts laughed. "You must not have been here in the Northwest when the Earth Liberation Front was active. That was their MO."

Quince looked more confused than embarrassed. "I thought their crimes were mostly arson."

"Yes, but they committed vandalism and sabotage too." Fouts turned to the monitor. "And half of those arrested were women, so I don't put much faith in the concept that he's likely a male."

"The ELF arsonists were different," Moczary argued. "They were environmentally and politically motivated, and most of them had no prior criminal histories."

"Our perps are environmentally motivated too," Fouts said.

River took charge again. "We have intel that says four men from ELF Lite met at Tony's Tavern the night of the bombing. Not only did they argue, but our UC says she overheard a conversation that indicated one of the members had gone rogue and planted the firebomb without the consent of the group."

"Then I'll modify my profile," Moczary said. "Teenage delinquent behavior, substance abuse, and low self-esteem coupled with seeing himself as an outsider."

"What about the letter he wrote to the owner of the bottled water company?" River asked.

"What letter?" Moczary squinted.

"I scanned it and attached it to an e-mail I sent you."

"Never got it."

"Damn." River dug through her paperwork, found the letter, and read it to the profiler. She was reminded of the personal threat of exposure.

"That's quite odd." Moczary played with his lips for a moment. "I think our perp has deep personal issues. He may be seeing a shrink and may have been sexually molested."

"How the hell do you get that?" Fouts' brows came together in a deep scowl.

"The phrase 'I know a lot more about myself' indicates counseling and new self-awareness," the profiler explained. "The threat to reveal what he knows about Rockman demonstrates that he feels shame and assumes others do too. I'm guessing sexual abuse."

"You think Rockman, the state senator, abused him?" River wanted clarity.

"Probably not." Moczary took a long sip of his bottled water. "But I believe the letter writer feels shame about something, and for men his age, it's often sexual."

"We appreciate your insight." River stood.

"Anytime. That's my job." The profiler gave them a little salute, and River clicked off the monitor.

"I'm not sure how that helps us, but I'll relay it to our UC." River looked at Fouts. "And we should go back through all the

Rock Spring employee files and see if anything new pops, based on the profile."

"What have you got for me?" Quince asked.

"We need more info on Crowder, but I'm still waiting for a judge to release his juvenile record. If you have any clout over there, please use it."

"I know the court clerk well." Quince smiled and River thought she saw a little blush.

Just as they were about to head out, River's phone rang. She looked at the ID: *Darrell Shoemaker.* Aka Special Agent in Charge from Alcohol, Tobacco, and Firearms. She put him on speaker. "Agent Shoemaker, we're in a task force meeting, so your timing is good. I've got you on speakerphone."

"I don't have much yet, but I wanted to let you know that the incendiary liquid in the firebomb was napalm, a mix of gasoline and aluminum salts."

"Something he could have made himself?" River asked.

"Yes, unfortunately."

After the meeting, River sat at her desk, thinking about the pro-filer's comments. She called Ted Rockman's office and told his receptionist she needed to speak to him right away.

"Mr. Rockman is being interviewed right now. I'll have him call you as soon as he's done."

"I have one very important question. It's about the arson at his plant. He'll want to take it."

"Just a minute. I'll interrupt him."

A moment later, Rockman came on the line. "Do you have a break in the case?"

"Maybe. Do you know a young man named Russell Crowder?"

A pause. "Off the top of my head, no. But I've been involved with Boys and Girls Club as well as Boy Scouts, so I've met a lot of young people and I can't remember them all."

"If you do remember him, please call me."

"I will." Rockman hung up.

River wondered who was interviewing him. A local reporter or had the network people hit town on the firebomb story? It was time to check in with Dallas.

CHAPTER 24

Friday, March 15, 8:30 a.m.

As Jackson entered the violent crimes area, Evans spun in her chair and said, "Happy birthday."

Oh crap. He'd completely forgotten and he wasn't prepared to deal with it. "Thanks. Would you keep it to yourself? I'm not in a mood to celebrate."

Evans' face fell. "What's wrong?"

"Katie's not doing well, but I don't want to talk about it. This case needs our undivided attention today." He'd texted his daughter first thing that morning, and she had ignored him as usual.

Schak walked up. "Are we meeting this morning?"

"We are." Jackson grabbed his case folder and coffee and headed for the conference room. Between worrying about Katie and wondering what he could have done to keep Todd Sheppard alive, Jackson hadn't slept well again.

He and Schak took seats, and Evans headed for the board. Next to Sheppard's name, she wrote *Killed/silenced?*

The scene from the night before flashed in Jackson's memory. The big man's body had not been assaulted in any visible way. They wouldn't know how he died until after the autopsy. The pathologist might find the killer's injection site, or maybe Sheppard had simply had a stroke or heart attack. Jackson hated not knowing, and it contributed to his foul mood.

"It has to be natural causes." Schak sipped his coffee. "I was watching Sheppard's unit, except for ten minutes or so when I went to find a restroom."

"But the killer wouldn't know that," Evans countered. "And if Sheppard and the killer know each other, maybe they talked and the killer got worried."

"Let's focus on the first death for now." Jackson turned to Schak. "Do you have anything new for us?"

"Sorry, no. I told you last night, the video was worthless, and I couldn't find any witness around the storage business."

"I came up empty yesterday too," Evans said. "I talked with the neighbors, and only one woman remembered seeing Maggie's truck on Tuesday. The neighbor thinks the truck was there when she came home at six. But that leaves Maggie still open for Cooper's time of death, except for her daughter's alibi."

Schak looked at the board. "Did you question Jenna?"

"We did," Jackson said. "She claimed they were both home watching a movie. We think the daughter might have Asperger's. I did a little reading about it last night, and the condition doesn't necessarily disqualify her as a suspect. It just means her emotional and social development are off and that she's probably smart in unusual ways."

"Patrick is our likely perp." Schak shifted, looking a little agitated. "We need to search his place before the damn jail releases him."

"Trang said he would have a search warrant and subpoenas this morning," Jackson responded. "So we'll be able to access his phone, banking records, and DNA too."

"About fucking time." Schak shook his head. "I should have done the paperwork myself."

Evans changed the subject. "In the meantime, we need to get the ME and go out to the crime scene again. We have to figure out how far away the killer was when he shot the arrow."

"Maybe we'll do it this afternoon, but Gunderson has an autopsy to participate in first." Jackson scanned his notes, knowing he had something else to share, and finally spotted a reference to the crime lab. "I have some good news. The pathologist found a tiny speck of trace evidence in Craig Cooper's wound. Joe said he would call this morning after he'd run some tests."

The door banged open and Sergeant Lammers burst in. "Why do I have to hear about a second body from the rumor mill?" She glared at Jackson.

"I'm sorry. I had planned to update you right after this meeting."

"Not good enough. A damned reporter called me first thing this morning asking if we had a serial killer going after homeless men in storage units. Why does she know about the second murder when I don't?"

Good question, Jackson thought. "If it was Sophie Speranza, she probably called the storage place looking for details on the first murder and got lucky and found out about the second death."

"Tell me who fucking died." Lammers didn't sit.

Having her looming over him made Jackson uncomfortable. "Todd Sheppard. He lived in another storage unit, and he's the one who found and reported Craig Cooper's body." Jackson stood to stretch his legs—and look his boss in the eye. "We went out there to question Sheppard again last night and found him dead. No obvious wounds, no signs of homicide. He might have had a stroke. He had brain damage from playing football."

"When's the autopsy?"

"I don't know yet."

Lammers glanced at the board. "What other suspects do you have for the Cooper murder?"

Had he forgotten to update his boss at all? *Crap.* "Patrick Brennan. He's a friend of Cooper's and admits to being in his storage unit around the time of death. As soon as the ADA gets us warrants, we'll search his place and his bank records."

"Do we have him in custody?"

"He was in jail as of five o'clock yesterday." Jackson knew he should have called again this morning.

Lammers rolled her eyes, but before she could say anything, Jim Trang, an assistant district attorney, walked in.

"I'm sorry for the delay, but I got called into court yesterday. I should have sent you a message." Trang's smooth face and dark eyes were tense with guilt.

"Thanks." Jackson took a stack of paper from him and stuffed the case folder into his shoulder bag, eager to get moving. What if the jail had released Patrick moments ago after the first round of arraignments? He stepped toward the door. "We have a search to conduct."

Schak stood too, and Evans reached for her coffee.

"I take it this meeting is over?" Lammers' eyes were still focused on Jackson.

"We have to get out to Patrick Brennan's place. I'll update you again before five today."

"Do that." She turned and left.

Trang glanced at each of them. "Is there anything else you need?"

"Not right now. Thanks."

On his way out, Jackson pressed speed dial ten and waited for a deputy at the jail to pick up.

"Lane County Jail."

"Detective Jackson. I need to know if Patrick Brennan is still in custody. I put a hold request on him." It hardly mattered now that they were finally on their way to search his place, but he still wanted to know.

"He was arraigned this morning and was processed for release about ten minutes ago." She didn't even bother to apologize. The deputies were tired of taking shit for a financial problem that wasn't their fault.

Jackson turned to his partners. "We have to fly."

They took three cars, suspecting Patrick Brennan had a lot of weapons to take into evidence custody, and it must have startled some of the residents on Wolf Creek to see them race by. Patrick's Bronco was parked near the cabin when Jackson pulled in. *Damn.* How long had he been there?

Jackson bolted from his car, carrying only the paperwork, and rushed to the door. Schak and Evans were right behind him. Jackson fingered his weapon with one hand as he pounded. "Eugene Police. Open up, Brennan! We have warrants."

Loud barking on the other side of the door obscured any movement they might have heard.

Fucking dog. Jackson pounded again. "Open up or we're busting this door down."

"He's probably in there shoving his arrows into the fireplace." Schak's eyes were intense, and he had his taser ready.

Jackson handed the warrants to Evans, then said to Schak, "Let's shoulder it together." He glanced at Evans. "Shoot the dog if you have to."

They positioned themselves and Jackson started a count.

"Wait." Evans' voice was right in his ear. "Did you check to see if it's open?"

Crap. Jackson reached for the knob and it turned. Embarrassment and anger added gas to the fire of his foul mood. He shoved the door open and yelled at the dog. "Get out!"

The dog did as commanded but kept barking. Once they were all inside, Evans closed the door. The living room was empty, the bow was still on the wall, and no fire burned in the woodstove. They began a search for the occupant, weapons drawn.

A moment later, Patrick called from the bathroom in a distressed voice, "I'll be out in minute!"

Jackson used a chair to reach the crossbow, a weapon he knew nothing about. He hadn't shot a bow and arrow since Boy Scout camp. He tagged the weapon, took it to his car, and locked it. The arrows were more important, but he hadn't spotted any with a quick look around, and he wanted to take the weapon before Patrick could complain.

A few minutes later, Evans found a stash of arrows in the closet of a small back bedroom. Jackson didn't hold any hope that one would have Cooper's blood, but if they could at least match these to the wound, it would add weight to their case. Schak found some illegal hunting traps, and Jackson found a stack of pornographic VHS tapes, but overall the search was a disappointment. Patrick had come out of the bathroom and sat at the kitchen table, listening to the radio and pretending they weren't there. He hadn't even asked to see the warrant, and when Jackson asked him to open wide for a DNA cheek swab, he complied without a word.

As Jackson bagged and tagged the sample, his phone rang. He couldn't rush the evidence collection, so it chirped in his pocket a few times. Evans was searching the kitchen cabinets and looked over at him. "Could be important."

"I know." He slipped the DNA sample into his shoulder bag, grabbed his phone, and answered without looking at the ID.

"It's Joe at the lab. I finally identified the trace evidence in Cooper's wound."

"Tell me."

"It's nail polish. The flake is so small that the color spectrum is hard to identify, but I think it's dark purple or black."

"Thanks." Relief quickly morphed into confusion. Jackson glanced at Patrick's hands just to be sure. The suspect's nails were stained, but sans polish.

Evans stared at him intently, and Schak hurried up the hall. Jackson moved out of Patrick's earshot and his team followed.

"That was the crime lab," Jackson whispered. "The trace evidence in Cooper's wound is nail polish, a dark color."

Evans' eyes flashed. "Maggie Brennan wore dark purple yesterday."

Jackson hadn't noticed, another blow to his ego. "Let's go pick her up."

CHAPTER 25

On the way out of the newspaper building, Sophie stopped in the restroom and checked herself in the mirror. The forest-green jacket and skirt complemented her red hair, and she'd swapped her favorite red leather bag for a black Coach purse. This interview with Ted Rockman was important. Not that she was impressed by his money or his little state senator position; she was just the first journalist he'd agreed to meet with in years. And the fire-bomb story—if it mushroomed like the old Earth Liberation Front movement—could be huge. It could be her ticket to a bigger paper, some of which were still hanging in there, despite predictions that they would have all gone under by now.

Still humming with excitement, Sophie pulled into the small parking area of R&L Enterprises. Once a Victorian-era family home, the building had been renovated with commercial siding, large windows, and a sign in the grassy front yard that read: *Rockman's Rule: Think globally. Act locally.*

His political office had its own entrance from the rear of the parking lot, but Sophie wasn't sure which way to enter. Rockman probably had a personal office in the middle, so it shouldn't matter. Sophie headed for the front and stepped inside. A warm, yeasty smell permeated the air. Were they baking bread? The bottom half of the sign out front had said Rockman Real Estate, so maybe it was just an agent/broker trick, some incense that made the place smell like an inviting kitchen.

The reception area was small and staffed by an older woman with short silver hair. Opposite her L-shaped desk were two padded chairs and a student-size desk with a computer. No one waited in the chairs. Sophie speculated that the real estate business was mostly about property investments and holdings. No walk-in clients. She introduced herself to the receptionist. "I'm here to see Mr. Rockman."

"I'll see if he's ready for you." The woman stepped through a closed door and came back a moment later. "He needs five minutes."

Sophie smiled. "What's your name?"

"Patrice LaRue."

"How long have you worked for Ted Rockman?"

"Three years. Why?"

"I'm just wondering if you like him."

"He's great to work for. Lots of flexibility. But I should be working now." The receptionist went back to her task and Sophie looked at her notes. She'd read Rockman's political bio, but it was standard fare about his college degree and his lovely wife and kids.

After a few minutes, Patrice led her into the second room, and Ted Rockman stood and shook her hand. Good grip, warm hands, nice smile. His dark hair was from a bottle, but he had a flat stomach and great posture for man in his forties.

"Thanks for taking the time to speak with me." She sat in a leather chair across from his oversize desk, pulled out her recorder, and clicked it on. "I'd like to get your quotes right." A set of tall windows could have let light into the room, but the curtains were closed.

Rockman looked uncomfortable, then nodded. "You understand I only have about twenty minutes?"

"That's fine. I'd like to start by asking about your political goals." Sophie really wanted to ask about the eco-terrorist who'd firebombed his company, but all in good time.

"I haven't announced this officially yet, but I plan to run for Congress. I'm not happy with my representation, so I can only assume other Oregonians aren't either."

Another scoop! She loved her job.

Rockman's phone rang and he excused himself to take a quick call. When he'd hung up, she got back to his campaign. "Do you have specific issues you would legislate for on a national level?"

"Yes, I'd like to end the war on drugs and restructure our prison system."

Too surprised to respond, Sophie scribbled a note and collected her thoughts. "Would you work to make all drugs legal or just to defund the prosecution of drug offenses?"

"Both. You have to start by dismantling the DEA, then work toward taking the profit out of imprisoning people just for getting high."

Holy shit! Was he really going to let her print this? If he did, he'd never get elected to Congress. "Is this a personal issue for you? Do you know someone who's in prison for drugs?"

"Several of my childhood friends have done time for posses-sion. But this is mostly an economic issue for all of us. We can't afford our prison system. The productivity loss is horrendous."

"Tell me more about your childhood and the friends who went to jail."

Rockman's eyes tightened, and Sophie thought he was going to shut down. He glanced at a photo on the wall. A smiling young couple. "My parents were addicts. My mother died in a car acci-dent, and my father died of a heroin overdose. I only had one relative and she wouldn't take me, so I ended up in a foster home from the age of thirteen to seventeen, when I finally had the resources to leave."

Quite a success story. "What was the foster home like for you?"

"Good and bad." Rockman seemed lost in memory again. "The foster parents had three children of their own and three foster kids. At first, I liked having brothers and sisters, but the crowding and backstabbing became really unpleasant. And the foster father was an asshole." Rockman waved at her recorder. "I don't want you to print that. But the experience made me very ambitious at a young age. I had to work several jobs just to rent my own place, and I vowed to never be dependent on anyone again."

Sophie noticed he'd said "the" foster parents, not "my" foster parents. "Did you stay in touch with your foster family?"

"No. The one foster brother I liked turned to drugs and crime and ended up in prison, and I never bonded with the parents. They were only in it for the money." Rockman shook his head. "Let's talk about something else."

"Why do you think your company was targeted by the firebomber?"

Now he looked irritated. "Some people think plastic water bottles are evil because they end up in landfills. But so do disposable diapers and old couches and everything else we throw away."

"I think the idea is that disposable water bottles are unnecessary." Sophie realized that was too strong a statement and backtracked. "I mean, in most situations, tap water is available and people can refill the same drinking container."

Rockman looked at the clock on the wall. "I have an online conference in a few minutes."

Disappointed, Sophie slipped in one more question. "I've heard that David Emerson is going to run in the primary. Are you worried about him as a challenger?"

"Not at all."

Sophie stood and realized she really needed to pee. She had several other stops to make before she drove back to the newspaper, so she asked, "Do you have a restroom I can use?"

"Sure. It's through this door and to the right."

The hallway opened into a kitchen on one side, but Sophie resisted the urge to look around. She used the restroom, stepped back into Rockman's office, and closed the door to the hall. Across the office, the door to the lobby opened, and the receptionist came through. "Mr. Rockman, someone is here to see you. He says it's urgent."

Rockman, who stood near his desk, said, "Not right now. I have a conference in a moment."

A young man with a mohawk haircut rushed up behind the receptionist and shoved her forward.

CHAPTER 26

Dallas started her car and ran the heater for a while to keep warm. She'd woken at sunrise, stiff and thirsty, and had made a quick trip to a nearby Dutch Brothers for coffee and a restroom break. She hated leaving her post in front of Russell Crowder's house, but she was human and his car hadn't moved all night. By now, she was ready for him to do something. As much as she loved undercover work, she wasn't that fond of surveillance. Her gadgets could only keep her entertained for so long, then she had to move. Maybe she could risk a quick walk. She shoved her tablet under the car seat and grabbed the door handle, feeling disappointed that River hadn't given her any information about Russell. Was he using an alias? Or was just too young to be in the system? Were her instincts wrong?

The rumble of an engine caught her attention, and she looked back at the target's driveway. Behind the wheel of the Subaru,

Russell headed out. Glad her own car was already running, Dallas waited thirty seconds, then pulled out. She forced herself to hang back. The worst of the morning traffic had already found its way to work and she was more worried about being spotted than losing him. She popped in her earpiece and called River on her work phone. Her supervisor didn't pick up, so Dallas left a message: "I'm following Crowder and he's headed downtown. Do we know anything about him yet?"

Dallas tried to keep only one car between her and Russell, but as they neared Willamette, a car cut in front of her. Dallas resisted the urge to honk, but she was boxed in and couldn't see the Subaru.

The minivan made a sudden left turn and jetted out of her way as quickly as it had interfered. Ahead two blocks, Russell's Subaru moved into the right lane. Dallas waited for a count of five, then eased over too. Russell turned on the next cross street just as she had to stop for a light. *Damn!* She practically bounced in the seat waiting for the light to change. When it did, she hit the gas, then had to slam the brake for an idiot on a bike who crossed in front of her. What the hell was he thinking?

She raced up to Mill Street and careered around the corner. The street was empty except for a car in the distance, at least six blocks away. Where was Russell's car? Pulse racing, Dallas forced herself to slow down. She had to check parking lots, driveways and alleys, because he must have turned off. But what if he'd turned on to another street and was moving quickly away?

Dallas scanned in both directions, then crossed Fourteenth Avenue and didn't see him. *Damn!* Picking up speed again, she passed large old houses but didn't see the green car. Reluctantly, she crossed Fifteenth, then moments later spotted Russell in a small parking lot. Dallas passed by, noting the sign out front: R&L

Enterprises. As soon as she was out of his line of sight, she pulled to the curb, climbed from her car, and called River.

Her boss answered this time. "Hey, Dallas. Sorry I missed your earlier call. I was in a task force meeting. What's the update?"

"Russell Crowder just pulled into R and L Enterprises. Can you get me something on that business?"

She heard River draw in a sharp breath. "That's Ted Rockman's office. He owns the bottled water plant."

"Holy shit. What is Crowder up to?" Russell was going through the front door, wearing a bulky jacket. "He's going in. I think I'd better too." Dallas started to run. She passed two large houses, most likely occupied by students, then came to the R&L business.

"This could be a confrontation," River warned. "Fouts and I are on our way. Let me know if we need more backup."

Dallas scrambled for how to play this. If Russell saw her, he'd know she had followed him. Could she bullshit her way through this and keep her cover? She ran up the sidewalk and tried to push through the door. It was locked. What the hell? Had Russell locked it behind him?

Her pulse escalated and she struggled to think straight. If Russell had locked the door, his intentions weren't likely peaceful. There had to be another entrance. Dallas redialed River as she ran around the building and through the side parking lot. "Crowder's inside and he's locked the door behind him. I'm looking for another entrance." She saw the back door with the State Senator Rockman political sign. "I'm going in the back, but I'll leave us connected." She shoved her phone in her pocket, grabbed the doorknob, and pushed inside.

A young woman was taking off her jacket and preparing to sit down at the desk. She looked startled to see Dallas. "Can I help you?"

Dallas pointed at the other door in the small, spare office. "Does that connect to the front?"

"Yes, but it leads to a private space." The woman shook her head, looking alarmed. "You can't go through there."

"I'm FBI. Please leave the building."

Dallas didn't wait to see if the woman complied. She had to get to Rockman as soon as Russell did. Should she pull her weapon? Or was it premature? Dallas had no idea why Russell was here. Maybe it was just a meeting, and if she blew her cover, they might never catch Russell, or any of the others, in the act. She decided to get her Kel-Tec out of its compartment and have it ready. Dallas dug to the bottom of her bag and grabbed the zipper. It didn't budge. *Shit.* The fabric was caught. She tugged but only made it worse. Instinct made her keep moving. Her pepper spray and knife were handy, and she would slice open the damn purse to reach the gun if the situation called for it.

On the other side of the door was a galley kitchen, and she raced through it with only a glance. The end opened into a short hallway with two doors. The first one she tried was a bathroom. Dallas stopped, took a deep breath, and tried to figure out how to keep her cover if Russell turned out to be Rockman's nephew or something. Her cover was a grant writer, so she'd come up with something. Dallas grabbed the handle of the second door and twisted. It opened, but a force pushed back.

Russell shouted, "Let go of the door and get out of the building."

Dallas slammed her shoulder into the door, knocking it open a few more inches, then slipped through. Russell grabbed her upper arm and shoved her into a wall, then quickly locked the door. The blow stunned her for a moment, but she glanced around the room. In a quick second, she took it all in. The large office had a corner desk, several guest chairs, and draped windows on the wall facing the street. Two people sat on the floor against an empty wall, a middle-aged man with jet-black hair and an older woman with short silver hair. She recognized Rockman from photos, but not the woman. Why were they on the floor? Dallas snapped her head toward Russell.

His bulky jacket had come off, and he wore a vest with a bomb taped to it. *Jesus H. Fucking Christ.*

In her pocket, River's voice squeaked, "Dallas? What's going on?"

"Give me your cell phone!" Russell screamed and held out his hand.

Dallas hung up her call and handed him the phone. "What are you doing, Russell? I don't understand." She would keep her cover as long as she could. If Russell realized she was an FBI agent, he might try to kill her. Could she get to her gun without jeopardizing all of them? Dallas scanned him up and down. He had a knife in one hand, but no other weapon she could see. Except the bomb.

Russell tossed her phone on the desk next to the others, then grabbed her purse and threw it down too. *Shit!* Dallas was glad for the knife in her pocket, but had no idea what she could do against a man with an explosive device.

Russell pointed at Rockman. "I'm trying to get this scumbag to admit to what he really is." He turned back to Dallas with narrowed eyes. "What are you doing here, Fiona? Did you follow me?"

"No. I came to see Mr. Rockman about writing a grant for him. He wants to refit his factory to be more environmentally responsible." The lie might not save her or Rockman, but it might mitigate Russell's anger.

The bomber turned to Rockman. "Since when do you care about the environment?"

Rockman did his part and didn't look at Dallas. "I have always cared, Russell. You think I don't remember you, but I do. You were one of my Boy Scouts."

"And one of your victims." Russell gestured at Dallas to go sit next to the others. She had no choice but to comply. Trying to take Russell down could get them all killed.

Rockman looked genuinely confused. "What are you talking about?"

"No more bullshit!" Russell touched his vest. "We'll deal with that in a minute, but first you have to call your factory and send everyone home." The terrorist took a cell phone from his pants pocket. "Give me the number of your foreman and I'll dial. Then you get on the line and tell him to close down."

Rockman closed his eyes in distress.

"Don't even think about resisting," Russell threatened. "We're just getting started."

CHAPTER 27

River charged down the hall to Fouts' office and stuck her head in. "We've got a situation."

Fouts was on his feet and moving without asking questions. As they jogged to the elevator, River updated him.

"Did you alert EPD?"

"Yes, patrol units are on the way, but they're on standby mode. I'm worried that we have a hostage situation."

"Damn. That's a little crazy even for an environmentalist."

"And our crisis negotiator is speaking at a conference in Atlanta." They stepped into the elevator and rode it down to the lobby. "We need intel on Crowder," River said. "I'll call the juvie judge again and press for access to his record."

"If he has one."

"You know he does."

"Yeah." Fouts pulled on his coat. "Did you call Quince?"

"Not yet. But I will."

The elevator doors opened and they ran for their cars.

After River mentioned "potential hostage situation," the assistant put her on hold while she tracked down Judge Kramer. As River turned left on Mill and spotted a patrol car ahead, the assistant came back on the line. "The judge signed your subpoena and I'll fax over the documents in a minute."

"I need a digital file. I'm on my way to a crisis scene and need immediate access to information that I can use to negotiate with the hostage taker."

"I'll have to ask. We don't usually send files that can be printed or shared."

"I'm a federal officer; just the send the file, please." River clicked off.

The patrol car parked sideways in the middle of the street, and the officer began putting out orange cones to stop traffic. *Someone must have called 911*, River thought. Not seeing any parking spaces, River pulled up behind the police unit and shut off her car. A pang of anxiety tugged at her chest. What if this was a false alarm and Crowder was simply talking to Rockman? The media would be on this situation soon, and she didn't want both departments to look foolish. She remembered the thumping sound from Dallas' call, as if she'd been against a wall. *Every decision is correct in that moment*, River reminded herself.

River jumped out and flashed her badge at the uniformed officer. "Agent River. This is my case."

The officer nodded, picked up the cone, and moved it behind River's car. She didn't see Fouts, but two dark-blue patrol cars sat side by side in the street outside R&L Enterprises, blocking the driveway. A green car was parked next to the walkway to the front entrance. River jogged up and tapped on the trunk of one of the patrol vehicles. The officers jumped from their cars and hurried toward her.

"Agent River, FBI. The perp is Russell Crowder, who we think set off the firebomb Tuesday night." Agent Fouts rushed up as she briefed them, so she introduced him, then continued. "Rock Spring has its business office here, and we think the owner, Ted Rockman, is inside with the perp. We have an agent in there too, but I lost communication with her. They might both be hostages."

"Is the SWAT unit on the way?" The female officer's lips were set in a grim expression. She probably had kids at home and didn't want to be on the front line.

River didn't blame her. "They're on standby, but we're not sure what we're dealing with yet."

"Our report is that it's a bomb threat," the officer said.

No wonder they were parked out in the street. "Have you seen the perp? Does he have any other weapons?"

"No, ma'am." The male officer shook his head. "No activity so far."

River set her briefcase on the back of the patrol car, popped the case open, and took out binoculars. She focused on the small front window with blinds pulled up. She could see the edge of an unoccupied reception desk and the space in front of it. No people, no movement. A large multipaned window on the other side of the door had closed curtains, but River could make out a figure and some movement. Along the side of the building was another window that seemed to open into a kitchen. Also empty. Wooden fences bordered the parking lot on the left and back. Private homes sat on two of the surrounding lots. They needed to evacuate both residences and the chiropractic business on the right.

What the hell did Crowder want and how mentally ill was he? River wished she knew what the hell they were dealing with. Environmentalists were not known to take hostages, so this had to be personal. She needed to check her e-mail for Crowder's court file.

Finally, River said, "I see movement behind the big windows on the right. The other rooms look empty." She nodded to the officers. "I'd like you both to circle wide to the back side of the building, take cover, and hold your position until the snipers get here. The perp is young with a mohawk haircut. If he comes out, notify me."

Fouts drew his weapon. "We'll cover you."

The officers split up and ran through the adjacent properties. River lost visual contact with them and glanced back to the street. Patrol officers had blocked traffic both ways. She grabbed her tablet computer from her briefcase, clicked it on, and checked her e-mail. Nothing from the juvenile court yet. *Damn.* River willed herself to be calm. Even if the file didn't arrive in time, this could still turn out well. She had crisis negotiation training, just like every other agent. The key factors were to empathize and stall. It was time to contact Crowder and find out what he wanted. "I'm going back to my car for a bullhorn."

Fouts looked worried. "What if we don't have anything to negotiate with?"

River knew what he meant. "We pray that Rockman cooperates with whatever Crowder wants."

CHAPTER 28

Jackson pushed the speed limit but resisted using the siren to move traffic out of his way. Maggie might not even be home. If she wasn't, he'd put out an attempt-to-locate and they would stop by the restaurant where she worked. Searching her house for the nail polish and bow/arrows was their next priority. Schak had stayed at the department to produce the warrant and take it to a judge. Evans was following him so closely, she would rear end him if he braked too hard.

At the trailer house, Maggie opened the door a few inches. "What do you want now?" She sounded weary and resigned, as if the fight had gone out of her.

"We have more questions. Open up."

"I'm working the lunch shift today and have to leave soon."

"This won't take long." A blatant lie. But Maggie had lied to them, and it was just part of the job.

A long sigh, then the door opened and Maggie stepped back. "I don't know what else I can tell you."

Once inside, Jackson did a quick visual search and sensed Evans doing the same. He planned to take Maggie into the department for questioning this time. Maybe the small space, harsh lighting, and video camera would persuade her to tell the truth. Now that they had the leverage of the trace evidence, a confession was a good possibility.

Maggie wore a pullover sweatshirt with a Ducks logo and kept her hands in the pouch pocket.

"Show me your hands," Jackson commanded.

"What?" Maggie held them out. "You think I have a weapon?"

Her nails shimmered with dark polish. Jackson couldn't tell if it was purple, blue, or black. He suspected it didn't matter. "The pathologist found a chip of your nail polish in Craig Cooper's wound. So you're coming with us to make a statement."

Panic filled her eyes. "That's crazy. I didn't kill Craig."

"I'd like you to come with us peacefully. Otherwise, we'll have to cuff you."

"I want to call a lawyer."

"You'll have a chance later if we arrest you." Jackson stepped forward to take her arm, and a book on the coffee table caught his eye. *The Hunger Games.* A weird chill shot up the back of his neck. He'd watched the movie with Katie a month ago. The story was about a teenage girl who hunted with a bow and arrow. It all came together in his head. "Whose book is that?" He nodded at the coffee table next to Maggie.

"Jenna's. Why?"

"Where is she?"

"She's taking a film class downtown at Lane Community College. Why?" Maggie's lip trembled.

Jackson suspected she knew. "Jenna went out the night Craig Cooper was murdered, didn't she?"

Maggie's eyes glistened with tears. "I don't know. I fell asleep during the movie."

"Does Jenna own a bow? Or practice archery?"

"I don't have to tell you anything."

Jackson sympathized. He would probably react the same way if Katie were in trouble. And the likelihood of that had never been greater. "Turn around and put your hands behind your back. We're taking you in for questioning." He couldn't let Maggie call her daughter and warn her.

"This isn't necessary." Maggie burst into sobs, and Jackson felt like a prick. Still, he cuffed her and led her to Evans' car.

Once the suspect was in the backseat with the door closed, Evans asked, "Should I put out an ATL?"

"Yes, and put Maggie in an interrogation room. I'll stop by the community college and see if I can locate Jenna."

Evans' brows pulled together. "We knew they resented Craig Cooper, but the timing of the murder puzzles me. Why would Jenna wait six weeks after he got out of jail?"

"I don't know." Jackson was eager to get moving.

"I think we need to know more about Craig and Jenna's relationship before we question the girl." Evans headed for her driver's seat. "I'll make some calls."

Lane Community College had recently completed construction of a new auxiliary campus across from the library. The building occupied most of a square block and housed students on the upper floors. For nearly a decade before that, the lot had been a deep pit where a previous developer had started to dig a foundation—an ugly blight surrounded by a chain-link fence. Slowly, the downtown area was making a comeback, but the problem of transients and troubled teenagers had escalated. As Jackson parked across from a group of street kids, his mind turned to Katie. Was it obsessive to call again? He really wanted to hear her voice, but he sent a text instead: *I love you.*

He entered the building and stopped at the information desk, where he showed his badge and asked the young man to help him locate Jenna Brennan.

The young man seemed excited by the task. "I'll see what her schedule is."

It only took a few seconds. "Jenna had a class this morning, but it's over, so I don't know if she's still in the building. You could check the student lounge." He pointed to the left. "And there's more seating on every level."

Jackson checked the lobby area, then trotted up the steps, feeling a familiar tug. Would he ever get past this pain? A twenty-minute search of the many reading nooks and computer stations proved to be a waste of time. Jenna wasn't in the building.

Jackson grudgingly made another trip out to the trailer park and bounced across the speed humps to Maggie's place near the back. The first thing he noticed was that the little truck was gone from the driveway. Had Jenna come home and taken the car?

Jackson called the department and added the car's make and model to the ATL Evans had called in for Jenna. The girl wouldn't get far. He pounded on the door and looked in the windows just to make sure Jenna wasn't hiding inside, then got back in his car. If patrol units didn't spot Jenna this afternoon, he'd stop by the house again later this evening.

Before driving off, he put in his earpiece and called Schak. "How's the search warrant coming?"

"I'm entering the courthouse with it now."

"Good. We think the killer might be Maggie's daughter, and the sooner we search the better. I'm still at their house, and I'll just wait here for a while. Maybe Jenna will show up or you'll get the warrant signed and meet me here."

"Why the daughter?"

"Jenna is a fan of *The Hunger Games*."

"What's that?"

Jackson visualized Schak scratching his head.

"It's a story about a young girl, far in the future, who kills competitors with a bow and arrow. The book was made into a movie, and it started an archery craze among teenage girls."

"That's wild. But what's the motive?"

"Jenna blames Craig Cooper for her father's death, which she witnessed." Jackson knew it was weak, but the evidence was mounting.

"I'll keep you posted on the search warrant," Schak said. After a pause, he asked, "Have you heard the buzz on the EPD radio?"

"What's happening?"

"A possible hostage situation with the perp who firebombed that factory."

"No shit? Where?" Adrenaline surged in Jackson's veins. He envied those involved. Despite the danger, cops lived for those high-intensity scenarios. It beat the hell out of sitting in a trailer park waiting to arrest a troubled teenager, who'd likely killed a man she once called *uncle*.

While he waited to hear about the search warrant, Jackson knocked on doors to ask about Jenna. He needed to know if anyone had seen her leave that night. Only two neighbors were home and neither had noticed cars coming or going Tuesday night, but one woman said she'd seen Jenna shooting a bow and arrow in the small space between the trailers. Jackson searched the area and found straw on the grass near the back chain-link fence. Jenna must have used a bale of hay for her target, but it was gone now. Had she tossed the bow as well?

Jackson took photos of the area and bagged some of the straw as evidence. It started to rain, so he headed for his car. His phone rang and he didn't recognize the number. He almost didn't answer, then changed his mind. He was just killing time anyway.

"Detective Jackson? It's Jane Niven, Craig Cooper's sister."

"Hello, Jane. How are you?" Dumb question, but it was polite habit.

"I'm grieving . . . and wondering if I should hold a memorial service for Craig. There would only be a few of us there." She paused and took a deep breath. "Have you made any progress in the investigation?"

"We'll probably make an arrest today. I can't tell you anything more."

"Is it someone I know?"

"When we've made the arrest, we'll release the name. Sorry." Jackson was curious about which of Cooper's acquaintances Jane knew, or if she had ever met Jenna. "Who do you think would attend Craig's memorial?"

"I'm not sure. Probably Patrick Brennan. I think they're still friends. And maybe Patrick's ex-wife. Maybe even Craig's foster brother would come if I contacted him."

Surprised, Jackson asked, "Craig was in a foster home? You didn't grow up with him?"

"Our family was together until I was seventeen and Craig was thirteen. Then Dad died and Craig started getting into trouble. Mom couldn't handle him and he went to Skipworth." Jane choked up and started to cry. "While Craig was incarcerated, our mother moved back east. I stayed here with a friend, but Craig ended up in a foster home. He did okay for a while, but then he started using drugs and stealing to support his habit. He was in and out of treatment and jail for years. Then he committed the robbery."

All Jackson could think was: *How could a mother abandon her children?* Yet it was a familiar story. Jackson was glad Jane didn't blame herself. "What do you know about Craig's relationship with Danny Brennan's daughter?"

"Jenna? He loved that girl and used to babysit her so Danny and Maggie could go out drinking. And when Danny was in jail for a stint, Craig was like a father to her."

"What happened?" Jackson had heard it from Maggie, but it was always good to check with other sources.

"Jenna was with Danny when the police shot him. Jenna eventually blamed Craig for getting Danny hooked on drugs and never spoke to him again. It broke Craig's heart."

"Have you seen Jenna lately?"

"Oh no. Not since Craig went to prison. Why?"

"Just wondering." His phone made a beeping sound, and Jackson looked to see who was calling. Schak. "I'm getting another call, but I'll keep you posted."

He clicked over. "Did we get the warrant?"

"Indeed. Judge Volcansek has seen the *Hunger Games* movie. I'm on my way."

CHAPTER 29

"Get on the floor, both of you! I have a bomb!" the young man yelled.

Sophie heard the word *bomb* and instinctively dropped to the floor. Had the crazy man seen her? She crawled under Rockman's desk. *Oh hell.* Why hadn't she run back into the little hallway? *Because the door behind her was closed and she wouldn't have had time.* If the man had a gun too, he might have shot her in the back as she ran.

The crazy man yelled, "Give me your cell phones! Now!"

Under the desk, Sophie held her breath, waiting for him to come around and discover her. Instead she heard the cell phones slam down on the desktop over her head.

Now what?

Carefully, she shifted until she was sitting with her back against a wall of drawers and her legs bent in front. For the first time in her life, Sophie was glad to be short. She slipped her cell phone out of her jacket pocket and tried to decide if she could risk dialing 911. No, she couldn't speak out loud without giving herself away. But she could text someone and let them make the call. Her first thought was Jasmine, her lover, who happened to work for the public safety department. But Jaz didn't check her messages very often. Sophie scrolled through her recent texts. Brian Jones, a newspaper photographer, was fifth on her list. Hands shaking, she muted her phone, then keyed in the message: *At R&L Ent. Man with bomb. Hostages. Call 911.* She pressed send.

A moment later Sophie panicked. What if Brian thought it was a joke? She quickly sent another text: *No joke! Call!*

The bomber yelled at someone to get out of the building. The shout was followed by a scuffle, then the sound of someone being slammed into a wall. Who had he hurt? Sophie's heart pounded so hard she felt her pulse beat in her ears.

A woman's voice asked, "What are you doing, Russell?"

The crazy man had a name, and a third hostage was in the room. A young woman who knew him. His girlfriend?

Sophie heard the name Fiona, then the young woman said something she couldn't hear. After that Mr. Rockman and Russell talked about environmental issues and Boy Scouts. *What the hell?*

Sophie remembered the recorder in her purse. She scrambled to dig it out and get it turned on. She slipped the recorder into her pocket, where it could be effective but not seen. She had to assume the bomber would discover her eventually. When she tuned back in to what Russell was saying, she realized he wanted Rockman to shut down his factory. Russell was the eco-terrorist who'd firebombed Rock Spring!

She had to keep contacting people until someone responded. Sophie scrolled through her list of recent calls and found Agent River. She pushed the text icon and keyed in: *Terrorist at R&L with bomb. Hostages!*

Or that's what she intended it to say, but her shaking hands made errors and she had to correct the word *bomb*. Sophie left the other typos and pushed send. She hated releasing copy with mistakes, but now was not the time to be anal. It was, however, time to be a reporter.

Sophie tapped open the Twitter application on her phone, from which she posted Willamette News updates, and keyed in: *Hostage situation at Rock Spring office. Eco-terrorist demands shutdown. Tweeting the action from inside the building.*

She couldn't believe she said all that with 140 characters. In the room, she heard Rockman make a call and tell someone to send everyone home and close the factory. Sophie hoped that would alarm the foreman enough to call the police.

She checked her text messages to see if Brian or River had responded. Not yet. Sophie concentrated on the voices beyond her space under the desk. She heard Fiona say, "Why don't you let Patrice, the receptionist, go? You have no reason to terrorize her."

"When I've heard that the factory is shut down, I'll think about it."

Rockman spoke next. "You wrote the threatening letter, didn't you?"

"Of course. Why?"

"I think your issue with me is personal and we can work through it."

"Work through it?" Russell sounded stunned and angry. "Like it's some employee grievance?"

Rockman stayed calm. "What did you mean by revealing what you know about me?"

"You know what I'm talking about, and today you'll admit your guilt. But first, you have to burn down your factory, so it will never produce another plastic water bottle. If you don't, I'll blow us all up."

Holy shit. What a great video clip this would make—if only she could find a way to capture it on her cell phone. She would even send the clips to her competitor, Trina Waterman at KRSL, just to break the story.

"That's insane." Rockman's voice wavered with anxiety.

"So is arguing with a man wearing a bomb."

A long silence followed. Sophie checked her text messages while keeping one eye on the floor beside the desk, watching for the terrorist's feet. So far he'd stayed in the open area of the room.

Brian, her coworker, had responded: *Seriously?*

She texted back: *Yes! Come get pics. No visuals so far. Only tweets. Check Twitter for story.*

Footsteps came her way and Sophie's breath caught in her throat. The footsteps retreated. She quickly sent her next Twitter post: *Terrorist, Russell, demands Ted Rockman burn Rock Spring bottled water factory to the ground. Threat: 4 hostages will be blown up.*

A moment later, a text came from Agent River: *Is young woman named Fiona or Dallas there? Is she OK?*

Fiona or Dallas? That was weird. And how would Agent River know who was in the building? Unless the FBI had been following Russell and Fiona was an agent. Sophie texted: *Fiona is here and OK. Rockman, receptionist, and me. I'm under desk. Russell doesn't know I'm here/sending.*

A moment later, another text from River: *What kind of bomb?*

Good question.

* * *

Dallas studied the bomb taped to Russell Crowder's chest, trying to determine how powerful it might be. It looked simple, like sticks of dynamite connected to an igniter made from a timer.

He had set off a small firebomb at the Rock Spring factory, so she had to assume Crowder knew something about explosives and was willing to use them. But making a vest bomb with a trigger detonator was another level of skill—and bravery. Crowder acted nervous enough for the part, pacing and sweating and sounding emotional. Dallas hoped to maintain her cover for as long as she could, just to protect herself, but as soon as she'd seen the bomb, she'd stopped thinking of him as Russell. Given an opportunity, she would kill him to save the others.

Crowder's demand that Rockman order his foreman to burn down his factory didn't surprise Dallas. What better way to put a bottled water company out of business? What surprised her was Rockman's reluctance.

"It's just a building," she whispered to Rockman. "Four people could die in here."

Rockman ignored her and continued to engage Russell. "What if I put a twenty-cent return value on every bottle? Ninety-five percent of them would get redeemed and recycled."

"But that won't solve the whole problem. I want to send a message to bottled water companies everywhere. I want to shut down the whole industry."

"You can't do it from here," Rockman argued. "It's a global business. You'll have to think in bigger terms."

"Think globally. Act locally." Russell smirked at his own comeback, then shifted moods again. He grabbed Rockman's phone from the desk and pressed a key, then held it to his ear. "Is this the Rock Spring foreman? Is everyone out of the building?"

A pause, while he listened to the response.

Russell raised his voice, "Almost isn't good enough. When the building is empty, pour gas everywhere, then throw a flame and run." Russell made a satisfied sound. "Take pictures with your phone and send them. I want to see it burning before I let anyone go."

Another brief pause.

"You can talk to Rockman, but he'll tell you the same thing. Because he doesn't want to die." Crowder's voice grew loud and weird at the end, like an announcer for a creepy movie.

Dallas was reminded that he was still a kid. As a young male, his frontal lobe hadn't fully developed, and he hadn't yet processed how badly this would turn out for him.

Russell handed the phone to Rockman, who was practically hyperventilating. "Do what he says," Rockman commanded. "It's not just me in here. He has two women hostages as well. Get the fire department out there on standby. Nobody gets hurt and nobody's property will be damaged but mine."

Dallas wondered if the foreman would actually go through with it. Her next thought was: *Where the hell is the team?* Shouldn't River or a crisis negotiator send a cell phone up to the exterior door so Crowder could communicate with them? They had little remote-controlled units to do that kind of thing. But this was a unique scenario. The person who could meet the terrorist's demands was already in the building, making it happen. Russell wouldn't need anything from law enforcement until it was time to escape. What the hell was his plan?

"While we wait for the pictures, we can talk about what you did to me." Crowder fidgeted with the phone, slapping it against his palm.

"I really don't know what you mean." Rockman sounded like a man with no options.

Dallas felt sorry for him. Crowder was clearly off his rocker.

"Are you talking about the Boy Scout camping trip you took with my sons' troop?" Rockman shook his head. "That was the only time I ever saw you before this."

Russell's face darkened with rage. "You molested me!"

The furious accusation caught them all off guard and they sat back against the wall. Dallas stopped looking at the bomb and studied Crowder's face. His looks were distorted by the anguish in his eyes and the tight set of his mouth.

Next to her, Rockman jerked back. "What are you talking about? That's just crazy."

* * *

Russell hated when people called him crazy. Just because he'd been diagnosed with borderline personality disorder and had been sexually abused by every male father figure he'd known didn't make him a nutcase. He was trying hard to get closure, to get well, and to make a difference in the world all at the same time. Those weren't the actions of someone still in denial. He accepted what had happened to him, but he couldn't move forward until Rockman admitted it and went to jail. Or to hell, if that's the way it worked out.

Russell's therapist believed that confronting Rockman was essential. She thought Russell wouldn't be able to let go of his anger until Rockman was publicly exposed as a pedophile. Exposed and punished! Russell understood that sending Rockman to jail as a sexual predator would make his own life better, but it would be a setback for his environmental cause. While Rockman served his time, his company would go right on bottling water in plastic containers, and nobody would have the authority to make the important changes that would benefit the environment.

Russell had dreamed up this plan to force Rockman to deal with both issues. But he hadn't counted on these two women being in here. He had wanted to keep it simple, and if Rockman had refused his demands, Russell had been prepared to trip the detonator and blow them both up. He was ready to die for his cause, rather than live an angry pointless life of shame. But now he had these two other hostages. He hoped it put pressure on Rockman as well.

Russell strode to the desk and searched for some paper. "I want you to write out a full confession," he called over his shoulder as he lifted yellow folders and stacks of spreadsheets. "Where is your paper?"

"In the top drawer on the right." Rockman's voice changed volume halfway through his statement.

Russell spun and saw that the pedophile had stood and so had Fiona. "Sit down!" He held out the knife. "Don't make me hurt you or your secretary."

"I'm sorry, but I have bad knees. I had to stand."

Russell laughed. The man had bad knees? It wasn't nearly enough karmic justice. "Stay on the floor." Russell had a roll of duct tape in his pocket and he would use it on Rockman as soon as the pervert wrote out his confession. He would have to tape the women now too because he needed time to get out of the state. He already had new ID and would head for Colorado. They had an active environmental group there and some progressive ideas about livability.

"I can't confess to something I didn't do," Rockman whined.

Russell glared at the liar. "You have to! I need closure."

He hadn't counted on having three hostages, but since he did, Russell was glad he'd decided on the bomb instead of a gun. He'd worried that Rockman wouldn't take a gun seriously, that the pedophile would dare him to shoot him before he commanded his foreman to burn down the factory. But everybody took a bomb seriously.

Next to Rockman, Fiona studied him intently. Russell was still mystified by her presence. Especially the way she'd shoved herself in the door. At first, he'd thought she might be some kind of federal agent. But he'd glanced in her wallet, and her ID said Fiona Ingram. She even had a library card and a business card for a grant writer. Still, he was keeping an eye on her. But with a bomb taped to his chest and a knife in his hand, Russell didn't expect anyone to come at him.

He moved around the desk and reached for a drawer. Something caught his attention. Was that someone tapping a cell phone? He stepped back and stared down at the leg-space cavity under the desk. A petite redheaded woman was tucked in there. *Shit!* Where the hell had she come from? Another hostage to deal with.

"Come out of there!" Russell glanced over at the others. No one had moved this time.

The woman scooted sideways until she cleared the desktop, then stood. She was pretty and dressed nicely, and Russell thought he'd seen her somewhere. "Who are you?"

"Sophie Speranza."

"Why do I know that name?"

"I write for the Willamette News."

"You're a reporter?" Russell's stomach churned. This was not going as planned.

"Yes, and it's a good thing for you." Her eyes looked scared, but her tone was cheerful and confident.

Russell glanced at his hostages, then motioned for the reporter to move to the other side of the desk. "Why is it good?"

"Because you want Ted Rockman to make a public confession. I can help you."

"You mean you'll print it in the newspaper?" The idea gave him renewed hope that this mission could be salvaged.

"I can do better than that." Sophie's eyes glinted with energy. "I can record his confession on my cell phone and send it to the media. We can make him go on TV and tell the world what he did."

"I didn't do anything!" Rockman cried out.

Russell ignored him. His brain scrambled to work through the consequences. "But I don't want the police to come here. I need to get away."

"You still can. Recording his confession will take less time than writing it out. And the TV people can hold the story until you're safely gone."

Russell liked the idea. It was much better than his plan to mail Rockman's written confession to all the news organizations once he'd left town. "Let's do it."

Sophie pulled her cell phone from her pocket. "You can make a public statement too, Russell. This is your chance to get your message about plastic water bottles out there to the whole state." The reporter locked eyes with him. "I think you should do that first. You want people to know this is really about your cause."

Excitement and confusion overwhelmed him. Russell desperately wanted to bring his message to a wide audience. But he didn't want his face to be publicly known. It could hurt his chances of starting a new life in Colorado—unless he radically changed his appearance too. But he could do that by growing a beard and letting his hair get long. "Okay. Give me a minute to think about what I want to say."

Russell spun back to Rockman. "You get ready too. You're going to confess to sexually molesting me on that camping trip. And if you've molested others, I'm sure they'll come forward after this." He heard the reporter tapping her cell phone. "What are you doing?"

"Just letting Trina Waterman at KRSL know I'll be sending video." She looked up and smiled at him. "Professional courtesy."

CHAPTER 30

River checked her cell phone to see if Dallas had made contact. Instead she had a text from Sophie Speranza: *Terrorist at R&L with bomb. Hostages!*

"What the hell?"

"What is it?" Fouts asked.

She showed him the text. They were still behind the patrol cars, waiting for the SWAT unit.

"Who sent it?"

"Sophie Speranza. She's a reporter for the Willamette News. She's covering the incident at Rock Spring and called me three times this week. But I never returned her calls, and I have no idea how she knows what's going on here."

Fouts scowled. "She must be inside."

River tried to process everything at once. "Why would Crowder let her send a text? And why haven't I heard from Dallas?" A sense of dread washed over River. Was Dallas dead?

River texted back: *Is young woman named Fiona or Dallas there? Is she OK?*

"Where is the SWAT unit?" Fouts lamented. The EPD special operations team typically gathered at the training center where the big vehicles were kept, then went out as a unit from there. It took time.

River sent another text: *What kind of bomb?* Damn, she wished she were communicating with Dallas.

Detective Quince trotted up. "What have we got?"

"A hostage situation." River kept her voice calm. "Crowder has a bomb."

"Shit! Is the EPD bomb unit on the way?"

"Of course." But in this situation, there wasn't much the explosive experts could do until it was over. They typically dealt with small devices that perps had left and walked away from. Or devices that people found in their deceased loved one's back closet. None of them had ever dealt with a situation like this— a bomb used to terrorize hostages into meeting demands. Panic flooded River's chest and she recited her calming mantra to keep her heart rate steady.

"What is he demanding?" Quince asked.

"We don't know yet. We believe Ted Rockman is in there, and that Crowder likely wants something from Rockman, probably having to do with his bottled water factory."

"Rockman is the only hostage?"

River shook her head. "No. I think our UC followed Crowder inside and a reporter, Sophie Speranza, is in there too. Believe it or not, she's sending texts." River glanced down at the phone in her hand, willing the text icon to light up.

"That is odd." Quince glanced at the tall windows. "Does Crowder even know we're out here?"

"We don't know. We're hoping he'll contact us." River's bullhorn was on the trunk of the patrol unit, but she hadn't used it. Why alert him before snipers arrived?

River glanced at her phone again. She had a text! From Sophie: *Fiona is here and OK. Rockman, receptionist, and me. I'm under desk. Russell doesn't know I'm here/sending.*

River turned to Fouts and Quince. "He has four hostages, Ted Rockman, our agent, a receptionist, and Sophie Speranza. The reporter is under a desk and Crowder doesn't know she's texting."

"At least we've got some intel," Fouts said. "Ask her what he wants."

River texted again, then glanced across the parking lot at the two officers watching the back door. She had an obligation to let them know what they were dealing with. She waited for Sophie's response to the bomb question.

It came a moment later: *Taped to his chest. Maybe dynamite? Only saw it for a sec.* River relayed the information, then called her boss and gave him a brief report. He offered to get federal marshals on the scene and to fly a hostage negotiator down from Portland.

"I don't think we need either," River said. "EPD is sending out a SWAT unit that includes a hostage negotiator and snipers, and their bomb unit is responding as well. It'll be a madhouse here soon."

"Keep me posted."

As they waited for Sophie's next text, the wind picked up and the sky grew dark and threatened rain. River was glad for the cool air. It would keep the team from seeing her sweat. Two more patrol units arrived, and out of her peripheral vision, she saw men and women in blue uniforms knocking on doors.

A loud rumbling caught her attention, and River turned to see a large armored vehicle stop at the perimeter of the scene.

Uniformed men with rifles and Kevlar vests poured out of the truck and gathered around a patrol car, waiting for instructions. A tall man with a crew cut jogged their way.

River glanced at her phone. Another text from Sophie: *Russell wants Rockman to burn his factory. And confess to sex crimes. Knows I'm here now. Sending out video soon.*

"Good glory." River showed the text to Fouts.

"Sex crimes? Then it's personal for him. That makes him more dangerous."

River agreed. The profiler had nailed it. She grabbed her tablet and checked her e-mail. The court had finally sent Crowder's juvenile record. As she opened the file, the SWAT commander reached them.

"Sergeant Bruckner. Glad to have you here." They'd met at the Rock Spring firebombing.

"What have we got?" His massive chest and shoulders seemed too big for his Kevlar vest.

River pointed at the tall windows. "We believe the terrorist is in that front room. He has four hostages, including an FBI agent. His main target is Ted Rockman, and I'm hoping we can get him to release the others."

"Any contact with him yet?"

"We were waiting for your team to get in place."

"Excellent. Are the houses evacuated?"

"Yes."

Bruckner's jaw tightened. "We'll get snipers in place. If we get a shot, we have to take it."

River understood his position but wanted a better outcome. "We hope to talk him out. Who's your crisis negotiator? Ours is out of town."

"I am." A sandy-haired woman in her late forties walked up. She was the only SWAT member not in a uniform. "Libby Miller."

After a round of introductions, River said, "One of the hostages is communicating with us." She remembered the court file she'd received. "And I may have new information about the perp that we can use. Give me a minute."

"I'll get snipers and the hasty team in place." Bruckner trotted back to his men. No women were on the crew because the physical requirements were too rigorous.

River scanned the lengthy file. Russell was only nineteen, yet he had pages and pages of court appearances, charges, and evaluations from social workers and psychiatrists. Russell Crowder's troubles had started at twelve when a friend of his mother's had molested him. Crowder had been caught with alcohol at thirteen and had vandalized his middle school at fourteen. He'd been incarcerated at the Serbu campus for sixth months and diagnosed with borderline personality disorder. At seventeen, he'd been arrested for trespassing at an LTE protest in front of Rock Spring. Somewhere in there, the lost and volatile young man had found a cause and a family with Love the Earth. River sighed and closed the file.

She summarized the information for the group, directing most of her attention to Libby Miller, who might be doing some of the negotiation. River said, "I understand this young man. I'd like to communicate with him first."

"I'm trained for this," Miller said.

"So am I." River needed every resource available to her, but she wasn't turning over command of this scene. "I have an agent in there too, and I'm responsible for her. Let's work together."

"I'll get the hailer," Miller said. "We'll send in a phone with it."

"Okay, I'll contact my insider again and see where we're at."

River keyed in a new text to Sophie: *Has Rockman met demands? What is Crowder's plan?*

Scrolling back through previous communications, River saw the phrase, *sending out video soon.* Was Crowder recording a public statement? Did he crave attention? While she waited to hear from Sophie, River watched a SWAT sniper enter the house to the left. The upstairs window would make a good vantage point. River asked the universe to keep Russell Crowder alive. He wasn't a psychopath, just a mentally ill teenager who'd had some tough breaks and fallen in with some misguided activists.

River heard shouting and turned. A white media van parked in the street just beyond the patrol-vehicle barricade, and a blonde woman argued with a uniformed officer.

River's phone beeped and she opened another text: *Video going live soon. KRSL.*

"Oh hell." She showed the message to Fouts, then Miller.

"We need to keep the station from airing it," Miller announced. "It's the only leverage we have to get some hostages released."

"Good luck with that." River glanced at the white van. "I'll bet that's a KRSL reporter. If she has video, her station will run it. We need to negotiate for the release of some hostages now."

Miller prepped a little remote-controlled unit, sent it up the walkway to the door, and handed the corresponding microphone to River. "Let's see how you do."

River spoke softly, knowing the sudden intrusion of a loud voice would startle the eco-terrorist. "Russell, this is Carla River with the FBI. I'm here to help you accomplish your goals."

The wind died at that moment and an eerie silence enveloped the scene. River held up her binoculars and watched the curtains on the occupied room. A hand clutched one edge in the center, then pulled it back enough for the person to peek through. A quick look was all he needed. The hand disappeared and the curtains came back together.

River tried again. "Russell, there's a mobile unit outside the front door with a cell phone. Grab the phone and call me. I want to help you and you need to talk to me."

Another long silence. The door didn't open. Finally, River's phone rang. An unknown number. "Agent River here."

"This is Russell Crowder. Sophie gave me your number."

Yes! He was communicating. "I'm glad you called. This is an unfortunate situation, but we can resolve it, if you let me help you."

"Why should I believe you?"

"I was a homeless teenager once. I know what you've been through. And I know you don't really want to hurt anyone."

"Not true. I want Ted Rockman to go to jail. Or maybe burn in hell."

"If he assaulted you, I will press charges against him, no matter how long ago it happened. But you have to let the other hostages go."

"Not yet."

"What are your demands, Russell?"

"I asked Ted Rockman to burn down his factory and make a public video confession of sexually assaulting me."

Good glory. "You can't really expect him to burn it. That would be dangerous."

"He already gave his foreman the order. I'm just waiting for the pictures to prove it's done."

That might be a long wait, River thought. "What about the confession video?"

"He recorded it and Sophie sent it to the TV station. But Rockman is still denying to me that it happened. So I don't have closure."

River understood that need. "Some people never admit their guilt, Russell. You have to find closure another way." She grabbed her computer and clicked open her browser.

"That's not what my therapist says."

Miller, the EPD crisis negotiator, mouthed *hostages*. River ignored her. "I think your therapist might be wrong. What if Rockman won't tell you he's sorry? How long can you stay in there? And do you really want to blow up three innocent women? That's not who you are, Russell."

"You don't know me."

"Anyone as concerned about the environment as you are is also concerned about people. Your grievance is with Rockman. You need to let the other hostages go." River googled KRSL. The website showed a broadcast of Russell talking on the phone. The video had been made with a handheld camera, probably from a cell phone. Was Sophie recording and sending out everything?

"Why should I?" Russell said.

"Because you want to escape, don't you? You want us to let you out of there? We can't do that unless you send out the hostages."

"I'll send out one and think about the others."

"Think about what I said about closure too. You don't need Rockman's admission for closure. You just need to make peace with who you are. Maybe even forgive him."

"I'll call my therapist and see what she says." Crowder clicked off.

CHAPTER 31

Schak arrived with a search warrant, and Jackson eagerly climbed from his car. He was tired of being cooped up and ready to find some tangible evidence that Jenna Brennan had killed Craig Cooper. He wanted to wrap up the hardest part of this case so he could focus on his daughter. Jackson's heart went out to Jenna. She was only a couple years older than Katie, yet emotionally much younger. He doubted if Jenna fully understood what she'd done, and he wondered how the district attorney would handle the case. With murder, DAs liked to charge anyone over fourteen as an adult. And Jenna had lied to the investigators, indicating she understood she had something to hide. Jackson hoped the family could find a decent attorney to work pro bono. Maybe Jenna's therapist could testify to her mental condition and emotional immaturity.

The house was locked as expected.

"Busting open the door would be so easy," Schak said. "These old trailers give like cardboard."

"I don't think it'll be necessary." Jackson looked around for a spare key and found one under a ceramic bunny in a planter box.

Schak looked disappointed. They went inside and Jackson called Evans and updated her.

"You think Jenna is hiding from the police?"

"I don't think she even knows we're onto her."

Evans hesitated. "Should I question Maggie, instead of just leaving her sitting there?"

The original plan had been to wait and question the mother and daughter at the same time, to play them against each other. Jackson wanted information *now*. "Go ahead. After we've searched the house, we'll let Maggie go. Jenna will turn up."

"Do you think Maggie helped Jenna with the murder or just lied to us about whether Jenna left the house?"

"Throw it at her and see how it goes."

"I'm on it."

Jackson turned to Schak. "I'll start in Jenna's bedroom. You check closets and storage spaces for the bow and any arrows she might have."

"Will do."

Jenna's bedroom was decorated in lime green and purple, with posters of her favorite movies, one of which was *The Hunger Games*. The room was also stacked with clothing, books, games, and old toys. Not necessarily messy, but it clearly belonged to someone who couldn't let go of anything. The thought of searching through all of it overwhelmed him.

Where would she keep a bow-and-arrow set? If she hadn't tossed it when she got rid of the hay bale she'd used for practice.

Jackson searched the closet first, sorting through old coats, Halloween costumes, a hula hoop, roller skates, and various other recreational items. At one point, he dislodged a karaoke machine from the upper shelf, and a pile of sweaters and CDs crashed down on his head. One of the disks contained videos of archery instructions. With gloved hands, Jackson slipped the disk into an evidence bag and labeled it. Enough circumstantial evidence could add up to a conviction.

The bow wasn't in the closet or under the bed, but he found the dark polish in a little lime-colored basket on top of the dresser. Jackson bagged several bottles of polish, not certain of the colors. He would check Maggie's room and the bathroom too, and bring in every container of nail polish that was even remotely dark.

The drawers turned up nothing interesting, but Jackson bagged all the clothing in the laundry hamper, on the off chance Jenna hadn't washed the clothes she'd worn Tuesday night and Cooper's blood might be on her shirt or jacket. He stepped out of the bedroom just to get a break from the bright colors and overwhelming collection of stuff.

Schak was coming toward him. "Nothing so far."

"I think I've got the nail polish." Jackson pulled out his phone. "I'm calling the ME to see if he has postmortem results for Todd Sheppard."

"You think Jenna killed Sheppard too because he saw her with Cooper that night?"

"I don't know. Probably not." Jackson didn't get an answer so he left a message.

Schak looked at him. "What now?"

"It's a trailer with three feet of crawl space under it. I think we should look under the house. But I need to spend a few more minutes in Jenna's room."

"Yeah, right. You just want me to do the dirty work." Schak knew he was claustrophobic.

Jackson gave him a twisted grin. "I'll join you in a minute."

Back in the room, he noticed a collection of stuffed animals on the bed. Would Jenna hide something inside her favorite comfort toys? Only two had zippers, a small orange-striped tiger and a fuzzy pink cat. The tiger was stuffed with white clumpy bedding material, and the cat contained a pair of matching slippers. A large brown teddy bear sat on a little chair in the corner, looking dusty. The stuffed animal was matted with wear, and one ear was torn. The bear looked like something Jenna might have had since she was a toddler. Jackson picked it up, thinking of Katie's favorite comfort toy, a stuffed panda she'd left behind six months ago when they'd moved out of her childhood home.

The teddy bear felt surprisingly heavy. On reflex, Jackson shook it. Something shifted inside. Thinking Jenna had hidden something from her mother—maybe drugs or a banned movie—Jackson set it down. He pulled a utility knife from his carryall and slit open the stuffed toy along its back side. He'd also cut through a thick plastic liner. Jackson stuck the knife into one of the interior slits and opened up the plastic.

Stacks of cash filled the bear's belly.

Holy crap. The bank robbery money. Jackson pulled out a stack and flipped through it. All hundreds. He shoved it back, grabbed his camera, and took various shots of the bear and the money. He wanted to count it as badly as he craved pizza after a five-mile run—but he would log it into evidence at the crime lab and let Joe or Jasmine do the honors.

"Holy shit. Is that what I think it is?" Schak came into the room and stared.

"I think so. It looks like stacks of hundred-dollar bills."

"Well, hell. I was pretty excited about finding a bow and some arrows stashed under a sheet of cardboard under the house, but you win. This is a better find."

"The real question is: Did Jenna know the money was here?"

"Wouldn't she have told her mother? And wouldn't her mother have spent it by now?"

"Probably." Jackson realized he'd have to go to his car for a large evidence bag. "I'm guessing Danny Brennan stashed it in the bear nine years ago, then was shot by police detectives before he could grab it and get out of town."

"I suppose the bank will get it back." Schak's voice held a note of regret.

Jackson thought about Katie's future and the potential cost of long-term therapy and substance-abuse treatment. He buried the thought as quickly as it surfaced. "Yes, it will."

"Should we count it before we turn it in? Keep the lab people and the prosecutors honest?"

"We'll count it at the crime lab with several people present. I don't ever want anyone to question the amount of money."

Schak gave him a wistful grin. "Sometimes it sucks being one of the good guys."

CHAPTER 32

Sophie's hands finally stopped shaking. Russell seemed quite taken with her idea to go public with his demands, and somehow she was slightly less scared now. He just wanted attention for his cause and justice for what had been done to him. He hadn't threatened to blow them up in a while. Sophie glanced at Rockman. His public confession had been flatline, and so far, Rockman wouldn't give the crazy young man a personal apology. His denial of the sexual abuse charges seemed sincere, but she knew that didn't mean anything.

"Are you ready?" Russell asked.

"Sure." Sophie held up her phone and focused the camera on the man with the bomb. She and Russell stood in the middle of the room, and the other hostages were against the wall. Russell had wrapped Rockman's wrists in duct tape, but he'd left the women unbound. Sophie hoped to capture a few seconds of video of the hostages without Russell knowing. "We should probably do this in short sections, so the files are smaller and easier to send."

"Okay. Signal when I should stop each time."

Sophie nodded, pressed record, and signaled Russell to begin.

"This is Russell Crowder, a member of Love the Earth. But I'm acting on my own here to shut down Rock Spring, a bottled water company. Here's why. Bottled water has become the worst environmental hazard we have. Thirty-six billion plastic bottles end up in landfills every year."

Sophie signaled for him to stop. The room was silent as she attached the video clip to a text and sent it to the TV station. It took almost ten seconds to clear her phone. She said a silent thank you that satellite reception was working here in the building. She pressed record and signaled Russell to start again.

"In addition, two million tons of plastic are used annually to make water bottles. That requires seven hundred and fourteen million gallons of oil. The amount of energy used in that production is incalculable. The fossil fuels burned transporting those bottles to consumers contributes significantly to global warming. And it's all unnecessary. Tap water is cleaner, safer, and available almost everywhere. In fact, tap water is what's in most of the bottled water sold."

Sophie made him stop again. It was better to keep these clips manageable. The last thing she wanted was her phone to freeze up trying to send a huge file. While the message was going out, Russell's phone rang.

She only heard his end of the conversation, but it was clear that someone in law enforcement was trying to talk him into letting hostages go, maybe even giving himself up. Russell referred to his therapist several times, and Sophie wondered if Russell was taking medication. More accurately, if he'd gone off his meds recently.

While he was talking, Russell took his eyes off her. She quickly pressed record and panned her phone over the hostages.

It would make a great clip, and KRSL would likely play it over and over. Fiona's eyes widened and she gave a tiny shake of her head. Sophie brought the phone back to Russell just as he looked up at her again. She ended the video and sent it too.

Russell made another call to someone named Charlotte and left a message. When he'd hung up, Fiona said, "You should let Patrice and Sophie go. You don't need four hostages. The police won't work with you unless you send out a hostage."

Russell cocked his head and stared at Fiona. "How do you know that? And why aren't you asking for your own release?"

Sophie aimed her camera without lifting it and started recording again.

Fiona said, "Everyone knows you have to release a hostage to get something in return."

"Don't you want out of here?" Russell seemed skeptical of Fiona, and Sophie wondered if he realized Fiona was with the FBI.

"Of course I do," Fiona said. "But I can tell that Patrice is more freaked out, and at least I know you a little."

Russell nodded. "Okay, I'll let Patrice go." He motioned for her to get up.

CHAPTER 33

Charlotte Diebold brought her client slowly out of hypnosis. While the girl was in a meditative trance, Charlotte had spoken to her subconscious with simple, powerful self-esteem messages. The technique had proven effective with other young people, and Charlotte hoped it would help Emma feel good enough about herself to say no to sexual pressure. Emma was only sixteen and she'd already had a dozen sexual partners, but it was the shoplifting that had landed her in juvenile court.

"I want you to keep the diary this week, Emma. It's important to process your thoughts and commit them to paper."

"I don't like writing."

"Do it on your phone then. There are plenty of apps for taking notes. Think of it as texts to yourself."

"I'll try that. Is my time up?"

Charlotte smiled, even though it hurt her feelings for Emma to be so eager to leave. "Not quite, but you can go. I'll see you next Friday."

As soon as the girl was gone, Charlotte checked her cell phone. Russell Crowder had called and left a distressed message: "Ms. Diebold, I need you to call me. I'm in a situation here. Turn on the news and watch KRSL if you can."

Oh dear. What had the young man done now? The panic in Russell's voice, combined with the reference to the news, made her pulse quicken. Charlotte turned to her monitor, clicked over to TV mode, and found the station. Trina Waterman had cut into their regular talk-show programming to give a breaking news update. Charlotte caught the last half of a sentence.

". . . has four hostages in an office on Mill Street, owned by local business owner and state senator Ted Rockman. Crowder alleges that Rockman sexually assaulted him sometime in the past and has sent the station a video clip of the senator confessing to the assault. As you can see in the clip we're about to show you, Rockman seems distressed and it's likely he made the confession under duress. One of the hostages, a newspaper reporter, has been sending updates and tweeting news from inside the building. She claims Crowder has a bomb taped to his chest. We'll cut now to footage from inside the hostage crisis."

A bomb? Oh dear God. Charlotte's pulse pounded in her throat and little rockets of pain went off in her chest. She reached in her purse for her blood pressure medicine.

On a dark and shaky video clip, she watched Ted Rockman admit to sexually assaulting Russell Crowder during a camping trip seven years ago. His face was impassive and his voice deadpan. Not a hint of remorse. The station cut back to blonde pretty Trina Waterman.

"Our inside source tells us Russell Crowder also demanded that Ted Rockman burn down his bottled water plant. The eco-terrorist plans to keep the hostages until he's seen proof that the factory foreman has met the demand. Eugene police and the FBI are at the scene and are negotiating with Crowder. What we've learned so far about this disturbed young man is that he's a member of Love the Earth, an environmental group that has been active locally."

Charlotte muted the sound, unable to listen anymore. Russell had not seemed that disturbed. During the year she'd been treating him, he'd shown tendencies toward irrational thought and impulsive behavior, but she'd believed they had that under control with olanzapine.

Taking a long gulp of oxygen, Charlotte heaved herself from her chair. She had to go down there and talk to Russell face-to-face, to convince him to let the other hostages go. She didn't care what happened to Ted Rockman, but she cared about Russell, and she had misjudged the depth of his pain and anger. She'd also had no idea that Russell's interest in environmental issues would become so obsessive.

Charlotte hurried, but every heavy step was a laborious effort and her knees and ankles cried out with pain. Once she was inside her SUV, Charlotte called her young client, pulled out of the parking lot, and hoped she wasn't too late.

CHAPTER 34

River tried to visualize the room where the hostages were held. Were they on the floor? Had Crowder bound them? What she really wanted to know was if Dallas had a gun or other weapon. If she did, Crowder may have taken it from her. Bomb trumped gun every time. River texted Sophie: *Is anyone tied or taped?*

Waiting was excruciating. Snipers with high-powered rifles had taken spots in three surrounding buildings, including one on the roof of the business across the street. SWAT members with automatic weapons were also in place, tucked behind cars, shrubs, and fences, just waiting for the go command. But Crowder had a bomb, and neither she nor Sergeant Bruckner wanted to risk him setting it off. They had to convince Crowder to release the hostages and give himself up. River hoped his conversation with his therapist was productive. With Fouts, Quince, and Miller standing by, the small group took turns leaning against the patrol cars and pacing in a small circle, throwing out ideas.

River checked her tablet again to see if the TV station had any new clips from Sophie. She caught one of Russell making a statement about plastic water bottles and their effect on the environment. Good. Once the perp got his message out there, he'd feel better and maybe start to cooperate. Fouts and Miller stood shoulder to shoulder with her, watching the video.

"Crazy motherfucker," Fouts mumbled.

River couldn't disagree. She watched Crowder carefully, looking for signs of weakness. His message played in chunks that were spliced together. The station cut to the blonde newscaster again. "Our reporter inside also captured video of the hostages, who seem terrified but unharmed." A short clip showed three hostages—two against a wall, and one leaning on a file cabinet. Rockman's wrists were duct-taped, but only the silver-haired woman looked really scared.

"The young woman on the right is our undercover agent, Jamie Dallas," River said, for the others. "Crowder knows her as Fiona. The older woman is probably Rockman's assistant."

"Is your agent armed?" Bruckner asked.

"I don't know. If she's not carrying a gun, I'm sure she has a knife or pepper spray." River turned to face him. "Our perp has a bomb. It's not really safe for your snipers to take a shot, let alone for Dallas to try and overpower him."

"If they get a clear shot, I'll give the order. We can't just sit here waiting for Rockman to burn down his factory." Bruckner tried to stare her down.

"The shot is too risky."

"They won't miss. One kill shot to his head and he'll die instantly."

"What if the bomb goes off when Crowder hits the ground? And it kills all the hostages? Or levels this city block?"

"Our bomb experts have looked at close-ups of the video footage," Bruckner countered. "They say it's made of three sticks of dynamite, which may not even destroy the building. If we can get the hostages away from him—"

River cut him off. "Give the negotiations a chance."

They waited in silence for a few minutes, then Bruckner said, "We can get the utility company to cut off the power. If it gets cold in there, he'll get uncomfortable."

"Not yet," River said. "I want the lights on." She turned to Fouts. "Call the Rock Spring manager again. We need to find a compromise, a way to show that the plant is disabled without actually burning it down."

They heard a door open, and they all spun toward the R&L building. The older woman burst out the door and ran toward them.

As River got an arm around her, the woman burst into tears. They waited while she got herself under control.

"What's your name?" River spoke gently.

"Patrice LaRue. I'm Ted Rockman's administrative assistant." She was still shaking, and Bruckner sent one of his men to the armored unit for a blanket.

"How many hostages?"

"Three left. My boss and the reporter who was interviewing him when Crowder came in, plus some woman named Fiona who pushed her way in through the interior door."

"What interior door?"

"Mr. Rockman's office connects to the center of the building, where there's a kitchen and a bathroom. On the back side is his political headquarters."

"Is anyone in the other half of the building?"

"I don't think so." Patrice glanced at the parking lot. "An intern works there part time, but I don't see her car."

River turned to Bruckner. "We need to get SWAT guys into the back office."

"I'm already there." He touched his radio and gave the command.

"Crowder locked the interior door," Patrice said. "And there's no visibility into the office from the hallway. But I left the front door unlocked. He told me to lock it after I went through, but I couldn't make myself stop and do it."

"Good to know. What else can you tell us? Does he have any other weapons?"

"He's got a knife." Patrice started to cry again. "He says he won't let anyone else go until Mr. Rockman burns down his factory."

River walked the woman to a patrol officer on the perimeter. "Get her into a car where it's warm and give her a phone so she can call her family."

Bruckner got a report on his radio, but River didn't hear anything clearly, except the word *therapist*. That caught her attention.

"Charlotte Diebold is here on the perimeter and wants to speak with the perp," Bruckner reported. "She says she's his therapist and can talk him out of this."

"Bring her to me."

CHAPTER 35

Charlotte couldn't keep up with the police sergeant, but she tried. She was a big woman and moved slowly, even on her good days, but once she had momentum on her side, she picked up speed. Still, her heart raced, her back ached with tension, and she felt lightheaded. Sergeant Bruckner led her to a cluster of people standing behind two side-by-side cop cars in the street.

A tall woman with a pleasant face stuck out her hand. "Agent River. Thanks for coming."

"Charlotte Diebold." Charlotte often declined to shake hands because of her arthritis, but this was the FBI. "Russell called me and left a message. I tried calling him back but he didn't answer. But it's best I speak with him in person."

"We have the hailer." Agent River pointed at a portable microphone sitting on the trunk of the patrol car. "Or you can try him again on his phone. Keep the conversation low-key and personal."

"I want to go in there and talk to him face-to-face. I'll tell him to release a hostage and I'll take her place."

"We can't let you do that," the agent said. "He has a bomb."

Charlotte understood their thinking, but they didn't understand her responsibility. "Where is he?"

"The room on the right."

Charlotte pulled her phone from her pocket and pressed redial. Russell cried, "Charlotte. Thank God you called. I need your help."

"I'm here, Russell." She watched the closed curtains and saw the center move a little. He'd seen her. Without another word, Charlotte charged toward the building, moving as quickly as her thick legs and heavy body would allow.

"No!" A chorus echoed behind her and large hands grabbed at her shoulders. Charlotte shook them off. With her weight, once she got moving, there was no stopping her. What would they do? Shoot her to keep her safe? The thought almost made her smile.

The sergeant grabbed at her again, but the FBI agent in charged yelled, "Let her go. Crowder might be watching."

That's right, Charlotte thought. *Don't piss off the man with the bomb by assaulting his therapist.*

She reached the door and pushed it open. Until the moment she stepped into the building, she'd felt determined and a little numb. Now her legs were weak and her chest felt as if someone were sitting on it. If she survived this, she promised herself she would get her stomach stapled and lose a hundred pounds.

Across the lobby, an interior door opened and Russell yelled, "We're in here."

Winded and with pain shooting up her calves, Charlotte made her way across the room and stepped into the hostage crisis. The bomb taped to Russell's chest caught her attention first, but the fact that Ted Rockman was in the room filled her with panic. And rage.

Charlotte turned and stared down at the man who'd degraded her, robbed her of her self-confidence, and trapped her in this hideous body. He looked rather helpless, sitting on the floor with his wrists duct-taped together. The young woman next to him was wide-eyed.

"Hello, Ted."

He looked confused, but nodded. Of course he didn't recognize her. It had been thirty years. And her face was buried under a thick layer of fat now. Charlotte pulled her attention back to her misguided client. She would deal with Ted later. "Russell, this has to stop now. You made your statements, now let everyone go. This can't end well for you."

"I want Rock Spring to burn. I want to see the ashes."

"It won't change anything. You'll still go to jail, and Mr. Rockman will rebuild the factory. Even if he doesn't, there are dozens of bottled water plants. You can't burn them all. You can make more of a difference with legislation." That chance was remote now, but she had to give him hope.

"But he's a pedophile. And I'm not letting him go until he apologizes for molesting me."

This was what Russell's behavior was about. If she hadn't planted those false memories, Russell would have been content to protest in front of the factory and gather petition signatures.

From the floor, Rockman said, "I didn't molest you." He sounded weary, as if he'd given up trying to be convincing.

Now was the moment. Charlotte took a deep breath. "He didn't molest you, Russell. Someone named Chet did. But Rockman didn't."

"Why are you saying that?" Russell's voice pitched with an edge of panic.

"I helped you come to believe Ted Rockman was one of the men who sexually abused you. I wanted you to go to the police and file charges. But not to strap on a bomb and threaten innocent lives."

"What?" Russell's face twisted in confusion. "What do you mean you helped me? How?"

"During some of our hypnosis sessions I planted false memories." Charlotte realized she would need a good lawyer.

"Why? I don't understand."

She heard Rockman make a noise behind her, but Charlotte ignored him. "Because he raped me when I was a teenager and I never had the courage to accuse him. So I wanted you to. I thought it would help you get closure as well. Since the man who assaulted you was long gone, I thought Ted Rockman would serve as his proxy." Anguish threatened to overwhelm her, and Charlotte fought to keep her composure. "I'm sorry, Russell."

For a long time, Russell was silent, and his face registered a range of emotions: confusion, anger, fear. While he worked through them, Charlotte relived the years. As a young teenager in a foster home, she'd felt powerless. Back then, the children's advocacy service had not existed, and no one would have believed her if she claimed her foster brothers had both raped her. As she'd grown older and fatter, she'd been afraid to press charges for what people would say. Cops and social workers would have looked at her and thought: *Why would anyone rape her? She's hideous.*

So much time had passed that Charlotte had given up on the idea that Ted and Craig would be prosecuted, but she'd followed both their lives and rejoiced when Craig went to prison. But Ted Rockman's life had been blessed. When she'd read that he was considering a run for Congress, she knew she couldn't let a predator assume a position of power.

Charlotte noticed the short redheaded woman sitting on the edge of the desk, holding out a cell phone. Was she recording? "Shut that off!"

The woman didn't even look up. She turned the phone on its side and keyed in a message. Charlotte resisted the impulse to grab her phone and crush it. She had to stay focused on Russell.

Rockman stood and came to her. "Who the hell are you?"

She pulled in breath for courage. "Charlotte Diebold. Your foster sister. Remember? You and Craig both raped me."

She watched Rockman's eyes fill with recognition.

At least the bastard remembered her. His sexual assaults had filled her with self-loathing and she'd begun to eat for comfort. Even when she was free of the foster home, she couldn't stop. She'd attended college on a grant and studied psychiatry to understand her own issues, but she'd never come to terms with her rage or her appetite. Then one day at the courthouse Russell had come along—after being arrested at Rockman's factory—and Charlotte had visualized a way to be free of her past and bring justice to one of the men who'd condemned her to a lonely life of bitterness. She'd given Russell's aunt her business card and prayed she would call.

Rockman shook his head. "No, Charlotte. We had consensual sex while we were drunk. I came to regret that because you were so young. But I was young too. One of your foster fathers may have raped you, but I didn't."

Memories flooded her brain, and faces blurred together. Charlotte pushed it all aside. "Liar!"

"No, Charlotte, you've got it wrong."

CHAPTER 36

Jenna braked to cross the speed hump and spotted two dark sedans parked outside the trailer. *Uh oh.* The cops were here again. She didn't want to talk to them. She hated lying. Jenna put the truck in reverse, backed into a neighbor's driveway, then drove out the way she'd come in. At the curve in the narrow street, she allowed herself to look in the rearview mirror. One of the detectives was on the porch, watching her drive away. *Damn.* She pinched herself on the back of her hand. She hated swearing too.

Out of habit, she turned right and headed toward downtown. She would go to the library and get online for a while, or maybe to the student center at LCC's campus to see if one of her friends was there. She hadn't had many friends in high school, but she'd met several new people in her film class, and she still had Brianna, a friend from middle school. Jenna hoped the cops would be gone when she got back.

She drove faster than she usually did and it made her nervous. Mom couldn't afford to have an accident on their insurance.

Her mother didn't like Jenna to drive, but she let her use the truck sometimes when she was working, as long as Jenna agreed to run an errand or two. Jenna glanced in the rearview mirror and didn't see the dark cars. A sense of relief made her giggle. Then she felt bad about being silly. She understood their investigation was serious and that what she'd done was serious too. But she was a protector now, someone who looked after others who were shy or picked on or afraid. She used to be one of the picked on, but not anymore. Katniss had shown her how to be a warrior. Then Arrow had shown her what she needed to do.

Jenna's phone rang and startled her. She fumbled in her backpack, looking for her earpiece. She wasn't supposed to talk and drive, but she did sometimes anyway. She managed to get her earpiece in. "Jenna speaking."

"It's Bri. Have you seen the news?"

Just the sound of her friend's voice made Jenna feel better. "No. I went to the post office for Mom. Why?"

"That therapist you go to? The fat lady named Charlotte? She's on the news. She's talking to a guy with a bomb."

"Get out!" Jenna thought Brianna was teasing her.

"I'm serious. Do you have your Kindle? They're showing the clip on channel three."

"Yeah, but I'm driving."

"Well, pull over. You have to see it." Brianna was practically yelling at her. "The shrink kind of messed with the guy's head during their sessions. I don't think you should see her anymore."

Oh no! Her head was already messy enough. "I'm stopping now." Jenna pulled into a parking lot on West Thirteenth, a few blocks from the library. After she shut off the truck to save gas, she pulled her Kindle Fire tablet out of her backpack. Her grandma had given it to her for Christmas. Jenna liked its name. The fire reminded her of Katniss and Peeta. "You said KRSL?"

"Yes. Trina Waterman is reporting. She's awesome." Brianna wanted to be a newscaster. Or an actress.

"I'll watch it and call you back." Jenna hung up. Sometimes her phone didn't work well next to another wireless device.

She searched for the TV station and clicked open the video with Trina Waterman. The reporter stood on the sidewalk on a street near campus. Behind her were police cars. Trina was talking about Jenna's therapist.

"For those just tuning in, the breaking news in the hostage crisis is that a therapist named Charlotte Diebold entered the building where the hostages are being held and confronted Russell Crowder, the eco-terrorist with the bomb. After failing to convince Crowder to let the hostages go, Diebold confessed to planting false memories of sexual assault during Crowder's therapy sessions. We'll cut to the video again so you can see it for yourself."

False memories? What did that mean? Jenna felt queasy.

A dark, low-quality clip began to play. Jenna watched, fascinated, as her therapist confronted the man with the bomb. When Ms. Diebold said she'd put ideas into Russell's mind during hypnosis, Jenna felt sick. During her own sessions, she'd recently recovered memories of being molested. Memories of Uncle Craig doing disgusting things to her. Jenna could see the faded green couch and the little rug she played on with her toys. The memories seemed so real.

But were they? She watched the rest of the video, the sickness filling her belly. Russell had been molested, but not by the man he thought. *Oh no.* Had she made a horrible mistake? Jenna had thought she was protecting other young girls from a predator. Ms. Diebold had said Jenna needed to report Craig to protect other children. But Jenna didn't like the police, and her way had seemed simpler and better for everyone.

Had Ms. Diebold tricked her? She had to find out!

Jenna googled R&L Enterprises, the office the reporter had mentioned, and found the address. Anxiety mounting, she put her tablet on the seat beside her, started the truck, and pulled out. A few blocks later, she turned on Mill Street and ran into a roadblock. Cop cars parked in the street, and a white van straddled the sidewalk nearby. A police officer motioned for her to turn around and leave. Jenna did as he instructed, then drove one block over and into an alley. She pulled off in a gravel turnout, stuffed all her electronics into her backpack, and left the truck. She realized the cops wouldn't let her get close to the office where Russell and her therapist were, but Jenna could talk to Trina Waterman. The news people had someone on the inside reporting, and Jenna wanted to see Ms. Diebold's face when she confronted her.

At the end of the alley, she turned right and spotted the white van. Jenna ran straight for the reporter, pushing her way through a small crowd. "Excuse me. Excuse me." It was important to be polite.

The reporter looked up and Jenna realized she was being loud. She often couldn't tell.

"Ms. Waterman, I'm Jenna Brennan. Charlotte Diebold is my therapist too." Her mother had taken her to see Ms. Diebold after Jenna had hit one of her classmates who made fun of her. She'd learned how to calm herself, but what else had happened during those sessions?

The reporter signaled the cameraman, then motioned to Jenna. "Come over here, please."

Jenna took tentative steps forward, suddenly self-conscious. Would they put her on TV? She hoped she didn't get tongue-tied. This was too important.

"What brings you down here?" Trina held out the microphone.

"I saw what Ms. Diebold said about putting false memories in Russell's head. I'm worried she did that to me too."

"You're one of her patients?"

"I'm her client." Ms. Diebold said that she didn't see patients because patients were sick, and her clients were not. But that didn't matter. "I want to talk to Ms. Diebold. I want your reporter in there to put the camera on her face when I call her." Jenna couldn't always tell what people were thinking, but she was getting better at it.

"What are you going to say?"

"I'm going to ask her if she did that to me." Frustration bubbled up and Jenna yelled a little. "I need to know! Please help me see her face when I ask."

"Let's see what we can do." Trina Waterman pulled out her phone and keyed in a text message. "It may take a moment. It's pretty tense in there, and I don't know if our reporter is still able to record."

Jenna glanced nervously at the crowd watching her. She didn't like to be around this many people. She wished her mother were with her.

Trina smiled and patted her arm. "Thanks for coming down. I think your question is important."

Jenna bit her lip. The reporter had no idea how important.

The reporter's phone made a noise and she said, "That was fast." Trina read the text, then signaled the cameraman again. She turned to Jenna. "We're on. Do you have a cell phone to call in?"

"Of course." Jenna resisted the urge to scowl. She dug for her phone, looked up her therapist's number, and pressed call.

Trina pointed to a laptop she had on a portable stand. "The video will come up on that monitor as soon as Sophie sends it. It's not really live, but it's close."

Ms. Diebold suddenly answered in her ear. "Jenna, I'm glad you're here."

The sad tone of her voice gave her away. Jenna knew the truth. She didn't need to see Ms. Diebold's face or even ask the question. Her therapist had tricked her too. "Why did you do that to me?"

"I wanted to empower you and to help you heal. You had so much anger. And yes, to help myself too. Because Craig Cooper hurt me, and I wanted to hurt him back. I used you and I'm sorry. But I just wanted you to press sexual abuse charges." Ms. Diebold closed her eyes, as if she couldn't bear to think about what Jenna had done instead.

"So Uncle Craig didn't molest me when he was my babysitter?"

"Not that I know of."

"I hate you." It was childish, she knew, but it was all Jenna could think to say. She hung up. She still hated Uncle Craig too, for making her father a drug addict and bank robber, but she understood now that he wasn't a danger to other young girls. What had she done?

The reporter plugged her phone into the laptop, and a minute later, a video of Ms. Diebold talking on the phone came up on the monitor. She looked scared and sorry, but Jenna couldn't watch. She felt too sick.

Someone touched her elbow and Jenna turned. One of the cops who'd been at the house was standing there. He looked tired and sad, and she knew he was here to arrest her.

CHAPTER 37

Jackson didn't understand the full implications of Charlotte Diebold's video, but the gist of it was clear. Jenna had somehow been manipulated by her therapist into killing Craig Cooper. Revolting! What terrified him was that he had sent his daughter to see Charlotte Diebold for therapy. How had someone so unethical become so recommended? Jackson wanted to call Katie and tell her they had to keep looking for a counselor, but he had to deal with Jenna first. The poor girl was so young, so unprepared for the consequences she faced. He hoped the DA would extend Jenna every possible break.

"Jenna Brennan. I need you to come with me."

"I will. But can we stay and see what happens to Charlotte? I need to know." Jenna stepped toward him and held out her hands.

Jackson had never felt worse about cuffing someone.

"What are you arresting her for?" Trina Waterman held out the mic, as if he might answer.

Jackson turned to Schak, who'd walked up while the video played. They had followed Jenna from her home and had watched to see where she was going, in case she led them to evidence they could use. Jackson had been stunned to see her end up here at the hostage crisis.

Schak said, "Let's see what's happening. If Jenna knows the therapist, maybe she can be helpful."

"I don't want to help her," Jenna said, her voice as deadpan as ever.

"Not her, the other hostages." Schak grabbed Jenna's other elbow, and they walked toward the yellow tape stretched across the sidewalk. Jackson wanted to know what the hell was going on too.

Behind them, the reporter talked to her viewers. "In yet another odd development, Jenna Brennan, the young woman we just heard from, has been cuffed and led away."

A patrol officer approached them as they stepped under the tape. "I know you're EPD, but I was told no one gets in."

"Is Agent River in charge?" Jackson asked.

"Yes. Our SWAT unit is here too."

"Tell 'em we're coming." Jackson and Schak kept moving.

As they approached the command center, River called out, "What's going on, Jackson? Why are you bringing a civilian into this scene?"

"She's a patient of the therapist who's in there with the hostages. And another of Diebold's victims. I thought she might be helpful."

River looked a little rattled. "I don't see how."

"Why don't you update us?" Jackson said. "Maybe we have some insight."

River gave them a quick rundown and concluded with, "Now our hostage taker is freaking out. Crowder seems to have shifted his anger to Charlotte Diebold and won't answer my calls. I need to get Sophie and Dallas out."

"Sophie Speranza is in there?" Jackson was surprised, but realized he shouldn't have been. If a story was breaking, Sophie was there.

"She's been sending out the videos." River's phone beeped, and she tapped her earpiece and listened for a moment. "Release Sophie and Fiona, and we'll clear out and let you walk away."

After another moment, River responded, "Send them out, then we'll talk details." She hung up.

Miller, the EPD's crisis negotiator, asked, "What does he want?"

"He wants us to clear out, so he can get away." River rolled her eyes. "And he wants a helicopter to fly him out of the state. I told him I wouldn't discuss details until he sent out the reporter and my UC."

"Good," Miller said. "We need to free as many of the hostages as we can, then get Crowder out into the open."

"What about the therapist?" Detective Quince asked. "I think he might kill her. He looked outraged when she told him what she'd done."

"We worry about everyone else first," Sergeant Bruckner said. His eyes never left the curtained front windows. Jackson remembered another hostage scene they'd experienced together. Bruckner and his team had been incredible that day.

Jackson looked up and around to see if he could spot the snipers, now feeling guilty about bringing Jenna into this scene. He started to tell Schak that he would take the girl into the department for questioning, but they heard the front door open.

Jackson spun back and saw Sophie come running out, clutching her phone, her purse still strapped to her shoulder.

CHAPTER 38

Dallas watched Sophie go and wondered if Russell would send her out too. Unless she brought up that she was a federal agent, she would be the next to go. But she wouldn't do that. Crowder might come at her with the knife he clutched. Her gun was still in the bottom of her purse, which was on the desk eight feet away. She felt so damn useless. The reporter had facilitated the conversations and sent out intel, while Dallas had just sat there, watching and waiting. She'd been prepared to make a move at any point, but with Russell's nervous fingers never far from his bomb, Dallas hadn't had an opportunity to go for it.

Now Crowder was asking River for a helicopter. The crazy man actually thought he was going to escape. He had bound the therapist's hands and mouth with duct tape and told her she was going with him. He planned to use the big woman as a shield when he left the building. Could he actually get past the snipers that way? She knew they were out there, hiding in the upper floors of the surrounding buildings.

"Fiona, I'm sending you out too." Crowder motioned for her to get up.

She stood, knowing this was her only chance. "Rockman needs to go first. He's suffered enough for something he didn't do."

"Why do you care?" Crowder glared at her.

"I'm just that kind of person. Let him go. You can't take two hostages with you."

Russell thought it over.

Dallas pressed him. "I'm not leaving until after he does."

Rockman stood, his wrists still duct-taped. "We'll go together."

"Shut up and go." Dallas pushed him toward the door.

Rockman stumbled but didn't argue and didn't stop. She heard him running across the front office.

It was time to make her move. Crowder was crazy and might kill the therapist as soon as Dallas was gone. Or he might realize he wasn't going to get away and set off the bomb, killing the shrink and himself to avoid a life sentence in prison. Dallas glanced at the pull-string for the curtains. The edge of the window was about five feet from the door. One long leap over. Russell didn't expect anything from her and wouldn't know what to think for that split second. That was all the time the snipers needed.

One leap over and one leap back, Dallas corrected. She would still run like hell from the building. Who knew what would happen when Crowder hit the floor?

"Get out now!" Crowder had been highly agitated since his shrink had admitted she'd fucked with his head and used him like a windup toy. Dallas felt a little sorry for him.

She took two steps toward the door, then lunged sideways for the curtain cord, yanking down as she landed.

The drapes pulled open more slowly than she'd visualized, but the room flooded with daylight. From the outside, Crowder was now visible through the floor-to-ceiling windows. An easy target. Dallas spun and sprinted for the door.

The crack of a high-powered rifle boomed, joined by the shattering of glass. Dallas kept running. As she reached the outer wall, she heard a thud. She yanked open the door and rushed outside, filling her lungs with sweet, damp air as she charged across the street.

A chorus of cheers sounded and Dallas looked up, feeling like she was moving in slow motion. She took in the patrol cars and the group of law enforcement people behind them. Their relieved faces said it all. The hostage taker was down and the bomb had not exploded.

CHAPTER 39

Late that afternoon, Jackson and his boss walked over to the federal building. He'd briefed Sergeant Lammers earlier, but now they had a meeting with Agent River. Charlotte Diebold was in federal custody, and River wanted Jackson to have a chance to question her.

"Where is Jenna Brennan?" Lammers asked.

"She's at the Serbu campus. I convinced the DA to keep her in juvie lockup until he decides what charges to file. Slonecker wants to meet with forensic psychiatrists and hear what Charlotte Diebold has to say."

"I hope the DA and the feds both go after that quack. Yet I suspect Diebold will only do time for criminal negligence or maybe manslaughter."

"You're probably right." Jackson couldn't bring himself to admit he'd taken Katie to see Diebold. "The therapist has already expressed public remorse. Plus her foster care childhood and history of sexual abuse will make jurists sympathetic to her."

"Not me. She's a predator as far as I'm concerned."

Jackson had mixed feelings. So many criminals had once been victims.

They went through federal security, got on the elevator, and rode up to the FBI's headquarters on the third floor. After identifying themselves through a speaker, Agent River came to the door and let them in.

"Quite the day we've had." She led them to the conference room. "I'm sorry to report that Charlotte Diebold is refusing to answer questions. I finally let her call a lawyer, then had federal marshals pick her up. They're taking her to the county jail, so you can try to question her again later."

Jackson was glad Diebold was being booked in by a marshal. Federal prisoners weren't released because the feds paid for those jail beds, no matter how crowded the jail was. "What about Rockman?" he asked.

"We debriefed him and sent him home. It's up to the DA whether he wants to file rape charges."

"I don't think he will." Jackson didn't know what to believe. It was a case of he-said-she-said from thirty years ago. Considering how screwed up Diebold was, Jackson was inclined to think the therapist was confused and maybe mentally ill.

They sat down at the conference table. River, Fouts, and Dallas were already there. Jackson admired the young undercover agent for her coolheaded bravery.

"We're still expecting Bruckner and Quince, but we can get started." River smiled at the group and sat down next to Dallas.

"What happens with your Downdraft case now?" Lammers asked.

"We think we can make a case against Adam Greene for the JB Pharma sabotage," River said. "But essentially, the investigation is over. Dallas will head back to Phoenix, and we expect Love the Earth to go back to circulating petitions."

"Too much federal and media scrutiny for them," Fouts added. "But we'll still keep an eye on them."

Quince came in, took a seat, and asked, "Do we know how Russell Crowder got into the bottled water factory?"

River shook her head. "My best guess is that he watched Candy Morrison type the code a few times. There's a place to hide in that smokers' shelter right next to the door."

"Was it a real bomb on his chest?" Lammers asked.

"Oh yes." River patted Dallas' hand. "I'm sorry we couldn't save him, but we had no civilian casualties, and everyone on the team was excellent today."

Jackson's phone beeped and he looked at the ID: *Katie*. His chest tightened and he quickly opened her message: *I love u. Happy Birthday!*

His heart burst with joy. Katie still loved him. He had to believe their relationship was salvageable.

Jackson texted back: *Thanks. Want to have dinner?*

Katie responded: *OK. I signed up for a treatment program today.*

Thank God. He texted again, keeping it casual: *Happy to hear that.*

Katie got in the last word: *I saw the news. That counselor you took me to: what the hell?*

Jackson laughed. Humor was the first step. His daughter was on her way back.

ABOUT THE AUTHOR

L.J. Sellers is a native of Eugene, Oregon, the setting of her thrillers. She's an award-winning journalist and best-selling novelist, as well as a cyclist, social networker, and thrill-seeking fanatic. A long-standing fan of police procedurals, she counts John Sandford, Michael Connelly, Ridley Pearson, and Lawrence Sanders among her favorites. Her own novels, featuring Detective Jackson, include *The Sex Club*; *Secrets to Die For*; *Thrilled to Death*; *Passions of the Dead*; *Dying for Justice*; *Liars, Cheaters & Thieves*; *Rules of Crime*; and *Crimes of Memory*. In addition, she's penned three stand-alone thrillers: *The Baby Thief*, *The Gauntlet Assassin*, and *The Lethal Effect*. When not plotting crime, she's also been known to perform stand-up comedy and occasionally jump out of airplanes.

Made in the USA
Charleston, SC
17 September 2013